'A dark and gripping debut with sinister undertones from the very first page. I loved it.'

Sophie Flynn, author of *All My Lies*

'A perfect romantic-noir – a crime story wrapped up in a love story. The characters draw you in to their world and make you root for them, until a creeping sense of dread makes you cower as you wonder where the fatal blow is going to come from. Well-crafted and chilling!'

S.E. Moorhead, author of *Witness X*

'The minute I started it I was absolutely hooked… This is a terrific debut and I for one cannot wait to see what this author comes up with next. It's an absolute 5★ read without a doubt. If I could give it more I would.'

Jackie's Reading Corner

'It is a testimony to the writer's skill that one becomes lost in the emotion and pathos of the story to such an extent that it is easy to forget that the novel consists entirely of a monologue… A great debut novel that explores love, loss, friendship, motherhood and betrayal. It is engrossing throughout and ends with a shocking and unexpected twist. Enjoyable and highly recommended.'

Mystery People

'A psychological thriller that spins around a couple of modern themes, touching on mental health and even migration and Brexit. The characters are plausible and intriguing and the reveals are clever and satisfying.'

Crime Time

TWIN TRUTHS

JACQUELINE SUTHERLAND

A Point Blank Book

First published in Great Britain, Australia and the Republic of Ireland by
Point Blank, an imprint of Oneworld Publications, 2023

Copyright © Jacqueline Sutherland, 2023

The moral right of Jacqueline Sutherland to be identified as the Author of this
work has been asserted by her in accordance with the Copyright, Designs, and
Patents Act 1988

ISBN 978-0-86154-405-9
ISBN 978-0-86154-406-6 (ebook)

Printed and bound in Great Britain by Clays Ltd, Elcograf S.p.A.

Oneworld Publications
10 Bloomsbury Street
London WC1B 3SR
England

Stay up to date with the latest books,
special offers, and exclusive content from
Oneworld with our newsletter

Sign up on our website
oneworld-publications.com/point-blank

For Euan.
Love you always.

Friday 15 December

Sea temperature: 9.1 degrees.
Air temperature: 6 degrees.

Colder than yesterday with a wind from the east, the sea was a grey churn that sucked and spat on the sand. Nancy Barfoot, my daily swim buddy, was already on her way out to the shallows. She saw me there on the beach and raised a hand in a salute before submerging. Knowing she was now safe to go in. That somebody would keep a lookout for her. Just as she would keep an eye on me. I waved one swim-gloved hand back at her and pulled the other glove over my fingers, looking for other members of the Southwold Sea-girls. The stalwarts. The dailies. There weren't many of us that stuck it out throughout the winter, the majority being a spring-to-autumn gang. A quick survey from pier to marshes told me it was nobody but Nancy and me that morning, just as I had thought. The WhatsApp group had been silent for weeks, the only chat being the two of us arranging times to meet the next morning, or talking of tides. Once the clocks went forward in spring, the other members would appear again as if by magic. But this morning, I didn't mind the lack of others. It meant the North Sea was practically empty. Nothing between me and Holland. It was mine. Suddenly I couldn't wait to get in.

I started my swim watch – ten minutes and no more, not at this time of year – and walked steadily into the waves. There was no point stopping or deliberating, this bit just had to be endured. The strips of shingle pricked lightly at the soles of my booties, the bars of sand gave a reprieve. The water streamed icy into my wetsuit, flooding the gaps between suit and skin. As soon as it reached my lowest rib, I pushed forward: no going back. I submerged everything except my head and struck out into a breaststroke even as the cold stole the breath from my lungs. I gasped and felt it tear deep inside me. It was only dangerous if you were submerged, and I knew to just swim steadily until the cold-water shock had passed. Reach, pull. Reach, pull. Reach, pull. Nothing else until my breath was steady, in and out. No other thought audible over the rush of blood and surf in my head. I was acclimatised by swimming every day, more able to withstand this than most, but it was always the same. You could see why it was dangerous for people unaccustomed to the temperature; this literally robbed you of thought. It incited panic. Reach, pull. In, out. I kept close to the shore until I knew that the cold-water shock had passed, that I was functioning, that I was alive.

The current was gentle, not the lateral pull that sometimes held me swimming in place, and I struck out towards the pier. Should be able to make it halfway there and back in the time. I lowered my face now too, felt the burn of the salt and the cold on my cheeks, worth it for a better stroke. I cut through the water with my arms, felt the expansion of my lungs, the kick of my legs, my personal float trailing behind me. Every part of my body pulsing with blood, with charge, with life.

Later, as I peeled off my goggles and my wetsuit in our beach hut and towelled myself pink, I felt the endorphins kick in. I'd done it. I loved it. It was my favourite way to start my day. The torture was always worth this. I needed this rush, this buzz. I craved it. I was addicted to feeling this alive.

This is the time the Sea-girls would normally laugh and hug goodbye, some of them dancing on the beach, full of happy chemicals, smelling of the sea. I pulled on my thick onesie and zipped myself in, feeling the softness of the fleece against my skin. I hung my wetsuit on its hanger on the back wall and stuffed my sandy wet towel into my rucksack. I could have run home in my wetsuit really – it was only two minutes to South Green – but I liked to get wrapped up, to take my time. To enjoy it.

After all, David would be at work by the time I got back, so I wasn't in a rush. He'd planned to go in early today, what with it being the last day of term, so that he could finish on time and break up for the holidays at the end of the school day. It would be good for him to have a rest; Christmas term was full-on with mock examinations and fundraising fairs.

I locked the beach hut with tingly fingers and put the key in my pocket. The promenade was still empty, a lone dog-walker ahead of me marching towards Walberswick. I'd have to take Dodge out later, once I'd showered and dressed. Otherwise he'd follow me around the house carrying his lead until I gave in. The sky promised rain, so I might as well get it over and done with this morning. My trainers crunched and I stopped. Glass littered the walkway underneath a streetlight. Looking up, I saw the hole in the glass canopy. There'd been a spate of vandalism recently apparently, according to the town council. At the last meeting,

3

I'd taken the minutes while the councillors bemoaned bored kids taking aim at streetlights and CCTV along the front and on the pier. I'd listened to the fact that the kids also kept stealing the coloured cones marking repair sites, and had smiled to myself, thinking they'd probably ended up as drinking trophies in someone's bedroom. The ones on the northern side of the pier had to be replaced twice over the previous weekend. While I didn't agree with it, I could sympathise with the kids. There wasn't a lot for teenagers to do in Southwold. Our twins had started yearning for nightclubs a few years ago and they'd had to go further afield.

I snapped a photo of the unit number for the streetlight from its column to report it online, and moved the breakage carefully to the side with my foot. I'd call Geoff, the street cleaner, when I got home. I had his number on the council contacts.

There was a delivery van outside the Red Lion. George, the landlord, was lifting boxes from the back and stacking them on the bench table nearest the door.

'Good swim this morning, Belle?' he called.

'You should try it for yourself, George!' I called back with a grin.

'Believe me, it's better I don't!' he said. 'Nobody wants to see me in my budgie-smugglers!' I couldn't help but laugh as he turned back to the driver to sign the paperwork.

Otherwise, South Green was empty, so different from the tourists, cricket games and picnics of summer. When the holidaymakers came it was always nice to see it being used, and when they left it was a relief. A rest. Now it sat as a green buffer, between the land and the sea, quiet and waiting.

My shoes squeaked on the stone steps up to number 28. I didn't pause, in case Morag called me from her basement flat, not wanting to get caught up. My key slid into the lock of the front door as though oiled, a perfect fit, having been partners for over twenty years.

I ran through a checklist in my head. Shower. Walk Dodge. Finish off the website content for a medical client I'd won, promoting their practice in Norwich. The last job before I put my out-of-office on for the Christmas holidays. Send out a few invoices for copy written earlier this month. Write the town-council minutes. Notify the county council of the need for CCTV for the pier. Then I was done – almost. I mustn't forget to register the most recently broken street-light, although it probably wouldn't get fixed for a month as it wasn't an emergency.

A surge of excitement rushed through me. After those chores, all I had to do was get the house ready for the girls. The twins were coming home for the first time since we dropped them for Freshers' Week and my arms ached to hold them as much as they had when picking them up from infants' school so many years ago. It wasn't just their first time away from us, but their first time away from each other. Kit had chosen Bristol and Jess Exeter, and I felt a deep urge for us to be all together again. Phone calls were good, FaceTime was better – I could read their expressions – but I wanted to see them in the flesh, smell their skin, hug them to me. We had them for a whole week, all to ourselves, supposedly to celebrate my fiftieth birthday. But in truth, no present could top them coming home.

The phone was ringing as I opened the door. I slung my keys into the bowl and ran to answer it.

'So, would you mind if Ivo came back with me?'

It was Kit on the phone and I could imagine her biting her lip the other end, waiting on my decision.

It hadn't taken her long to get to the reason for her call. A quick hello, a question about my morning swim, expression of how excited she was to be coming home. I'd kicked my trainers off and climbed into the corner of the window seat, looking across South Green as she chatted. Just hearing her voice on the other end made me realise how much I'd missed her.

'What, tomorrow?' I said, playing for time, trying to work out how I felt about the request.

Ivo was apparently the new boyfriend. She'd mentioned him once or twice on the phone. But we'd never met. Did I really want a strange boy in my house for a whole week?

'Yeah. Thought he could stay with us and join in the fun?'

She was trying to sell it to me. Make it sound like it was all about him coming to join in my birthday celebrations. I hesitated. I'd been so looking forward to seeing her and Jess. To having them home in their beds for a week, just the four of us – and Morag, of course. Couldn't forget her, much as I'd like to sometimes.

'Doesn't he have family of his own that are missing him?' I asked, answering a question with a question.

'Does that mean no?' she said immediately and I heard the hurt in her voice.

'I'm not saying no…' I said, trying another tack. 'I just didn't realise you'd got that serious?'

It must have been a month ago I'd heard her mention his name for the first time. Ivo. It was unusual enough for me to ask about it. Where did it originate from? Kit had snorted. She had 'no idea, but it's cool'. Since then, many of her texts or calls had his name in them. They'd been to a pub. They'd watched a band. He'd driven her home.

'Well we're not getting married yet, if that's what you're asking.' She sounded sulky suddenly, not getting her way. Typical Kit. She'd always been up and down as a child. She either shone bright or darkened the room.

'Tell me a bit about him?' I said to get her back on side, tucking my legs underneath me, leaning back on the cushion. Dodge padded into the room and lay down beside me.

'He's gorgeous.' She giggled.

'I'm sure he is.' I laughed, stroking the dog's silky ears. 'Tell me.'

'He's a mature student,' she said. This was the first I'd heard of it. Images of a bearded hippie flooded my mind.

'How old is he then?' I asked, as casually as possible.

'Twenty-four.'

Relief washed over me. Not old at all. In fact I wasn't even sure the word mature would apply, but I'd wait and see.

'He works at our student union, but doesn't go to Bristol Uni,' she said, humouring me. 'He goes to UWE over the other side of the city.'

'What's he studying there?' I asked.

'Photography,' she said. 'He sees things in a really different way.'

'He's arty then?' I said.

'Really creative,' she said.

'And he works at your bar?' I repeated.

'They'd filled all the jobs at his,' she explained. 'You have to get in quick.'

'So is that where you met?'

'Yep, he gave me free shots all night,' she said and I could hear her smiling. I knew her dimples would be deep into her cheeks. My eyes flicked to the photos on the mantelpiece, the toothy grins of her and her sister. From babes in arms through the pigtail years, to holding Dodge, newly rescued, between them after their first day at secondary school.

Dodge thumped his tail on the carpet, bringing me back to the present, and I sank my free hand into the hair of his coat.

'Would he even want to come back with you?'

'He'd love to,' she said, decisively. 'Says he came to Southwold as a really young boy and has never been back since.'

So they'd already discussed it. That made it awkward to say no. Kit had a tendency to do this. Arrange things and expect everyone to fall in with her, which they normally did. Especially Jess, who was happy to go with the flow. Although Jess had been born as twin number one, she'd followed Kit in everything ever since.

'What about Jess?' I asked then and heard Kit pause.

'What about her?' she said.

'She's not bringing a friend back with her,' I said, not wanting Jess to feel left out.

'She'll be okay.' Kit laughed. 'She met him last weekend, she liked him.'

'Where did she meet him?' I asked, confused.

'We went to Exeter for a gig and Jess joined us for drinks.'

I felt a pang for their life without me. The fact that they didn't need me for lifts, or arrangements. They cooked their own teas, put themselves to bed. I hadn't plaited a braid or steadied a bike for years. But simultaneously I felt pleased they'd seen each other. They'd always been so close. The fact that they chose to see each other without me prompting them made my heart swell.

However, this was the first I'd heard of their meeting and I'd spoken to them both earlier in the week, at least once. It made me think they'd all discussed the holidays when they were together and come up with a plan of attack. Nothing like being the last to know.

'Well, suppose I'd better go,' I said, giving in to the inevitable, hoping David would go along with it too. 'Now that I've got to make up the spare room...'

I wouldn't refuse her. Although I'd been looking forward to it just being the four of us for the week, it would be good to meet the new boyfriend. Maybe he might last longer than the last one. Kit always had boys in tow; they seemed drawn to her. She, however, had a low boredom threshold and went through them like a knife through butter. David used to sing 'Another One Bites the Dust' every time she dumped someone.

'Mum, really!' she said with a very teenage groan. 'There's no need to do that.' So they were sleeping together too.

'Not sure Dad is going to like that, Kit,' I warned.

'You can talk him round, Mum,' she said. 'Come on, I'm eighteen.'

'You're still his little girl,' I said. 'And what about what Granny will think?' I could picture Morag's face already.

'Seriously Mum. We're grown-ups,' she said, and then giggled. 'And we're shagging like bunnies down here.'

I laughed. Classic Kit.

'Can't wait to see you,' I said. '*Both* of you.'

Saturday 16 December

Sea temperature: 9 degrees.
Air temperature: 6 degrees.

The current was strong this morning, running parallel to the shore. I had to pull harder with every stroke, kick more fiercely with my legs, to push through. It was like swimming against a force, an underwater energy holding me back. My thighs were burning from both exertion and cold by the time it was halfway-time in my swim, and I'd only reached the level of the lighthouse, tucked on land between tiny cobbled streets. I decided to push on in the same direction for another minute or two, knowing that as soon as I turned, the current would get me back to my starting point in half the time.

Nancy and I were the only ones in again this morning. The water was empty, blank, ours. The sky was a low rumble of gunmetal grey, the threat of rain not far away. Wading in had brought the inevitable involuntary gasp and then the thrill of being part of the sea.

I'd left David in bed with a coffee to enjoy his first morning of the Christmas holidays. He'd waved from his pillow and said something about making us brunch for when I got back. That would be nice. He'd prepare muffins with crisped bacon and poached eggs; a full coffee pot and the newspapers. It was one of the luxuries of having grown-up children. No early mornings anymore. David able to watch the Formula One at the weekends without having to pick someone up or drop them off somewhere. No interrupted meals. Mind you, it would be our last meal on our own for a while; the girls should be here by early afternoon. And the boyfriend, of course. Ivo.

I checked my watch again. Time to turn. I circled, and took a moment to lift my head and check Nancy was where she should be, then scanned the sea ahead for other swimmers, obstacles, buoys, boats. Nothing. The coast was literally clear. Now on my every fourth stroke I saw watery glimpses of the beach, the promenade, as I snatched my next breath. From my position in the sea I felt separate from the land, the town. I felt strong. I felt free.

Everything was ready for them to come home. David had laughed at me when I mentioned making up the spare room. 'It's fine,' he'd said, with a shake of his head, 'she's old enough to do what she wants.' Although when I'd mentioned his mother, he'd agreed that perhaps we should get Kit to keep up the pretence of spare rooms, rather than give Morag a heart attack.

The fridge was full of things David and I hadn't bought since the summer. The pear cider that Jess loved. The Brie that Kit ate with grapes. The tub of mixed olives with feta, even though I knew they'd only eat the green ones. The babyish things they'd never grown out of. Banana Nesquik to mix into their milk. Frube yoghurts that they sucked straight from the tubes. All their favourites, to make them smile. It would be so nice to have them home. Although they'd probably be driving me mad and treating the house like a hotel within a few hours.

The current was behind me now and my strokes were easier as it powered me towards home, which was suddenly where I wanted to be. I made my marker in just a few minutes and waded out, just as Nancy did the same a few feet down the shingle. We grinned at each other in triumph. Nancy punched the air and whooped.

Five minutes later I was dressed and walking back to South Green. The warmth was retuning, the buzz was kicking in. Every cell of my body hummed with its own energy. I was alive. I was excited. I was on top of the world.

'They're here,' I shouted, too loud, to David, who was only five feet away in his armchair by the fire. He jumped and Dodge barked at the level of my voice, reflexively. I'd been on the window seat for the past hour, craning my neck to look into any strange cars that drove past. We'd not set a specific time for the girls and it was a good four- or five-hour drive, so I knew their time of arrival would be totally governed by what time they had woken that morning. After brunch I'd cosied myself in the corner of the window with a book, pretending I wasn't waiting. Aware of every approaching motor. Trying to determine whether they slowed as they came past or were carrying on towards Ferry Road. When finally the battered, bottle-green VW Polo pulled in to the parking spot outside and I saw Jess waving from the back window, I sprang from my spot.

Dodge danced round my legs as I opened the front door. David was there with me and suddenly there was Morag at the bottom of the steps, out of her own basement door, between the car and us. She must have been watching from her window, too. Trust her to get there first.

The car doors spilled open and Jess tumbled out, dragging a canvas holdall the size of at least three washing loads. She was barefaced, hair caught in some kind of dark-blond bun, trendy tortoiseshell glasses dwarfing her face.

'Hi Gran.' She kissed Morag, who then held her at a distance with both hands, to get a proper look.

'You're a sight for sore eyes, Jessie,' she said, pulling her back in for a hug. Jess grinned at me over Morag's shoulder and rolled her eyes.

'I've only been away for a few weeks, Granny,' she said, lugging her bag towards me.

In fact, it had been a few months. Three actually and it felt like longer, to me anyway. But when she got to me and we hugged, it all melted away.

'Hi, Mum,' she said into my shoulder, smelling of apple shampoo and soap as she squeezed me.

'God, I've missed you,' I told her, because it was true. She grinned and moved to David, who took her bag from her shoulders, dumped it on the step and wrapped her in a bear hug that lifted her feet off the ground.

Kit was out of the car now, heaving her laundry from the boot, swearing low under her breath with the weight of it.

'Your dad will help with that,' Morag said, stepping towards her and planting a kiss on her cheek. 'I'm so glad you made it back,' she said, clasping her hands together.

'I was only in Bristol, Gran,' said Kit, 'Not Antarctica!' She left her bag where it was on the road and bounded up the steps past Morag. I had my arms open already by the time she reached me, and held my other girl close for a few seconds, feeling the strength in her, the energy in her body.

She chuckled and whispered, 'Gran's still one for the dramatic, then?' into my ear and I smiled.

'Hi, darling,' I said into her hair, which hung long and wavy, slightly tousled, a shade or two darker than mine. She was already moving onto David, and my hand trailed off her arm.

It was then that I saw him. Ivo. He'd got out the driver's side and was leaning on the car roof, watching us. The first thing I noticed was the loose black curl of his own shoulder-length hair. It was beautiful. He caught it up quickly between his hands and wrapped it into some kind of man-bun at the back of his head.

Kit remembered him at the same instant and ran back down the steps. She led him round the car and into full view, their hands entwined.

'This is Ivo,' she said, and swung both of their hands endearingly.

Hi, Ivo,' said David, walking towards him, hand outstretched. They were of similar height, Ivo maybe just pipping him. They shook hands firmly, as men do. 'Good to have you here.'

'Thanks for having me, Mr Walker,' said Ivo, immediately earning himself Brownie points for manners.

'Call me David,' David said, and clapped him on the shoulder.

'You're Kit's young man, are you?' said Morag and both girls groaned, but Ivo put his hand out to her as well, with a good-humoured smile.

'You must be Granny,' he said with a grin. I sucked my breath, wondering what Morag would think of that, at the 'audacity', but she smiled back at him, even giggled. 'That's me,' she said.

Then he was looking at me and it was my turn. I felt oddly awkward under his gaze, this young man, handsome, unfamiliar. Dodge wound his way round the girls' legs, one after the other, as pleased as us to have them home. I joined them all at the rear of the car.

I put my hand out.

'Hi Ivo,' I said. 'I'm Belle.'

He caught my hand in both of his, a hold and a shake at the same time.

'Belle,' he said. We met eyes and his were black as night. 'Nice to finally meet you.'

Dodge barked and the girls laughed, bending to make a fuss of him as he wiggled and wagged around their legs. Ivo squeezed my hand and then let go, slowly, and I tucked it into my pocket.

David and Ivo managed the bags between them and dragged them out the back to the utility room.

'Easier to unload to the washing machine,' I said, predicting correctly that the girls would have brought back their entire wardrobes.

Kit, Jess and Morag moved through to the kitchen, the girls hanging coats on the bannisters as they passed, the same spot they used to hang their satchels after school. Chairs were pulled out around the old wooden kitchen table behind me, the girls settling with sighs of contentment. I wondered how it felt for them, coming back for the first time. Everything still the same. The table they did their homework on. Well-thumbed recipe books on the shelf. Dodge's wicker basket in the corner.

'It's nice to be home,' Jess said, stretching, as though reading my mind.

'Shall we have a cuppa, Belle?' Morag said, staying put, so I filled the kettle with water and put it on the Aga top as David and Ivo came in.

'It wasn't too bad. Jess stayed with us last night so we just had to come up from Bristol,' Ivo was saying. I noted the 'us' with a small smile.

'It's a long drive though,' David said, 'slower this end as the roads turn to single carriageway.'

They joined the girls at the table, Ivo sitting next to Kit, who immediately put her hand on his thigh.

'Tea or coffee, Ivo?' I asked.

'Tea,' he said. 'Please.' I lifted the big teapot from the shelf and chucked a handful of tea bags into it. Morag saw me and sniffed. She was a traditionalist for loose tea leaves. I couldn't be doing with it. Always picking a stray brown leaf from your teeth afterwards. Strainers and the like. I really couldn't taste the difference anyway. I set about putting mugs on the table, a sugar bowl, a milk jug.

By the time I placed the teapot on the table next to a plate of special cookies I'd bought, and sat down, the girls were chatting and laughing as if they'd never been away. Jess, next to me, was doodling on my notepad for council meetings. She'd found a clean sheet and was drawing a border of swirls and spirals, just like she'd done in her old school books.

'So, how's it going?' I asked her.

'Great, but I need a detox!' She grinned. 'Some good food and less alcohol!'

'Some people just seem to be able to party every night!' Kit agreed.

'Is that you then?' I asked her but she shook her head.

'But only because I can't afford it!' All three of them laughed.

'So social life is a big tick then,' I said. 'And work-wise? You on top of everything?'

Jess nodded thoughtfully at her doodle. She was studying English literature. She had been a bookworm from the day she learned to read.

'Great,' she said, looking up. 'The reading list is pretty heavy but I'm loving it.' She'd been set on the course since for ever, never interested in anything else. We used to find her, curled around a book, at all times of day or night – when she was meant to be getting ready for school, when she was meant to be asleep already – lost in another world in between the pages.

'Hard work reading books, isn't it Jess?' Kit laughed, and Jess smiled good-naturedly over her glasses.

'Next term we're doing a study of illegitimate children in literature, comparing authors through history – Shakespeare, George Eliot, for example.'

'That sounds interesting,' David said, probably while he wondered how that might help her get a job in three years' time. I flashed him a grin as he swilled the teapot and started to pour mugs of tea.

'It really is,' Jess said earnestly, going back to her drawing. 'I'm learning loads. And the people on my course are so cool. They just think like I do – reading... writing... and more reading! Perfect.'

'What about you, Kit?' I asked her across the table, passing the first mug of tea to Ivo and pushing the biscuits his way. 'How's the world of Public Relations?' Kit glanced at Ivo, bit the side of her cheek.

'It's okay,' she said with a shrug. 'But I'm not sure it's me.'

This was news.

David paused mid-pour and then forced himself to carry on. I knew this tactic of his. Never express shock. No matter what is said.

'Really?' I asked, tone neutral, handing the next mug to her. 'Why do you say that?'

'Well.' Kit twirled a strand of hair around her index finger. 'The people on my course are all quite shallow…'

Aha, so she hadn't made any proper friends yet. Maybe that was it. She wasn't really used to being on her own. She'd always had Jess as her wing-woman before. Jess who went along with pretty much anything she suggested, unless it went against any of her many campaigning topics – women, homelessness, abortion rights. The topic had changed regularly but she'd always been one for standing up for the underdog.

'What about the course, though?' David said, sitting back in his chair with his own cup. 'How's that?'

Kit lifted her shoulders, held them up round her ears and then blew out through her lips and dropped them again. An exaggerated shrug.

'Not quite what I imagined, so far,' she admitted, and I felt a tug of disappointment for her. Kit always had high expectations, and sometimes it was to her detriment. She tended to build things up in advance and then feel let down when they didn't quite measure up. She shook herself.

'Let's not talk about it now,' she said, making me think there was something more she wanted to say. 'We've plenty of time.'

She took a noisy sip of her tea to change the subject.

'But Ivo's course is really cool!' she said, making him the centre of attention.

'Ah, yes, photography?' David said, passing round cookies and probably again wondering how you make a living out of that.

'He's brilliant,' Kit said. 'And the assignments he gets are so interesting.'

Morag frowned at her tea before taking a very cautious sip. Anyone would think it was going to kill her.

'What sort of things?' I asked, nibbling on a pistachio-nut cookie.

Ivo turned towards me, leaned forward on his elbows. His skin was pale against the black of his hair, the dark of his eyes. But I supposed between working in a darkroom and in a bar, he didn't get much fresh air and sunshine.

'Different experiment every week,' he said. 'Designed to help you work out your style. So we've tried taking photos of the same thing every day in a different way, you know, like this teapot.' He put his hands on the teapot and moved it an inch to the left, and then a quarter-turn to the right. It still looked like a teapot to me, but I smiled and nodded, encouraged him on.

'We've taken portraits with eye contact and no eye contact. We've asked everyone who sits on a certain park bench if we can take their portrait.'

'And do they say yes?' asked Morag.

'About half the time,' said Ivo.

'Vanity probably.' Morag sniffed. 'Thinking you're going to make them look better than they do.'

Kit rolled her eyes, safe in the knowledge Morag couldn't see her, sitting next to her as she was.

'But we've also tried street photography – that's my favourite so far. When you take pictures of people when they are unaware. Catch them exactly as they really are.'

Kit reached for another cookie, her third, and crammed it into her mouth whole.

'Sounds fascinating,' I said.

'He's really good,' Kit mumbled round her mouthful.

'You've seen some?' David asked.

'Just the ones on his iPhone,' she said. 'The rest of his portfolio is at uni.'

'You hungry, love?' David laughed as she chomped noisily.

'Sorry, felt a bit travel-sick earlier, couldn't eat any breakfast when we stopped at the services.' She grinned. 'Big night last night.' She swallowed and wiped her mouth on the back of her hand.

'I remember the days,' David said with a grin at me.

'Show them the one of me,' Kit said, nudging Ivo. Jess snorted next to me.

'Might have known it,' she muttered with a smile.

Ivo took his phone from the front pocket of his hoodie and started to scroll.

'Don't worry, Dad, it's not indecent.' Kit grinned and I couldn't help but chuckle at the look on her granny's face. 'I've got all my clothes on.'

'For once,' Jess joked.

'That one?' said Ivo, flashing his phone for her approval. She nodded and he held it over the table to David, who peered at it. He rocked slightly back on his seat as he considered it, and then nodded to Ivo,

'Wow, you've really caught her.' He passed the phone to me.

There was Kit, laughing with another girl outside a café. Her head was thrown back, mouth open and eyes squinted shut. Her thighs were squeezed together as though worried for her bladder. She clutched at the girl's forearm for balance. I could almost hear her laughing. I could feel the joy. It was a great photograph.

'I love it,' I said. 'Could I have a copy?'

'Of course,' he said, genuinely pleased. 'I'll text it to you.' He reached to take the phone back from me, flashing me a glimpse of a tattoo on the back of his hand, half hidden under his sleeve. I recited my number and he tapped it in. The photo pinged across to me instantly. I heard its beep in the other room.

'That's why I like candid shots,' he said. 'You really catch the person.'

'Are there others?' I asked, finishing my tea.

He scrolled through his photo reel, lifted an eyebrow at the last one as though appraising it and then stood to bring me the phone.

'This?' he asked.

I leaned in. There we were, outside the house, not an hour ago. David stood slightly behind me. Jess was kneeling to pet Dodge. And in the foreground, at the top of the steps, I had my arms wrapped round Kit, my chin on her shoulder, my eyes shut with the sheer pleasure of holding her.

'You're good,' I said in amazement. 'You're really good.'

'Do you really think so, Belle?' he said. 'That means a lot.'

I looked up and he was standing so close I could see the shadow of his beard. I swallowed. He flicked a smile and glanced away.

A walk was called for, a chance to show Ivo around the town, to admire the Christmas lights. Everyone disappeared to find walking clothes, thicker jumpers, coats and beanie hats. Morag scuttled away downstairs to layer up, determined to come with us. I couldn't hold it against her, bless her, she'd missed them too. I rinsed the cups and stacked them in the dishwasher before running upstairs to get my gloves. The wind on the front would be biting.

I glanced out on to South Green as I rummaged through my drawers. Several families were already out, strolling towards the promenade or down to Ferry Lane to head to the dunes.

Dodge barked downstairs and I knew David would have picked his lead off the hook. The dog would be bounding around his legs, generally getting in the way. There was music playing in the house; one of the girls must have connected their phone to our speaker. There was a hum of conversation, a laugh somewhere, the bang of a door. I could feel the buzz of it. The life they brought with them. I hadn't noticed how quiet it had been, just David and me. We'd just got used to it over the past few months. Now it felt like there was a fizz in the air.

I found my gloves and pulled my bedroom door closed on the way out, and glanced into Kit's room automatically as I passed. They were both in there, Kit and Ivo, standing by the bed, kissing. His hand behind her head, tangled in her hair. Her eyes shut, face tilted to his mouth. I looked away, quickly, not wanting them to see me looking. A heat flooded my neck. It was so intense. Too private for me to see.

I'd seen Kit kissing before, obviously. It wasn't possible to be the mum of two teenage girls and not see them at some point 'snogging', as David called it. Outside the community centre discos at closing time, or on the beach at a BBQ. But they'd been teenage in comparison. This looked like a lot more than that.

Downstairs, I found a ball for Dodge and a spare hat for Jess, before they came down, Kit's lips glistening. Ivo threw his arm round her shoulder as we set off down the front steps to a waiting Morag at the bottom.

I was right. The wind nipped at ears and fingers. Kit led the way, pointing things out to Ivo as she went. The pub she had her first (legal) drink in. The bus stop she waited at every day for the school bus. The house her friend Tovey used to live in before they moved to Norwich.

Jess walked between us, chatting. Morag had taken up her usual position, next to David, marching along as if her life depended on it.

Turning right off the promenade, Kit led the way across Gun Hill to the dunes. As we turned into the wind Dodge strained at his lead, knowing he was going to be allowed off, and as soon as David released him he bounded away on to the beach. The girls followed him, drawn to the sea. The waves crested white in the darkness. We walked along the shoreline, listening to the rattle of the water on the stone, letting the wind blow our bones clean.

'Did you swim this morning, Mum?' Kit asked over her shoulder.

'Sure did,' I said with a smile.

Ivo was looking at me with his mouth open.

'Today?' he asked.

'Every day of the year,' David said, and pulled me towards him, tucking me under one arm, where I fitted perfectly.

'My God. That must be freezing,' Ivo said.

'You get used to it,' I said. 'Really.' It was true. Acclimatisation stood me in good stead. As long as I dipped at least a few times a week, I held my level of tolerance. But I preferred to swim daily. I had to, in fact. It gave me something I needed, a buzz, a feeling of euphoria. It was addictive.

He shook his head as if in disbelief.

'There's a group of us. The Southwold Sea-girls. We've done it for years. Ever since the twins were small.'

'Isn't it dangerous?' he said, looking at the horizon. A tanker headed north, far out to sea.

'Not if you know what you're doing, and we all swim with buddies at this time of year. You just need to know your limits. It's really good for you actually, physically and men-tally.' I said. 'Do you swim?'

He nodded and grinned. 'Just never in December.'

Kit took his hand. 'I have,' she said.

'We all have,' Jess clarified. 'The whole family used to take part in the Boxing Day Dip. It was good fun.'

'Even you, Granny?' Ivo asked and I had to swallow a smile, but Morag puffed her chest up in her duffel coat.

'Even me,' she said. 'Every year, without fail, since we moved here. I wouldn't miss it.'

'Granny's well known around this beach actually,' Kit said. 'She saved a boy from drowning.'

Ivo turned to Morag, giving her his full attention.

'Ach, that was a long time ago,' she said, loving it. She was right, it was a long time ago. Not long after we moved here together, her in the granny flat and us above, the only way to afford the beautiful house on South Green. When David was starting out as a teacher and Morag had just retired. When I first realised how isolated a seaside town could be in winter. Before boredom set in. Before babies. Before everything.

A boy had fallen off his lilo, way out further than he should be, and Morag had spotted him from the beach and run in. I'd been amazed at her confidence, her determination. By the time she reached him there was a crowd watching on the sand, the boy's mum among them, holding her own face in her hands, open-mouthed but unable to say a word as Morag towed him back safely to shore. She didn't even make a sound when Morag gave him CPR, breathing her own air into his lungs. Only when he coughed up a mouthful of water did a noise come out of the mother's mouth, a cry of relief like I'd never heard. Morag brushed the sand from her knees and stood up to a round of applause and claps on the back. I wrapped a towel round her.

'I can't believe you did that,' I'd said.

'I just did what I had to do,' she'd replied.

'Well, Granny,' Ivo said now. 'Glad to know I'm in safe hands.'

Morag flapped her hand at him, but when he looked away she gave Kit a little nod of approval and Kit beamed. The boy was doing well.

It was late but I didn't want the day to end. Dinner had gone down well, slow-cooked stew, one of my specialities. Bowls had been wiped clean with chunks of crusty bread. Candles burned low on the table, music played in the background. Rioja was passed round and poured, long after the food was finished. We lolled in our chairs, red-cheeked from our walk, the fire and red wine. Dodge snored in his basket. Morag hid several yawns behind her hand before pushing her chair back.

'I'm away to my bed,' she said. 'See you tomorrow.' Jess held her hand out to her as she passed her chair and Morag lifted it to her lips. David stood with her.

'I'll see you down,' he said, following her into the hall.

'Ach, I'm fine. I'm not old yet, you know.' We heard her open the front door and the smack of her kiss on his cheek.

'I'll just watch you from the top then, Mum,' he said, and it was a moment before he clicked the front door shut and slid the bolt.

Morag's leaving seemed to give the kids a cue to go too. Jess was off to watch something on Netflix on her iPad in bed. Kit and Ivo said they were going upstairs to chill. They made their way up the stairs, entwined already. Just as David and I thought we were in the clear to talk, soft feet padded back down and Kit slid round the doorframe.

'Thanks so much for letting Ivo come,' she said. 'He said he's having a great time.' She looked so relieved that I smiled.

'What did you expect?' I laughed. 'Of course we'd make him welcome.'

She shrugged, looked at her socked feet for a moment, and then raised her eyes.

'Do you like him then?' She bit her lip, waiting. David locked the back door and hung the key on its hook.

'He seems really nice,' he said, decisively.

'Mum?' she asked.

I took a deep breath.

'He's lovely, Kit,' I said and she let a grin spread over her face.

'Gorgeous-looking too, eh?' She laughed and I felt Ivo's hand on mine again. The soft hold of his fingers.

'Get out of here.' David rolled his eyes.

'Night,' she called as she turned back to the stairs.

Again, we listened for their door to click closed before David fixed me with a look.

'Well?' he asked, with a lift of his eyebrows. 'What do you *really* think of him?'

I laughed. It was the first time we'd been alone all day to sound out each other's reactions.

'He does seem nice,' I said. 'Good manners, well brought up.' He hadn't put a foot wrong all day.

'Kit's smitten,' he said, and I could only nod. The way she looked at him said everything.

'He likes Formula One too. Although he prefers Verstappen over Hamilton. Poor misguided boy.' He squeezed my shoulder gently as he passed and clicked the music off. 'Coming up?'

'You go,' I said, 'I'm going to sort this out first.' I nodded at the table, the debris of a good meal.

'Want a hand?' he said, as I knew he would.

'It's okay,' I said, looking at the shadows under his eyes. It had been a tough term. 'I'll be up in ten.'

It was nice to be on my own for a few minutes after the excitement of the day. I had a low-level glow of contentment in my tummy. A warmth that the girls were back, that we were together. I stacked the dishwasher, wiped the table, put Dodge out the back door into the black garden and stood at the kitchen window to watch for his return. The house ticked and settled around me, the immersion heater upstairs kicked in as David turned on the shower in our ensuite. Jess's door shut and her blinds were drawn above my head. The fridge hummed. All sounds I knew from the backing track of our lives. I peered into the dark for the dog.

Ivo's reflection in the window made me make a noise out loud, not a word but a sound. He was standing behind me in the kitchen, although I hadn't heard him come in. I spun to face him.

He was bare-chested, wearing only jogging pants that hung dangerously low on his hipbones and a chain that hung round his neck, glinting silver. His feet were bare too, white against the floorboards.

'God, you made me jump!' I said, trying to make a joke out of it, feeling ridiculous.

'Sorry,' he said with a grimace. 'Just wanted to take some water up, if that's okay?'

I nodded, opened the cupboard beside me and busied myself reaching for pint glasses, filling them, giving my heart a moment to return to normal. Looking anywhere but at him, very conscious of his lack of clothes. He was so close I could smell his skin. See the black hair on the tops of his big toes.

He reached out both hands to take the glasses, his tattoo now on full show. A symbol of some kind.

'Thanks,' he said, lifting the glasses towards me slightly in a mock-cheers.

'No problem,' I said, feeling better. The dog barked on the doorstep outside and I let him in, shutting the door quickly to keep out the cold. He ran to his basket, turned round three times in it before throwing himself down. Ivo chuckled.

'Night, Dodge,' he said, balancing on one leg and rubbing the dog's back with his bare foot. Then, as he turned to leave, over his shoulder he said, 'Night, Bella.'

Bella.

My mouth went dry and I could hear the roar of blood in my head like the surge of a tide.

'Ivo…' I said, before I could help myself. He stopped, eyebrows raised. 'Please call me Belle.'

He hesitated, confused. I tried to smile, but it trembled.

'It's just that nobody calls me Bella.'

'Sorry.' He grinned and nodded. 'My mistake. Night then.' Turning, he plodded up the stairs to Kit. I waited until I heard the click of her bedroom door before I breathed out.

I put a hand out to the sink to steady myself. The cold of the enamel felt good against my hot hand. I squinted my eyes shut, trying to block out the things I no longer want to see. Nobody calls me Bella. Not anymore.

I found the pub easily – corner plot, brick-built, on a back street in Aldeburgh. The wooden floor was gritty under my feet, the tables were scratched and sticky. I bagged a stool at the bar and ordered a double rum and Coke. Fran had said she'd be there by eight – her husband would drive her over after she'd put little Stanley to bed. I'd arrived a bit earlier, having caught the bus, my sighs fogging the window until I had to clear it with my hand to see through it to the dark, damp hedgerows. We would share a taxi home later.

It was nice to be somewhere different. A pub that didn't know me and I didn't know it. Exactly what I needed. It was nice not to recognise anyone. Because I didn't recognise myself much recently. I felt much more than a decade away from university. I felt a world away from my 'old self'. I felt like I'd lost myself in domestics and logistics and bills.

Our life in Southwold was one of marriage and in-laws and work. It had been almost ten years of routine since leaving university, ten years of working, saving and Sunday lunches since we'd moved here and bought the house. And somewhere in those ten years, I'd lost the spark of me.

I loved David. We had a solid marriage. A good one. But I longed for something more than slippers and TV series and Sunday trips to Snape Maltings. I felt dormant. I craved something to make me feel alive again.

I just wanted a night out. An evening to break the endless grey in my head. I couldn't remember the last light moment. When I'd laughed out loud, or woken up without a weight on my chest. Probably months ago, when the days were long and the air smelled sweet in the evenings with the jasmine on the back wall. Then every-thing had seemed possible, fun, good.

The pub certainly didn't smell sweet, but it smelled of life and my nostrils flared and sucked it in. My first drink didn't even touch the sides and I waved at the barman for another, ordering two when I'd got his attention, so that Fran had one waiting for her. I made them both doubles.

Recently, life seemed to consist of endless deadlines for work. My copywriting business had taken off but I was not enjoying my success. I was a victim of it. I had a range of clients – government organisations, medical foundations – who all kept me on a retainer to write their newsletters, opinion pieces, policies. I had contacts who helped me whenever I needed them – a freelance network – but we all worked remotely and there was no office banter, no lunches at the pub or drinks after work. The closest I got to a regular chat or a work colleague was with Doctor Sue every Thursday when I checked my copy for factual correctness with her before posting it on the medical website. We'd become virtual friends even though we'd never met face to face. I was lonely. Bored.

And when I wasn't working – once I'd turned off the computer and closed the home-office door – there was just a fridge that needed restocking, a spare room musty with damp washing on the airer. A mother-in-law downstairs. A tired husband who'd discovered motor racing and spent hours on the sofa watching noisy cars race endless laps. Evenings trapped me on the sofa with police dramas and soap operas. Bills got paid. Invoices sent. Hoovering done. The blankness of the sea horizon, the rural expanse of marshes and dunes and rivers all around, hemmed me in. I felt the sea holding me there, pinning me on the land in a tiny, isolated little town, with nowhere to go, nothing to do.

My phone beeped with a text. Fran.

'Sorry, Stanley has just projectile vomited. Stomach bug. Have to cancel. Will make it up to you. xx'

A flash of disappointment, anger even. I didn't want to go home. Tonight I wanted more. I took a long swallow of my drink.

A bass guitar began tuning up in the corner. A man set up microphones.

I checked my reflection in the mirror behind the bar, ran my fingers through my hair. It didn't matter what I looked like anyway. I just wanted to drink, listen to some music, feel some life around me. Dance if I got the chance. For the first time in for ever, a flicker of excitement made me lick my lips. I'd stay. A thrill ran through me at the thought of being alone. Unknown.

Soon, the pub was packed, more people than I'd seen in one place for at least a month. There was a buzz, a feeling of electricity travelling person to person. The guitar kicked in and I felt it right through my body. Every cell vibrated with the bass, my blood echoed the chord.

The band started up for real and the crowd clapped and surged towards the little stage. I turned on my stool to face it, but soon slid off and joined them. People around me, my hands in the air, eyes half-closed, I let myself go in the hope of finding myself again. The anonymity was a relief. For a while, I forgot about deadlines and mortgages and became just another person, in a crowd, dancing. Me.

At the end of the set I retreated, hot and thirsty, to the bar. Condensation ran down the inside of the windows, the floor was slippery now under my feet with spilled beer, but I was flushed, exhausted, feeling better than I had been in months. I ordered a drink and crunched the ice first to cool myself down.

I felt him next to me before I looked. The press of his thigh against my hip, the scent of him, wood and musk. He reached past me and the barman passed him a whisky on ice, a double. I raised my glass at him. Stubble over high cheekbones; tall, angular body.

'That was so awesome,' I said, nodding towards the stage.

His fingers were long, curled round his own drink.

'Saw you on the dance floor,' he said, his voice a hot smoke. 'You looked like you were enjoying yourself.' He gave the slight hint of a smile, more in his eyes than on his mouth.

I drank and then pressed the cool glass against my hot face, recognising the danger.

He called to the barman, who was wiping up, lifted his empty glass, and then nodded his head towards mine too. 'Another, for both of us, thanks.'

'Oh I'm fine, thanks…' I started to say, thinking that I should ask for a taxi number and start the process of getting home.

'Have one with me?' he said as the barman put it in front of me. Looking at him properly, I could see he was older than me. Not much, but a little. White squint lines showed in a tanned face. Bright, dark eyes fringed with lashes a girl would kill for. Hair long enough to be tied back in a ponytail. Something lit inside me.

I picked up the new glass and took a long swallow. Ice clinked a warning. He climbed up onto the stool next to me, his thigh keeping contact with mine. I should have moved it away but I didn't. A charge jumped between us.

'Felix,' he said, putting his hand out to shake. His tongue flicked at his lower lip.

'Belle,' I returned, putting my own hand in his.

'Nice to meet you, Bella,' he said, lifting his glass to his mouth.

Sunday 17 December

Sea temperature: 9 degrees.
Air temperature: 6 degrees.

The wind blew the grasses flat over the dunes and a slate-grey sky merged into the sea on the horizon. I paused momentarily on the sand, tucking my hair into my swim cap. Nancy strode ahead, in the water already, then submerged. Her bright neoprene swimming hat bobbed up and down with every breaststroke. I watched her as I pulled my gloves on to see if I could gauge any current, but she seemed to be steady-paced, consistent, as she settled into her swim.

There was nobody else swimming. A couple of dogs further up bounded after a ball, their owner huddled into the oncoming wind. A cargo boat sat low and heavy where the sea met the sky, heading towards the north. I set my timer.

The tide was on the turn and I felt the suck of it at my calves as I walked in, pulling me outwards, into the deep. The rattle of the stones told me they felt it too as they tumbled with the ebb. I submerged earlier than normal, at thigh level, wanting to join the water, empty my brain. The freeze, the shock took all my thoughts away, leaving the roar, the burn, the momentary panic until my breath eased, my body took over.

I'd left the household sleeping. Creeping along the landing, I'd felt almost awkward passing Kit's closed bedroom door, the thought of her sleeping with Ivo in her childhood bed. I wanted to be gone when they got up; I wasn't ready to see them undone like that, in their PJs or robes, unshowered, intimate. And I wasn't sure how David would cope seeing her like that, either. A woman. A sexual being. A lover. Hopefully by the time I got back from my swim, they'd be ready for the day.

Dodge had stood hopefully as I came downstairs, wagging his tail, but I put him out in the back garden for a pit stop and then encouraged him back to his bed with a biscuit. He could wait. I needed to clear my head.

It was probably the wine, a slight hangover, that tightened at my temples as I swam. The water accentuated it to start with and then the numb let it go. My breath got deeper, more regular.

I hadn't drunk as much wine as that for ages, but it had been lovely, a real treat, to sit, to talk, to have time with the girls. Jess's eyes shone behind her horn-rimmed glasses when she talked of books, telling me of authors I'd never heard of, stories I'd never read. When she stopped to consider things, she looked slightly upwards, as though she was picturing it there, in the air above her head. She smiled without showing her teeth, cheeks pink with the cider she preferred.

Kit had tucked into the wine, regularly topping up her own glass before passing the bottle to Ivo. She sat with her feet in his lap, or lolled against his shoulder, as though she couldn't bear to be apart from him. He responded with a hand on her neck, a massage of her feet, a twist of a strand of her hair.

David and I had been like that. When I thought of university, I remembered the buzz I got, the ache in the pit of my stomach when I saw him on campus. The long looks across the room at random parties, the late nights in smoky bedsits, as we edged closer to each other, pulled by force. After we finally spent the night together, I never went back to my own room. I just stayed, sharing his single bed that meant we slept like spoons, with hardly a breath between us. If he had a lecture, I'd read or write, propped in the corner of the bed, cross-legged, waiting for him to come back. And when I went to a seminar, he'd shop, buying jacket potatoes that he cooked in the shared kitchen, cider for us to drink, laying it all out before me when I opened the door. The ramshackle room, with its damp patch of plaster on the ceiling, the carpet that didn't quite meet the skirting, was the most exotic, erotic place my eighteen-year-old self had ever been. My eyes were constantly dark with shadows, my cheeks permanently flushed as we tumbled in and out of bed, sleeping late, loving often.

I reached my marker, checked my watch, noticed my drift outwards in the tide. Perfect timing. I turned, checked for Nancy ahead of me, strong-stroked and steady, the way ahead all clear. Head down, I stretched out again.

I loved thinking about the early days of David and me. It was good to recall how passionate we were, how much we'd felt, at the beginning. How intense we'd been. How amazed at ourselves and each other we were.

Last night at the kitchen table, I'd felt his hand on the back of my chair, several times, him laying it there, claiming ownership. And when we'd finally gone to bed, he'd turned to me and slung a heavy arm round my waist as he slept. Maybe he was affected by Kit's demonstration of love, too. Maybe it was catching.

Things had changed slowly and I wasn't sad about it, just sentimental. David and I still loved each other, deeply, and had got to this point, thirty-odd years later, with hardly a blip. But now our love was a softness, an intimacy, rather than a burn of passion. Those waves had morphed into comfort, or reassurance, and lovemaking was now a gentle ebb and flow. Still good, just different.

I spotted the cobalt blue of our beach-hut door on my breath stroke, and turned inwards towards the shore. It took a dozen strong final strokes against the force of the sea before I could stand, then walk jelly-legged towards the shallows. Nancy waved and whooped as she headed up the beach. Even then, the outgoing tide pulled at me still, not letting me go until my ankles lifted clear of the break. As my booties hit the sand, I saw Dodge race towards me, ball in mouth, and behind him, David. Scarf wrapped tight, collar up, he held out my Dry Robe and, when I reached him, he wrapped me like he used to wrap the girls after a bath. And I felt like they must have: warm, safe, loved.

Betty raised her hand to us from behind the bar of the Sole Bay Inn, and pointed to the best table – the round one in front of the window. I'd reserved it earlier in the week so that we could look straight out onto the lighthouse.

David led the way, peeling off layers as he went. The wind had called for gloves and scarves, and had driven the tears from the corner of our eyes. But it had been fresh, blown away memories, and turned the girls' cheeks pink. I diverted straight to the ladies' to remove my bobble hat and run my fingers through my hair. Everyone was seated when I got back, a space left for me between David and Kit. I squeezed in, hanging my coat on the back of the chair alongside the others, looking to see where everyone had ended up.

'Ivo was just asking about the lighthouse, Mum,' Kit said as they both gazed at its white tower opposite.

'We'll go in, and up to the top, while you're here,' I said to Ivo, who was next to Kit. It wasn't unexpected for him to be there, but it was Jess's normal seat. 'It's a good view from up there on the right day.'

'Not today, though!' Kit interrupted, turning back to the table. 'Ivo wants to go to the pier today. And there's only so much excitement we can take.' She laughed, rubbing her hand on his thigh. She'd give him a friction burn at this rate. She literally couldn't seem to keep her hands off him. He didn't seem to mind though, long legs relaxed under the table.

'True.' I laughed. 'Kit's right, Ivo. The pier is enough for one day.'

Drinks were ordered, ciders and wine, bottled beer for Ivo and Kit. Morag had a whisky.

'Make sure it's Scottish,' she reminded the waiter.

I noticed she'd taken the seat the other side of Ivo, poor boy, and kept holding his elbow to get his attention. I sipped my wine. Betty came over herself to take the order, fuchsia-pink lipstick bleeding into the lines around her mouth. I could smell the cigarette smoke on her from my seat. Pulling her pencil out from behind her ear, she licked its tip and shook out a new page on her pad. Morag put her external face on, puffing herself up in her chair. As predicted, Betty addressed her first.

'Nice to see you, Morag, how are you keeping?'

'Well, thank you, Betty. You all ready for Christmas?

'Booked solid, love, right up until the day. Pop in for drinks in the morning, will you?' It was a tradition, many years in the making. The girls opened their stockings, and we walked Dodge on the beach before a drink at the Sole Bay while the turkey roasted and browned at home. It was probably the only morning of the year I didn't swim.

'Of course we will, Bet,' Morag said as if it was her decision to make. I studied the menu, irritated.

'You all right, girls?' Betty asked the twins and they both replied, bright smiles, public faces.

'Not doing the pantomime this year then, Kit?' She teased and Kit blushed to the roots of her hair.

'Not doing that anymore, Betty!' she said with a quick glance at Ivo. So she hadn't told him about her love of the stage as a child, her endeavours to be famous. The embarrassment at the local pantomime when she fell through the trapdoor in the middle of a scene. Luckily nobody had been hurt, apart from their ribs from laughing. I glanced at Kit now and she threw me a warning glance to say nothing. I smiled a reassurance.

'Right, what's everyone having?' Betty asked and lowered her eyes to her pad. Orders were placed and she bustled off, saying something about 'quick service for the local hero'. Morag literally preened and nudged Ivo so that he knew it was another reference to her life-saving. I took a swallow of my drink and turned towards David, who was telling a story about school. After a few seconds I knew which one it was, but settled in for the laugh.

'It was year four,' he said, 'they're about eight years old, not even in my part of school.' His school was private, taking boys from four to eighteen, and he taught History in the upper school.

'I'd been pulled in to do PE because Stu was off sick. It's not normally the kind of thing I do, and I guess I'm a bit rusty with how these things work.' He took a pull of his pint, leaned forward on his elbows on the wooden tabletop.

'I'm at the front of the field, demonstrating how to do a drop-kick, and a pretty impressive one it was too,' he acknowledged with a grin. 'But when I turned round, half of them weren't even watching, they were passing balls to each other, trying to juggle, rolling on the floor. I'd forgotten about how to teach that age group. Their attention span is terrible. They have to be given precise instructions, just one thing at a time.' Someone tried to squeeze behind him on their way to the bar and David pulled his chair closer to the table.

'Anyway,' he started again. 'They're all lined up behind me, so I told them to hold their balls still while I showed them again. I did another drop-kick, not bad either, even if I do say so myself, and turned round to see fifteen boys all holding their privates in their hands – keeping their balls still!'

Even though I'd heard it before I laughed again, more at the cackle that came out of Kit's mouth than anything else. Everyone was laughing, even Morag, although she flapped her hand in David's direction.

'Dad's got loads of stories like that, haven't you, Dad?' Jess said. 'Like when you accidentally locked a student in the cupboard for an entire lesson?'

'Or when you were on playground duty and that seagull crapped on your head!' Kit snorted, reaching across me to grab David's sleeve.

'Or when he set himself on fire with our science kit, trying to show us how to do an experiment!' Jess said, to Kit now, and the two of them shared a laugh, which made my chest swell. They might not be sitting next to each other, but they were still connected.

'The best one was the sex education lesson, where you get the kids to call out all the slang words for their genitals to take the embarrassment out of it all, and you write them on the board' – Kit clutched at Ivo now, almost beside herself – 'and he only went and wrote them on the board in PERMANENT MARKER!'

'I was scrubbing at it for days,' David admitted. 'Trying to get rid of the word WANGER.' Kit wiped her eyes. Ivo laughed loudly. 'Teaching's a funny business.'

'Not always, though, Dad,' Jess said, wiping her eyes too and putting her specs back on. 'Remember that lesson your friend did on genes?'

David paused for a moment, remembering. 'Now that *was* awkward,' he said, shaking his head. 'I really felt for him when he told us about it in the staffroom.'

'What was that, then?' said Ivo, taking the bait.

'It was a lesson on recessive genes: how they determine things from parent to child, like eye colour.'

Ivo nodded, drank from his bottle of lager.

'There was one student who just couldn't get it, kept asking the same question again and again, so my friend went over to his desk to help him through it, using examples, while the other kids worked on their own, but he just kept shaking his head. In the end, my friend asked what colour eyes his parents had.' He looked round the table, building the suspense.

'"They both had blue," he said.' Ivo leaned in and David grimaced at him with the memory. 'The boy's eyes were the brownest eyes ever, apparently. Then my friend knew why he was confused. It was nothing to do with his teaching. It was the fact that the boy had just realised there was no way he could have been their child. I don't know how these things work but apparently it was scientifically impossible.' He blew out his breath, took a drink.

'That's awful,' said Ivo, looking horrified. 'What did your friend do?'

'Thank God he was saved by the bell,' David said, putting his hand over mine on the table. 'Never so glad to hear it ring in his whole life.'

I rubbed his fingers and he squeezed my hand back.

'That's terrible,' said Morag, tapping the table to get attention. 'That family tree now has another branch on it that nobody knows is there. A life built on lies.'

'We don't know that, Gran, the parents might have adopted him and they just hadn't told him yet?' Jess placated.

'Or they might have had to use a donor and just not found the right way to talk about it?' Kit added in.

'Whatever it was, it was a secret. And that made the lineage a lie.' Morag sipped her whisky with a very pursed mouth and there was an awkward silence, during which I saw Kit nudge Ivo's leg under the table.

'Gran's into family trees,' she said by way of explanation.

'Genealogy, to give it its correct term.' Morag sniffed. 'It's my love of history that probably gave David his.'

'Wow,' said Ivo and I smiled at his enthusiasm, bless him. 'Have you researched yours?'

It was the right thing to say and Morag gave him a smile and placed her glass on the coaster in front of her.

'Right the way back to the 1600s,' she said. 'It's important to know your ancestry. It tells you who you are.'

'So what do you know from yours?' Ivo said. 'Apart from names of who married who?'

'I come from a long line of Scots from the Western Isles. David's father came from the south-west of England, from a long line of farmers, but he was a vicar. I can trace bloodlines from the Stuart times right into the veins on the arms of those girls.' She nodded at the twins, pleased with herself.

'That's actually awesome,' Ivo said, nodding, and I felt a surge of appreciation for him.

'It's not easy to do, it's time-consuming and you've got to have real staying power,' Morag said. 'Belle started tracing her own family once, but didn't make it past the Victorians.' She sipped her whisky, smiling my way, and all my nice feelings disappeared. David squeezed my hand. 'But I've done loads of them. It's fascinating.' She cast a quick glance at the bar, nodded her head towards Betty pulling a pint. 'I've done hers,' she said and then dropped her voice to a loud stage whisper, 'she comes from a long line of publicans and prostitutes.'

Jess snorted and gulped at her drink.

'We could make a start on yours, Ivo, while you're here,' Morag carried on regardless. 'I wouldn't mind helping you.'

'I'm not sure we'll have time to get into that, Gran,' Kit tried to interrupt, but Morag wasn't to be put off.

'Well, I could do some for you,' she said. 'All I need is some basic details.' I wouldn't have been a bit surprised if she'd pulled out a notebook and started taking details. 'Tell me about your family?'

Ivo flushed. It crept out of his collar and up the side of his neck.

'Names and where they live?' Morag said, oblivious. Kit slid her hand onto Ivo's thigh and squeezed. Eventually he lifted his eyes from his bottle of beer.

'I don't have a family, actually,' he said. 'My parents are both dead.'

Betty's arrival with a tray of food came at exactly the right time, so that Morag could offer a flustered, 'Oh, I am sorry to hear that,' and then try to change the subject completely, remarking on the beautiful crust on her fish pie. David and I murmured similar thoughts towards Ivo, 'oh how terrible,' 'so sorry,' as we passed orders to the right person.

'You weren't to know,' Ivo said to the table, as though he was reading my mind.

I threw Kit a look, but she was too busy squeezing hands under the table with Ivo. Why hadn't she mentioned it on the phone? I had specifically asked about his family and whether they would be missing him if he came to us for the week. It would have been so easy for her to tell me then, so poor Ivo didn't have to be put on the spot like that. Honestly. Sometimes she was really thoughtless. Everyone picked up knives and forks and got stuck in. 'When did you lose them?' I asked Ivo, more out of sympathy than anything else.

'Dad died when I was ten. Mum never got over it, to tell the truth. She died a few years later.'

'That's really tough,' I said, blowing out a breath.

'Belle's parents died when she was young too,' David said and Ivo turned his eyes to me.

'In a car accident,' I said.

'Both at once?'

I nodded and he shook his head as though unable to take that in. 'But I was sixteen, almost grown. I moved in with my gran for a couple of years and then was away to university—'

'Where you met Dad…' said Kit.

'And lived happily ever after,' said Jess.

'I can't imagine losing parents as young as you did, though. Where did you live?' I asked Ivo.

'Foster homes', he said. 'Some really nice ones.' It was the word 'some' that I noticed. I bit my lip. Poor kid.

'Do you remember a lot about your parents?' David asked, cutting his steak.

'Mum worked at the bakers,' Ivo said with a smile. 'She smelled like fresh bread.'

'And your dad?'

'He loved music. Lived for it really. I remember him playing it so loudly the neighbours used to knock on the door and he'd have to buy them a box of chocolates. He said he should have bought shares in Cadbury's.'

'That's lovely,' Jess said. 'I remember Dad playing records and dancing with me, but I had to stand on his feet and he moved me about.' David grinned at the memory too.

'I love to dance. It's probably something I got from *my* dad. Like David got his history from Granny,' Ivo agreed.

'It's nice to have good memories like that,' I said to him, thinking of my own. My mum and dad swinging me between them by my hands, so that I could jump puddles.

'That's one of the reasons I want to go to the pier. I've had a plaque made for Dad there.'

The pier was lined with them, hundreds of little plaques the size of envelopes attached to the railings for posterity. All

expressions of love or remembrance or occasions marked for-
ever in brass. Birthdays, deaths, retirements, holidays. It was
one of the things that made the pier unique. We'd walked
there for so many years, reading them to each other, remarking on new ones, that everyone in the family had their own
favourite.

'That's nice,' David said, and then almost as an afterthought, 'But why here? Why not where you lived?'

'Dad loved it here, apparently. Mum said he lost his heart
to Southwold,' Ivo said.

'He's got something there,' said David, smiling.

Kit, Ivo and Jess walked ahead, chatting. Ivo had his arm over
Kit's shoulders and she anchored it in place by holding on to
his hand where it rested. Jess, walking next to her sister, swung
her arms to keep warm. Morag tucked her arm into David's,
and did her collar up to the neck as we stepped onto the
boards of the pier, round the side of the white-painted café
and out to sea. The wind had died down and the sun glinted
on the water. Waves broke gently against the iron legs of the
pier beneath us. The heavy metal chains linking stilts to deck
jangled. It was a perfect winter's day. Bright, cold, clean.

Jess checked her watch and then pulled at her sister and
they hurried off, Ivo in tow. A quick check of my own watch
told me the water clock was just about to pour, so my guess
was they wanted Ivo to see it. Visitors loved it: another reason
to visit the pier. The clock, which had originally been
designed as a lesson about water recycling, pumped water up
to its top from a well below, and powered a show every half
an hour when the clock chimed and two tin characters peed
out the water back into the well.

As we stepped on to the planks and made our way out above the shoreline, we almost had the pier to ourselves. Only a handful of other people could be seen.

We started up the northern side, where we would pass my favourite plaque.

'To Bert. Last of the Summer Wine.'

The kids were stopping to read them as they went. Past the shop, optimistically still open but empty of customers, to David's favourite plaque, the anonymous one that read: 'I wish it had been more.'

Morag commented on some of the memorial plaques, friends of hers who had died in years gone by.

It was right at the end, by the telescope you could rent for five minutes with a pound coin, that Ivo stopped. A new strut had been attached to the railings especially for the extra demand for new plaques. He put his hand on the rail and carefully wiped the brass with his sleeve. Jess hung back but Kit stepped in and I wondered if she should give him space, just for a moment. Her lips were moving, not that we could hear, but he nodded and closed his eyes for a second, tight. It felt too private to be watching and I tugged at David's arm to walk past. But as we did, Kit turned to us and beckoned us in.

'Come and see,' she said. 'It looks great.'

I wasn't sure how she could describe a memorial plaque as great, and was starting to question just how sensitive Kit was being. She'd always been close to the drama growing up. If there was ever a crisis, Kit was in it. Ivo, however, stepped back from the rails, made space for us.

'I think he'd like it,' he said, with a sad smile.

The plaque was obviously new. It gleamed in the winter sunlight, in comparison to the dull burnish of its neighbours.

It sat between a birth announcement for baby Poppy and a holiday memory, 'The Grays were here, for sun, sand and beer.'

We gathered round to read.

'For my dad. Until we meet again.' My eyes burned suddenly.

'It's lovely,' I said over the lump in my throat. I put a hand out to hold Ivo's forearm. He shut his eyes and I squeezed gently, sensing the emotion in him.

We left them there a while longer, just the two of them. Jess linked arms with her gran and marched her back off towards home, promising a cup of tea. Morag glanced my way as she said, 'A proper one this time?', which just made Jess giggle and roll her eyes. When I looked back to see if they were following, I saw Kit and Ivo standing in the wind at the end of the pier. Arms round each other, kissing and holding on like they'd never let go, lost to everyone else but each other.

Felix kissed me the first night we met. After the band had packed up and gone and the pub thinned out to a few blurred drunks, we moved to a corner away from the bar. We talked and drank, and all the time his leg scorched mine under the table, pressed, with a heat that I returned. For the first time in a long time, I felt a thrill. I felt interesting. I felt something. He looked at me as though my face was a thing to discover. He watched my mouth as I talked, studied my eyes like he was searching for an answer.

We spoke of writing. Not just the kind of words I wrote for work, the corporate, the informative, the educational. But about the words themselves, the shape of them in our mouths, the sound of them in the air, the impact of them on a page. He told me of a book he read that was one long, continuous sentence from start to end. I told him of an exhibition I'd been to where everything was made out of old books, which made him gasp in horror, and then laugh when I said: no books were harmed in the making of this artwork. He talked of music and closed his eyes when he sang a line, or drummed his fingers on the edge of the drink-stained wooden table. We talked favourite gigs. We named best songs for breakups, for funerals, for falling in love. He told me of summers listening to reggae, or winters discovering rockabilly. Trying out all kinds of music, finding some-thing in them all that made the hairs on the back of his neck stand, or his mouth dry. At closing time, the landlord turned the sign but let us sit on, turning down lights until we were lit by only our table candle and it felt like nothing existed out of the flickering glow. And still, his leg and mine, pressed together.

Eventually I checked my watch and reality began to kick in. I had to go home. The night had to end. I was to go back home, where I knew I'd lie awake, replaying moments of the evening when I'd felt attractive or funny or interesting. Where I'd not had to think about putting the bins out, or what to make for tea. I'd called a cab, with fingers that trembled as they dialled. I didn't want it to end. 'Tell him fifteen minutes,' Felix said. 'The beach will be beautiful.'

I knew as I nodded that I would follow him there, and that it would be the start of something, but I went anyway. We walked to the shore, listened to the waves build and fall, the stones rattle and drag. We put our faces up into the wind. I lifted my hair, let it cool my neck. It was as we turned back, the cab already flicking its indicator at the kerb, the driver reading a paper at the wheel, that he pulled me to him and kissed my mouth.

He tasted of whisky and his coat smelled of old leather and smoke and I was lost. When we stopped, he caught my bottom lip between his teeth, tugged at it softly and I felt it in my gut, in my groin and I didn't want to let go.

As I sat in the taxi and watched the dark fields rush past the windows, I rested my head on the back of the seat and pressed my fingers to my mouth. My lips pulsed with blood and I knew I would see him again.

Monday 18 December

Sea temperature: 8.9 degrees.
Air temperature: 7 degrees.

Nancy was ahead of me again, waving as I padded down the beach, and I watched her kick out from the dunes, moving forward faster than a steady breaststroke would normally take her, making me think the current was pulling her on. It must be strong this morning.

I could feel the set of my jaw, knew I was being rough with myself as I pulled on my booties, tugged on my gloves. I tutted when I couldn't do up the catch on my swim watch, kicked the sand as I walked. I needed to get in, work off the general feeling of annoyance that sat in my gut.

Morag never meant to upset me – or so she said. I should just laugh it off, David suggested. But she never missed an opportunity to make me feel slightly less, or a little worse, than everyone else. Although I didn't want to let it get to me, to spoil this one week that we had together, it stung. Like seawater on a scratch.

Last night it had been while we were playing Cluedo. Kit had been going through the old games cupboard next to the fireplace and pulled it out, the box torn at the corners. She held it up like a prize, shouted, 'Let's play,' and we all gathered round the kitchen table. Morag was still there, even though it was past teatime and she'd normally be downstairs with a soap opera or a documentary. The latest of her fads was *Who Do You Think You Are?*, where they traced the ancestry of a famous person. She'd recite it for you, generation by generation, the next day. But since the girls had come home, there was no shifting her. She'd been with us since the beginning, only returning to her flat for bed. Maybe the novelty would wear off today. Maybe she'd give us a bit of space.

I hit the shoreline and the water temperature made me gasp as I took the first few steps into the shallows. I didn't slow down. Pressing the timer on my watch, I pushed my shins through the low-level waves as they broke white against me.

Jess had selected Miss Scarlet, or 'Ms Scarlet', as she liked to call her.

'The modern woman,' said Morag with a nod.

Kit was Mrs Peacock, as always. She loved that particular shade of blue. 'The dramatic one,' Morag said. Kit blushed, rolled her eyes, not a scrap of make-up on her gorgeous face.

David asked for Professor Plum. That's what started it off.

'As you should be, son, being a teacher and all,' Morag said, passing him the purple character from the box in front of her. 'The intelligent one.'

'What about you, Belle?' She peered at me over the top of her half-moon glasses.

'Mrs White?' I suggested, not really caring to be green or yellow.

'Of course. The one everyone forgets. The housekeeper.' Morag handed over the piece with a smile, while everyone else started counting out cards and arranging their pieces. I took a deep, quiet breath.

'What about you, Ivo,' she said, moving along to hide the barb before anyone else noticed.

'Rev Green, please,' he said.

'Ah, the man that knows right from wrong,' said Morag.

He looked at her, thoughtful.

'I believe more in karma,' he said. 'What goes around comes around.'

I submerged now, face as well, mouth clenched tight, taking the hit all at once. The air left my body as I knew it would, the roar in my head and chest threatened to deafen me for a moment, until the calm broke through and I took a slow, steady stroke. Then another. I was right; the current was strong this morning, my body seeming to cut through the water with ease.

By the time I met my marker and turned, I'd realised just how strong it was. I checked ahead and saw Nancy, head down, powerful shoulders pumping her forward. I set off after her. It made my shoulders burn with every reach and pull. My legs had to kick harder to move me forward, inch by inch. The effort of every stroke emptied the anger from me. It drained away into the current. My thoughts were of nothing other than my body, my stroke, the rush of the water, the glimpse of the bluest sky starting to show on the horizon. My irritation had disappeared. My anxiety was gone. By the time I saw I was level with the beach hut and came out of the water, I was exhausted but charged. The water had let me go for another day.

Nancy was only just ahead of me on the sand – which was immediately wrong. She should have been already pulling on her Dry Robe or almost at her own hut. As I watched, her head lolled on her neck, and she staggered to the left and backward, as though drunk-dancing to some music I couldn't hear. Both her hands reached out to the sides as though searching for something to steady herself, and she staggered back the other way. Anyone watching would think she was absolutely out of her skin drunk, but I knew better. She was too cold, on her way to hypothermia. I'd seen the signs before. I'd been there before, myself, just once. It was too easy to do. Stay in a few minutes too long. Try to put your head under too early. Push yourself before you'd acclimatised. When it had happened to me was after a few weeks off due to a cold. I had thrown myself back in as though I'd never been away. Thankfully, a couple of the other Sea-girls had recognised my slurring speech while I was getting dressed. They'd layered me with blankets till I was too heavy to move, poured me hot tea and called David. It still took me an hour to stop shivering.

Now, catching Nancy up, I hooked my arm through hers, pulled her upright. She peered at me, confused, mouth slightly open, lips turning blue. I scanned the beach, but it was still just us.

'Here I am, Nancy,' I said, pulling her with me up the shingle towards the beach huts. 'Come on now, keep moving.' I got her to the steps of my hut – it was a few feet closer than hers – and yanked the door open, lowering her on to the wooden chair in the corner. I threw my Dry Robe over my wetsuit, knowing I had to be quick to help her, but I had to be safe myself too. I jogged down to her hut, only three doors away, and let myself in.

Her drying kit was laid out, just like mine, for speed and efficiency when wanting to warm up. Her towel hung on the hook with the Dry Robe, her fleece onesie on the back of the chair. I scooped the lot up and ran back.

'Right, what's your name then?' I asked as I crouched in front of her. It was important to ascertain how bad things were. Hypothermia victims couldn't answer the most basic questions. It was like they suddenly had advanced dementia.

She looked at me, an inner shiver starting in her core. For a second I thought she wouldn't answer, but then she gasped 'Nancy.' Good.

There was still no time for decorum though. I peeled down the zip on the back of her wetsuit and tugged the suit down over her shoulders to her waist. When her torso was bare I pulled her Dry Robe around her to keep her warm, and protect some of her modesty, so that I could yank the wetsuit free of her legs. She didn't have booties on, or gloves or a hat, and I wondered if that had been the issue. Her naked skin was goosebumped and faintly blue, the shivers so brutal they shook her whole body.

'It's okay now, Nance,' I was saying, as I tugged her onesie up her legs and body. She tried to help but her hands were clumsy, fingers incapable. I zipped her in, right to the neck. Grabbed my own woolly hat from the shelf and pulled it onto her head, and then wrapped her in the Dry Robe again.

'How's that then?' I asked as I rubbed her roughly, up her arms, across her shoulders, trying to stimulate the skin into warming itself. I was relieved to see her nod.

'So stupid,' she said through her chattering teeth. 'Cold feet.'

I ran back to her hut and found her Ugg boots, fluffy and warm, and soon manoeuvred her feet into them. I poured her some tea from my flask, pressed it between her clawed red hands, the colour of lobsters. Then I squished next to her and put my arms round her while she drank.

We sat looking at the sea through the open hut door until she stopped shivering. The sky was brightening, the blue winning out. Then I rang her husband Jim and said he'd best come to walk her home. Nancy managed a squeeze of my hand as he led her away.

I locked up my hut, then pulled her door shut, thinking I must text Jim later and tell him to come back to lock it up.

The tide was moving up the beach, depositing new treasures with each wave. The white frothy tips glistened in the sun and the water surged in its rush and pull. And I realised, again, the very fine line that existed in the sea. The line between feeling more alive than you've ever felt before, and feeling absolutely nothing at all.

Everyone had been ready to go to the lighthouse when I got back. I told them about Nancy and threw the towel in the wash and then hurried to get changed and ready.

We didn't have to queue at the lighthouse, it being off-season. It was a bright day, perfect for the view – the promised blue on the horizon at the end of my swim had claimed the sky and it was cold and crisp and beautiful. Seagulls wheeled and cried above us as we walked through the cobbled streets to the lighthouse entrance, hoping we might have chips for them to steal. They became confident thieves during the summer months, but it was slim pickings for them after the tourists left. Morag stayed home, not having wanted to climb the steps at the lighthouse, for which I felt guiltily grateful. I held David's hand as we walked, free to chat to him without her clutching at his arm the other side. He was on good form, relaxing into his holidays now, frown lines ironing out of his forehead with each day that passed.

Jess and Kit and Ivo took the wide spiralling stairs up the inside of the lighthouse as though they were nothing. They ran up, laughing. David and I followed behind, slowing as we rounded the upper curves, David pressing on his own thighs with each step as we approached the last landing. I noticed the heaviness of his breath and again considered whether I should have bought him a gym membership for Christmas. The kids were already up at the windows as we stepped in. We had the whole viewing platform to ourselves. I went to the nearest window, looking out at the pier, to stand, to see, to catch my breath.

The patchwork of roofs below us was broken by the little greens, the triangles, the strips and the grassy verges that separated the narrow lanes. The beachfront was lined with bay-windowed Victorian houses, steep-roofed, with tiled front paths. The terraces of smaller, pastel-painted brewery houses stood behind them, back to back, winding inland towards the church. I picked out my usual landmarks – friends' houses, the butcher's, the cheesemonger – as I let my breathing get back to normal. I knew David would be doing the same.

I loved the view, but it accentuated what I knew. The town was a tiny huddle in between the green, the marshes, the sea. It was surrounded by nothing on all sides. On a sunny day like today, it was rural, idyllic, a tiny hidden part of England. On grey days, you couldn't even see the edges of the town, and the feelings of isolation gnawed at my guts like an itch.

'How far can we see?' Ivo said, leaning his hands on the rail next to mine.

'At least five miles, on a good day,' I said, thinking of the view over the marshes. He turned away from the view towards the huge bulb of the lantern in the middle of the cylindrical platform.

'I suppose, more importantly, how far can the light be seen from?'

'About twenty nautical miles,' David answered for me. 'They upgraded it when they shut Orford Ness lighthouse.'

I smiled at him. We'd been up here and done the tour so many times, we didn't need the guide these days. David was like a walking fact-file.

Kit arrived beside Ivo, as I knew she would. She couldn't leave him alone for long. She lounged in front of him, leaning her back on his chest, and pulled his arms around her tummy.

'Good view of the pier from here,' she said with a casual flick of her head, but I saw something change on Ivo's face.

'How does it feel, knowing your dad's plaque is there now?' I said. He pressed his lips together before lifting his eyes directly to me.

'Like I've done the right thing,' he said, and I liked that. I'd always wanted to think that my parents would be proud of me, would approve of my choices. I guess he felt just the same.

Kit was half listening, tracing the tattoo on the back of his hand with her fingers. He watched her touch it.

'What's the tattoo mean?' David asked. 'Just fancied the design?'

'It's an Asian symbol for karma,' Ivo said, extending his hand so that David and I could see. 'The endless knot.'

David nodded politely. He hated tattoos. Always commented on them on the beach in the summer.

'Did it hurt?' I asked. 'When you had it done?'

Kit snorted. 'He didn't get it done,' she said. 'He did it himself.'

'No!' I said, shocked.

'Stupidly, yes. Just the outline, with a compass and some ink, last year of school.' Ivo grimaced. 'Then I got it coloured in later.'

I lifted his hand to look at the lines, seeing the varying thickness at some points, the slightly off symmetry. Close up, it looked amateurish. Suddenly I felt the heat, the heaviness of his hand in mine, looked up to see his face too close. I flushed and let his hand drop.

'God, that must have been painful,' I stammered.

Ivo rubbed it with his thumb, once, as though smoothing the skin.

'I'm getting one too,' Kit announced then, and David, beside me, nearly swallowed his tongue.

'What!' he barked.

'Keep your teeth in, Dad, I haven't done it yet.' She grinned.

'You need to think about it long and hard, Kitty,' he said, using her pet name to get through to her. 'You have to think, you're going to have to live with it for years—'

'I know that,' she said, mock-yawning as though she'd heard it all before.

'And you don't want some faded blue drawing on you when you're old,' he carried on, with a quick apologetic glance towards Ivo, 'Sorry Ivo, no offence.'

Ivo shrugged it off, smiled.

'I thought maybe a starfish here.' Kit pointed to the soft, white underside of her wrist. 'As I grew up by the sea.'

'I can see where you're coming from,' David appeased. 'But you have to think about the future. It might not look so nice on wrinkly skin, Kit.'

'Or a dolphin on the back of my shoulder?' Kit screwed her mouth to the side, thinking.

'You'd have to wear it for ever, Kit,' David warned. 'Can you imagine choosing a top to wear now for the rest of your life? That's what it would be like, apart from you can't ever take it off.'

Jess and Kit were both giggling by then and he realised she was winding him up. The girls could read their dad like a book.

'Don't panic, hassle-pants.' Kit laughed. 'I haven't decided yet.'

David gave a relieved laugh and then sighed. 'Just don't rush into anything,' he said.

'I knew you'd be like that about a tattoo,' said Kit, glancing at Ivo and then at Jess. My mum antenna buzzed. 'So I thought I'd start you off gently…'

Stepping towards David and me, she unzipped her coat and pulled the two sides apart. Lifting her hoodie clear of her jeans, she showed us her perfectly pierced navel. A jewelled stud sat in the dip, shining turquoise-blue against the pale tightness of her belly.

'Oh my God,' David cried, while I leaned in for a closer look, fascinated.

'Blue for the ocean, Dad!' Kit grinned.

'A permanent reminder of home,' Jess said, lifting her own hoodie and showing a matching stud. I couldn't help but laugh as they stood, arms round each other's waists, taut tummies out in the winter chill, my girls, my twins, closer than sisters could ever be.

'How could you do that to yourselves?' David was asking, shaking his head.

'I think it looks quite nice actually,' I said, admiring their gorgeous flat bellies just as much as the jewellery. It had been a long time since mine looked like that, even with the daily swimming and dog-walking.

'Could be worse, Dad,' Jess said.

'Could have been our nipples,' Kit said with a giggle, and I put my head back and roared.

As I wiped my eyes, and the girls hugged David from both sides, I noticed Ivo was quiet and saw him pressing his tattoo to his chest with his eyes fixed on the pier.

David carved the roast chicken, as was tradition. I cooked it, he cut it. I checked the accompaniments while he sharpened his knives like a master chef. Cauliflower cheese bubbled gently, carrots steamed and ran with butter. Yorkshire puddings were rising well. Jess had helped: chopped, stirred, chatted, and had pink cheeks from the Aga. She'd laughed about her flatmates, told stories about campus, enthused about her course. It was easy and lovely and everything I'd hoped their return would be. Everything apart from the fact that two of the party were missing.

'Do we need to text them, do you think?' I said to David when Jess popped to the loo, glancing into the dark of the back garden.

'They'll be here in a moment,' he said. 'You know what she's like.'

I tutted, irritated. 'You'd think they'd make the effort,' I said. 'Especially him – I mean, he is a guest here.'

David raised his eyebrows at my tone, but all of a sudden I couldn't let it lie.

'Don't you think he's maybe a bit overfamiliar?' I said, thinking of the way he looked at me, the way he seemed to stand just that inch too close. It made me vaguely uncomfortable.

Now David laughed.

'It's not funny, David,' I said. 'He had his top off the first night with me in the kitchen. And I found a really long dark curly hair in my hairbrush that looked like his.' It was true. I'd pulled it out and wondered why he'd do that. It made me shudder.

'Get over yourself, woman,' David said. 'You'd be annoyed if he was shy or stand-offish. He's friendly. He's nice.' He shrugged and I exhaled, gave up. He was right. I was just annoyed they were late. 'They'll be back soon. Stop stressing.'

Kit and Ivo had gone out for drinks an hour or so ago, and had said they'd be back by seven. It was now quarter past. Funny how quickly you forget how annoying people can be sometimes. But normally it was Jess that was late. Always had been, and it used to drive us crazy. She'd lose track of time reading. Kit on the other hand would be early everywhere, always at the front of any queue.

Just at that moment, the front door banged open and David threw me a grin. He was right. They were home.

I tipped crisped potatoes into a big white bowl and poured the gravy into jugs as we heard them taking off coats and throwing them over bannisters in the hall. Dodge hung around my legs hoping for a spill, until I sent him to his basket. He went with a slow wag, pinning me with disappointed eyes.

'Mum's roasts are legendary…' Kit was saying as they entered the room.

Ivo followed, rubbing his hands against the cold outside. Kit looked rosy, from walking and wine. He looked pale, tired. I wondered if he was coming down with something.

'So sorry we're late,' Ivo said to me, and David shot me a smug grin from the other side of the table. I rolled my eyes at him.

'Drinks,' Kit announced, heading straight to the fridge. She pulled out bottled lagers and a cider for Jess, who was organising music. It was nice to have it playing in the background; it was another sign the girls were home, music playing in several different rooms at once.

'Where did you go?' I asked as they pulled out chairs and sat down. Amazing how nobody thought to help with serving up, or to pour David and me a drink.

'The Lord Nelson,' Kit said, around the neck of her beer bottle.

'Thought you'd just pop to the Red Lion,' David said, no doubt thinking, as I was, that it was more convenient, only a few minutes' walk.

'Ivo wanted to see the Nelson.'

'Not the whole pub crawl then?' David said.

'Not tonight, Dad,' she said, but the glassy eyes told me they'd had a few.

I started loading the table and lit some candles while David uncorked a bottle of wine. Kit pulled the roast potatoes to her side of the table, staking ownership and smelling the steam coming off them. Morag appeared then, as if by magic, opening the front door and letting herself in. I gritted my teeth into a smile.

'Here you are, Mum,' David said to her. 'Perfect timing,' he added with a grin to me, knowing I could never fathom how she always turned up when all the work was done.

Plates were passed, glasses clinked, and everyone started to eat. I swear Kit waited until David and I both had our mouths full before saying, 'So I'm thinking university might not be for me.'

'What?' I stuttered, but felt David's knee nudge mine under the table, warning me not to overreact. He swallowed his mouthful and washed it down with a large swallow of wine.

'Oh?' he said. 'What's brought that on?' I let my breath out. His tone was just right. He sounded calm and curious.

I noticed Jess was still chewing, completely unsurprised. So she'd already known about it. I made myself spear a carrot, pop it in my mouth as if we were talking about the weather.

'It's just this whole public relations thing...' Kit said, screwing up her nose. 'It just doesn't feel right.'

I wiped the corner of my mouth with my napkin.

'What is it about it you don't like?' I asked, keeping my voice light.

'It's just so fake,' she said. 'Basically you're skewing the news. Putting out the good news, hiding the bad news.' She waved her knife in the air. 'It's a con.'

'It's about building a reputation though, isn't it?' I said.

'Yes. But who wants a reputation built on lies?' Ivo said.

I hid a frown. That wasn't helpful. I kept my eyes on Kit.

'Surely there's more to it than that? Knowing how to communicate with the media, the public?'

'Your shareholders, too? So they are happy with their investment?' David added.

'All correct,' she said. 'But it's just spin. It's not *creative* enough.' She glanced at Ivo, stabbed at a potato.

Aha. Now we were getting to the crux of it. She had a hankering after more of what he was doing. Maybe even thought it would be romantic to do the same course. She was obviously falling hard for him.

'So, it's maybe not university that doesn't suit you,' I suggested. 'It's just that you haven't found the right course yet.'

She crunched, considering.

'Maybe.'

'You could look at other courses then?' David said. 'Perhaps you could transfer your points across for this first term?'

'Maybe,' she repeated. 'Or maybe I should do something less *confining*.'

Jess bit her lip, then stuffed her mouth with another piece of chicken. Here it came.

'Like what?'

'Travel for a year or so?' Kit said, lifting her bottle. 'Ivo's thinking of taking a year to focus on travel photography.' She took a big mouthful of beer, flicked a look at Jess for backup, but Jess was studying her plate.

David put his knife and fork down and turned his attention to Ivo. 'Wow, that's a cool idea,' he said, giving himself time to think about what to say to Kit.

'Can you make that count towards your course?' I asked and Ivo nodded.

'I'm talking about it at the moment to the photography department. They think I can probably make it work as a module.'

'That's really flexible of them,' I said.

'University *is* flexible though,' David said. 'That's the whole point. So there are loads of options open to you, Kit. You could change course, or find a more creative one. One that suits you.'

'I'm not sure—' she started, but he cut her off.

'Or,' he went on, nodding at her, 'you could travel, take a year out, start again when you feel like it.' He'd pitched it just right. She thought he was taking it seriously, giving it consideration.

'Dad's right,' I interjected, smiling. 'You've got your whole life ahead of you. But you don't have to make a decision now, do you? Not today?'

'Let's just keep talking about it over the holidays,' David said, lifting up his knife and fork again.

'Plenty of time,' I said. 'We just want you to be happy, love.'

'Cauliflower's a bit soggy,' Morag said.

It was as I started clearing the table that Jess asked why Ivo had wanted to go to the Lord Nelson. David was stacking the dishwasher and I put the bigger pans in the sink to soak. The others, annoyingly, didn't seem to notice anything needed doing and sat cradling drinks, chatting.

'Kit said they have live music in there sometimes,' he answered, turning his bottle of lager round in his hands.

'More so in the summer though, when there are tourists around,' Kit quantified.

I placed the salt and pepper pots back by the Aga.

'My dad was in a band when he was younger,' Ivo said, 'he played around this area one year.'

'Sounds like your whole family was creative,' I said. 'Maybe that's where you get it from.'

'I was never cool enough to be in a band,' David said and the girls both laughed.

'Really, Dad?'

'You weren't cool?'

'I can't believe that!'

David smiled along, mellow with food and wine. He was tired and ready for the sofa and a film, or a book and bed. So was I.

'I wanted to see the places he might have played,' Ivo said. He'd pulled the nearest candle towards him, and was now licking his finger so that he could swipe it through the flame without getting burned. Kit edged closer to him to watch.

I leaned past to collect place mats; they'd need a wipe before going back in the drawer.

'You used to watch a few bands locally, didn't you, love?' David said to me. The words struck a memory I didn't want in my head. I felt the immediate fizz in my gut. I didn't like to think about it. I nodded with a smile, but then shook my head towards the table.

'About a gazillion years ago,' I said, apologetically as though to deny all knowledge.

'When she was young...' Kit said in a shaky old-lady voice, but Ivo didn't laugh.

'Maybe you knew them then,' he said, to me, over the top of the flame, with a look so intimate I felt a flush bloom on my throat.

I immediately dropped my eyes and shrugged in what I hoped was a casual way. I picked up the big white bowl – it now held only a few crispy crumbs of roasties – as an excuse to leave the table, and took it to the bin to empty. As I shook it over the mouth, and watched the remnants fall in, he said, 'He was quite well-known around here, the band was just on the up, I believe. Destined for bigger things.'

'Maybe we have heard of them, then. Even me, and I was never the musical one,' David said from the sink. 'What was the name?'

I took my foot off the bin pedal, let the lid drop.

'The band was called The Hush,' Ivo said as I turned. He unzipped his hoodie as he met my eye, showing the T-shirt beneath it. Big writing, red on a grey background. I'd seen it before. I'd worn one similar once.

'My dad was the lead singer. He was called Felix.'

The bowl slipped through my wet fingers and Kit jumped dramatically as it smashed on the tiled floor.

Morag broke the stunned silence with an exaggerated exclamation of dismay.

'I bought you that for your wedding present,' she said as I dropped blindly to my knees to start collecting the pieces. 'Should have known it wouldn't last.'

My mouth opened and closed like a beached fish. I concentrated on the broken crockery, the dagger-sharp splinters of white, as I tried to collect my thoughts.

'Mind your hands,' David said from the other side of the room, and I knew he was off into the utility cupboard for a dustpan and brush.

I gathered the bigger pieces together, taking my time and putting them on the corner of the table. I forced a swallow over the other realisation as it hit. Ivo's father was my Felix. And that Felix was dead. All this time and I never knew.

Only when David knelt beside me and swept the tiny slivers off the floor did I trust myself to say anything else.

'Sorry Ivo, The Hush?' I squinted at his T-shirt, pretending to read it again. 'No, I don't think I ever saw them. The name's not ringing a bell.'

He licked his lips slowly and ran his finger and then thumb across his tongue, wetting them till they glistened.

'Didn't think you would, really.' He pinched the candle out with a hiss.

After our first meeting, it was inevitable that I would see Felix again. I didn't even think about it. It lit me up inside, burned off the constant grey of the coastal mist that surrounded my life. The beep of my phone would make me press my lips together and my fingers would tremble as I replied. The excitement had a physical impact. It was like the first coffee of the day, that initial sip of wine at night, the pull of nicotine in an illicit cigarette. It was addictive.

Felix seemed to be always available. His gigs were at night, and he had the days to himself.

We would text arrangements and by the time I arrived, I'd be breathless with anticipation, stomach hollowed with wanting. Coffees in Aldeburgh, lunch in the pub at Thorpeness. Public places where I could claim he was a client if necessary. Where we'd talk and push food around our plates with hungry eyes, while our feet entwined under the table.

He'd talk about gigs, about a new song he was writing. He'd sing phrases to me in his low husk. Every one of his lyrics seemed to hold secret messages that only I would understand or recognise. Things that he could sing about because nobody knew about us. I told him I had the urge to write a book, something I'd always toyed with, and again it was so that I could put on paper what I couldn't say. I suddenly had the impetus to write and write and write, to let the imprisoned words, the pent-up feelings, be free. It felt like I was charged with creativity, with electricity, with potential. I could do anything, be anyone.

After talking we itched with the need to be alone, to touch each other, to kiss. We'd take to the dunes, the more isolated strips of beach, the woodland walks. We'd find the deserted paths, the forgotten benches. The weather didn't matter. The wind made it all the wilder. The cold made us hold each other tighter. The rain ran down my face like tears as I turned it up to be kissed.

I'd slip my hands inside his jacket, lift his T-shirt from his jeans, slip my hands against his skin. He'd talk against my hair, murmur into my neck, until we had to peel apart again for another few days of longing. Of waiting.

It shocked me how easily I became a person who relied on someone else to make everything okay. Break the grey. But I lived for it. I craved it.

I knew we would sleep together. It was just a matter of when.

Tuesday 19 December

Sea temperature: 8.9 degrees.
Air temperature: 7 degrees.

The water against my shins ripped the usual involuntary gasp from my lips, but this morning it seemed to come from deep within me. A noise that finally registered the shock of the night before. My eyes pricked hot behind my goggles and I pushed myself forward in the surf, wanting to get away from the beach, the house, the boy. Just wanting the nothing of the water around me, the sky above.

Nancy had messaged yesterday, saying she wouldn't swim today, citing a cold. I'd considered not swimming myself – it was dangerous without a buddy – but I needed it more today than ever before. It was worth the risk.

I submerged, felt the panic rise and threaten, the grip of it at my chest, the roar of it in my ears that made all thought black. When my breathing calmed, and my vision cleared, I struck out towards the dunes as hard as I could, smashing through the water with my arms, lungs bursting as I broke through the waves. So many thoughts in my head at once. Things I didn't want to remember. Names I didn't want to call myself. People I didn't want to be. And yet, at the heart of it, the shock.

Felix was dead. And had been for years.

It had been so long since I'd last seen him, but it didn't lessen the impact. Ivo's words in the kitchen had hit me like a sledgehammer, and I couldn't even react. I could never show how I felt. Nobody knew about Felix. I could only scrabble around on the floor for broken crockery and bite my lip to stop any sound escaping.

I'd wondered over the years what might have happened to him. After that last night, I never saw him again. I'd secretly wished him healthy and well. And happy. I'd never believed for one second that he would be dead. Even with what I knew.

I was swimming against the current, pleased with the way it made me battle. The force I had to use to make progress. It felt good to kick. To struggle. To lash out.

And Ivo. He was Felix's son. Now that I knew, I wondered how I hadn't seen.

It wasn't that they looked identical, but there were small tells, or tics, that should have warned me. The hold of his eyes. The wave of his hair. My stomach hollowed at the memory and I struck out again with my stroke.

But what were the chances? Why would I ever have guessed? A boy meets a girl at university on the other side of the country and comes home with her. Who would ever have made a connection between that and my life?

My hands were numb and I realised I had forgotten my gloves in my haste to get into the water, to escape. Damn. That would shorten my swim. But good job I'd noticed now, otherwise I might have ended up like Nancy yesterday. Too cold to function on my own. Needing David to come and get me home. I couldn't have that. I needed my wits about me today. So that I didn't say anything stupid, or let something slip. Nobody could know that I had known Ivo's dad.

It would raise too many questions. Things I never wanted known. I paused and checked my watch, careful of the minutes.

David had cleared up the breakage the night before, unsuspecting and helpful as always. He'd put the dog out in the garden and turned off the lights, letting me go up early, exhausted. He'd wrapped around me in bed later, one arm over my waist, tucking his hand on to the round of my belly. The softness that I hated, and that he loved. A reminder of the twins I'd carried and the mark they'd left on me. If I'd backed into him, or turned to face him, he would have made love to me, I knew. But I feigned tiredness, and listened as he drifted off to sleep, until he snored gently and his hand on me grew heavy. I lay there, for hours, weighed down by his arm, until my eyes were scratchy and sore. Thinking about what it meant.

Ivo was Felix's son.

The son I didn't know about until later. The boy who I'd had no idea existed. The secret that Felix kept from me.

I turned in the water, back towards the hut, let the current help on the home stretch. I knew what I had to do. I was clear. I just had to lie. I'd done it before and been good at it. And it wasn't as though it was for ever, let's face it; at the end of the week Ivo would be gone. And he and Kit probably wouldn't last, a typical university crush, over and done with by the end of the first year. I just had to get through this week with my secret intact. Then we'd never speak of Felix again.

The kitchen was buzzing when I got back, David drinking coffee at the table, Kit and Ivo at the stove pouring batter into a pan for pancakes. Jess was preparing the accompaniments, cutting lemons in half, slicing strawberries. The radio was on, although not our usual station; it was more music than talking. I hung my swimming togs across the radiators in the utility room, so that they would dry for the next day. I squeezed David's shoulder on the way past, helped myself to coffee, then joined him at the table. The hot liquid warmed my insides on the way down and I rolled my head on my shoulders, feeling better and looser in my muscles than I had an hour ago.

'Good swim?' David asked, and mussed the back of my hair where it hung salty-damp.

Kit popped the last of a pancake into her mouth at the stove with a kissing of the fingers. Ivo leaned in and wiped a smear of Nutella from her top lip. She grabbed his hand, laughing, and sucked the chocolate from his thumb. He let her. All of the anxiety that I'd lost on my swim started to nudge its way back in. He was Felix's. I never wanted our two worlds to be this close. The proximity was frightening. But at the same time, I couldn't take my eyes off him. He fascinated me. Even more so now that I knew who he was.

'Another?' he said to her and she shook her head, sticking her flat belly out and pretending to be full. He poured more batter into the pan, lifting the jug at the last minute so that not a drop was spilled.

'You're up, Jess,' he said.

Jess threw a strawberry across the kitchen to Kit, who caught it in her mouth to a small round of applause from Ivo.

Kit then threw one back to Jess, who missed it and laughed at the noise it made as it splatted on the tiled floor. Dodge ate it in one second flat. The dog always knew where to position himself. Jess had never been good at catching.

Ivo tossed the pancake in the pan, set it out on to a side plate and passed it to the table. Jess loaded it with sliced banana and squirted cream over the top, licking her lips as she rolled it and the cream escaped at the ends. She had her eyes half-shut as she took the first bite. Kit took her place at the chopping board as Ivo poured more batter into the pan.

'Have you had one yet, babe?' Kit asked him.

'Not hungry this morning, thanks,' he said. 'Right, next round.' Although he was smiling, he was paler again this morning, the shadows under his eyes a blue smudge. Maybe he wasn't sleeping well. I'd have to check he had enough pillows. 'Pancake?' Ivo asked David and he rubbed his hands together in anticipation.

'Strawberries and Nutella?' Kit said with her knife poised over the punnet.

'Oh, go on then,' David said and she passed it over.

'Ooh, exotic tastes,' Ivo said, tossing the next one. He was good at it, flicking his wrist decisively, catching the batter just right. I had to drag my eyes away. Knowing he was Felix's now made me look at him differently, made me want to study him, spot the similarities.

'Do you make these a lot in Bristol?' I asked.

'Pretty much live on them,' he said. 'Or jacket potatoes and baked beans.'

'What do you have on yours?' I asked.

'Depends on what's in the cupboard,' he said. 'Or how much money I've got left. I've had them with ice cream and apple one day and then with tuna and tomatoes the next.' Everyone exclaimed and he shrugged and said, 'It was surprisingly nice actually.'

Jess had finished and was wiping the plate clean of cream with her fingers.

'That was amazing,' she said. She'd always enjoyed her food. It gave her real pleasure, unlike Kit, who had always been a fussy eater.

'Belle? For you?' Ivo said.

I met his eyes across the kitchen. The same deep-brown eyes as Felix.

'If you've got enough batter left?' I said, not sure how many they'd had before I got back from the beach. He swilled the jug to check.

'Last one,' he said, pouring the last of the mix into the pan. 'Just for you.'

'What topping do you want?' Kit asked me from her chopping board.

'Just lemon and sugar please.'

'Bor-ing!' Jess said.

'I like to think of myself as *traditional* rather than *boring*.' I smiled, watching Ivo lift the batter at the edges of the pan to check it.

'Classic,' David agreed, putting his arm round my shoulders. 'My wife's a classic.'

'But you never try anything else!' Kit said. 'That's bor-ing!' She flicked the pips out of the lemon with the tip of her knife, ready to squeeze on to my breakfast.

'I think you'll find I have tried other pancakes, but I always come back to the original and best,' I said, laughing.

'Bor-ing,' both girls chorused, laughing at each other.

'My wife, loyal to the end.' David laughed as Ivo flipped the pancake, higher than he had the others. As it turned in mid-air, he pushed the pan out, not quite fast enough, to catch it and we all watched as it hit the floor.

The girls snorted and then laughed, looking at the broken batter on the tiles. David made an 'oh dear' sort of noise and made to stand, but Dodge made a dive for it and got there first. Ivo stood frozen, pan in hand, eyes on me from the other side of the kitchen table.

'Oops,' he said. 'Butterfingers.'

Then he laughed.

I'd have happily gone to the greengrocers for supplies on my own, just to get out of the house for a bit of fresh air, but the kids said they'd come with me. David gave us a lazy wave from the sofa. Dodge danced around our legs, generally getting in the way, until we were down the front steps, facing up towards the town.

Morag's door opened and I took a deep breath before turning towards her. Luckily, I spotted her slippers straight away – she wasn't planning on joining us. It made it easier to give her a real smile. She ignored me and waved to the girls.

'Just off to the shops, Gran,' Jess said. 'Do you want us to pick anything up for you?' She was a good kid. Well trained at having her gran live downstairs. Mind you. We all were.

Morag made a show of pulling her wrap round her shoulders, giving a big shiver. She pulled the front door behind her almost closed, to keep the hot air inside. I couldn't remember the last time I'd been in Morag's. She always came to us.

'I haven't really thought about dinner yet, Jessie. I'm just catching up on *Long Lost Family*,' she said. '*I'm not sure what I've got in.*' *Here we go*. I knew what would happen next.

'Mum's doing a chilli,' Kit said. 'Why don't you just come up for that?' Bingo. But even if one of them hadn't said it, I would have felt obliged to invite her. Morag wrinkled her nose and I knew then she'd say something about my cooking.

'As long as you don't over-spice it, Belle,' she said. 'You do have a tendency to make these things too hot.'

'It'll be fine, Morag,' I said, making a mental note to get the red bird's-eye chillis that would blow her teeth out. 'If it's too hot, we can always cool it for you with some sour cream.' I smiled. 'See you about seven?'

Even as I said it I knew she'd come up earlier. And I'd backtrack on the heat of the chilli. She waved us away, blowing kisses at the girls, playing the sweet old lady. I gritted my teeth behind my smile.

Dodge was surprised at the pace I set as we headed up the promenade, promising him a quick run on the beach before hitting the stalls to get what I needed. Jess walked alongside me, bobble hat pulled over her ears, cheeks pinking in the wind. Ivo and Kit walked behind, arms wrapped round each other, leaning together into the weather as one wall. Jess noticed my glance, nudged me with a grin. I let Dodge off the lead and Jess linked her arm into mine, her woollen mitten tucked through my elbow. I squeezed her closer.

'You okay?' I asked, thinking a lot of the conversation the night before had been around Kit. Her plans. Her university. Her life. I hadn't had a proper catch-up with Jess yet.

'Yup.' She threw a quick look over her shoulder before adding, 'They're so loved up, aren't they?'

'Do you think so?' I asked, trying to keep my voice steady as we shuffled into step together. '*Love?*'

'So she says.' Jess shrugged. 'He dropped the L-bomb last week, before they came up here.' That made sense, thinking about the late request for him to join her. It was obviously happening really fast. Which was precisely the last thing I wanted to hear.

'Wow,' I said. 'And she feels the same?'

'She's crazy about him. Literally. If he said jump, she'd ask how high.'

Jess had always been the more sensible one. She thought about things before she did them – bought knee pads at the same time as her roller skates, as opposed to Kit, who threw herself off the shed roof to see if she could fly.

'What do you think of him?' I asked, interested.

'He's all right,' she said. I had a feeling she was holding something back. I waited but she shrugged. 'He certainly seems to really like her.' It was not enthusiastic, but I shouldn't have expected anything else. Cautious Jess would be watching and waiting, just like her dad. And as long as he was good to her sister, she'd be happy.

'What about you?' I asked, changing the subject, not wanting to think about Kit and Ivo any more. 'Met anyone nice in Exeter?' I worded it deliberately carefully, leaving the conversation open, but she dropped her eyes, wrinkled her nose, the same expression her gran had used ten minutes before, but on her it was without malice and adorable.

'Not yet…' she said with a shrug. I wondered again if there was something she wasn't telling me. She never mentioned anyone she fancied, never had done. Not that it mattered. I just wanted her to be happy.

'Well, they'll be lucky to have you when you meet them,' I said with a nudge, and kissed her mittened hand.

'Mum...' she began, and I wondered if this was the moment she'd let me in, but the stamp of feet behind us made her turn and then say no more. Kit and Ivo caught us up, holding on to each other's hands as they ran, their faces a reflection of each other's happiness.

'Hot chocolates?' Kit puffed, pointing at the café serving takeaways. The girls were amazing, they just seemed to eat and drink and eat again and never put on a pound. I took the hint; I peeled a tenner out of my purse and handed it over. Jess and I sat on the promenade wall to wait while the others queued for our drinks. She chatted about a girl called Roberta on her course who had thrown up at a party after drinking cider and black, and managed to stain a whole bed-spread a beautiful shade of purple. She was now known on campus as Ribena.

When the hot chocolates arrived we stayed seated where we were, out of the wind. Dodge sat contentedly in front of us, watching the gulls as they wheeled and dived. A tanker sat low on the horizon. Every now and then a gust of wind blew us a snatch of music from the pier.

'This is where the Punch and Judy normally is,' Kit said to Ivo. 'I couldn't tell you how many ice creams we've eaten sitting here.'

She was right. Many a happy afternoon on the beach had ended there, in sandy flip-flops with salty hair and vanilla ice cream melting in the sun as we watched Punch get chased about by a crocodile.

'Closed for the season in September this year,' I said. 'Mainly because of that bad weather we had just after you went to university.'

'I'm surprised it's still going at all,' Jess said. 'I mean, Punch and Judy is so out of date, now, as a concept. I'm amazed it hasn't been shut down.'

'Oh you and your women's rights,' said Kit. 'Don't tell me you want to ban Punch and Judy?'

'It *is* a bit bloodthirsty I suppose,' I agreed, mainly to keep the peace, taking a creamy sip of my hot chocolate.

'It's not just bloodthirsty, it's domestic violence, Mum!' Jess said, shaking her head. 'I reckon in a few years' time, it will be a thing of the past. I can't believe really that people still think of it as entertainment.'

'I know, I know, but it's traditional,' I said. I could see her point, but wasn't it just a bit of fun?

'So we should carry on showing it – as an example to our children?' Jess asked.

'Don't be such a do-gooder.' Kit rolled her eyes. 'It doesn't *mean* anything.'

'But some people might say it promotes violence.' Jess was on a roll. 'Mr Punch mistreats his baby, beats his wife and kills the policeman.'

'But surely the point is that we all know he's wrong? We all shout at him,' I suggested, trying to calm the waters. I didn't want to patronise her, I just wanted to change the subject. She cared about human rights, women's rights, always had. A real stickler for right and wrong. Just like David. I'd just rather not have an argument.

Ivo, on my other side, nudged me.

'I'm with you, Belle. Don't see anything wrong with it myself.'

I heard Jess take a breath, ready to go again.

'I mean,' Ivo went on. 'What's wrong with smashing someone's brains out for some light entertainment?'

He jumped up and put on a Mr Punch voice, lifted his fist above his head and pretended to punch Kit in the face, one, two, three times. I gasped.

'That's the way to do it,' he croaked with each swing.

They all laughed, but something slid uneasy in my gut. It wasn't really very funny.

Morag fanned her face and blew out of her mouth like it was on fire every thirty seconds, even with a heaped spoonful of sour cream mixed into her chilli. Jess, sitting to her side, patted her back every few minutes and offered her a drink of milk.

'I'll cope, hen, thanks,' Morag said as though it was something she had to battle through. I looked away, refusing to be drawn. If she didn't like it, she needn't have come. David squeezed my thigh under the table.

'Delicious,' he said with a wink.

Soon, every plate was finished, even Morag's, although the theatre carried on for a good half an hour afterwards, with her wafting air down the neck of her tartan blouse and opening a window, 'before I expire'.

'Let's leave it for a bit,' I said, getting up from the table. 'I'll clear up in a while.' Nobody argued and we all made our way through to the lounge. Morag sat nearest the fire, despite the fact that she was 'burning up from the inside'. David tossed on another couple of logs and then sat next to me. The kids took the three-seater, although Kit and Ivo were only really taking up one space, her legs draped over his.

Jess was scrolling social media on her phone, shouting out the occasional update on people we all knew.

'Christina Morris is engaged,' she said, about a girl that they used to go to school with. I remembered her as a toothy teenager needing a brace. Jess flashed the phone around the room to show us a picture of a beaming Christina displaying an engagement ring on her finger.

'Lovely,' I said, thinking how well the brace had worked.

'Tiny ring,' said Kit.

Jess peered at the ring, shrugged and then scrolled on.

'Mike Daniels is home – maybe we'll see him.'

Mike's family lived in Walberswick, and we'd known them for ever. I sometimes bumped into his mum in the town.

'Hopefully not,' said Kit, who'd once gone out with him to a party and thrown up on his shoes. Jess chuckled and carried on.

'Gemma Matthews is in St Lucia for Christmas!' she said, turning the phone to us once again. I didn't know Gemma; she must be someone Jess knew from university. The picture was of a bikini-clad girl on a beach, the blue sky behind her unbroken, the sea sparkling in the sun. It was as far from Southwold promenade earlier that afternoon as it could have been.

'Oh my God, I'm so jealous,' said Jess. 'What I'd do for some sun!'

'That looks amazing,' Kit agreed.

'If you could be anywhere right now, where would you be?' Ivo asked the room.

David cleared his throat.

'I fancy a bit of skiing,' he said. 'Les Arcs, maybe. Nice wide routes, nothing too strenuous for my old knees.' We'd had a few good skiing trips when we were younger, before the girls came along. Then a few when they came with us but spent the days in ski school while we travelled the mountains together, a rare opportunity to be alone on holiday. We'd had hot chocolate or *gluhwein* in mountainside cafes and turned our faces to the sun. It had been wonderful. I nodded at him in memory. Maybe we should go again. Have a bit of fun together.

'No way,' Jess said. 'I want heat.'

'Where then?' Ivo asked her.

'Mexico,' she said. 'But not Cancun or anywhere *touristy*. Puebla or Chiapas. Somewhere off the beaten track.'

'I've never heard of those places,' I said and she crawled across the floor to lean against my knees, googling images to show me. Multicoloured terraced houses with iron railings and balconies bordered narrow pedestrianised streets. Waterfalls and ruins glittered in the sunshine. It looked gorgeous.

'Naomi and I are going to try to get jobs this term and save up enough to go in the summer.' It was the first I'd heard of that, but it didn't surprise me. Naomi and Jess had been best friends for years. She lived just up the road, and they'd been thick as thieves since secondary school.

'A holiday with Naomi?' Kit glared across at her. Jealous maybe? 'Wondered when we'd hear her name.' Jess lifted her chin in Kit's direction, defiant. I frowned. Something was afoot.

'I'm coming too,' David said with a grin, oblivious to the tension, looking over Jess's shoulder at the phone screen. 'Skiing can wait.'

'How is Nem?' I asked, to break whatever was going on between the girls.

'Good,' Jess said, turning to me. 'She's home tomorrow. Can't wait to see her. It's been ages.'

'Not that long, thought she came down to Exeter a few weekends ago,' Kit chipped in.

Again, the first I'd heard of it.

'It'll still be nice to see her,' Jess said. Kit looked away.

'What about you?' Ivo asked me. 'Bell-e.' I flinched, but he smiled. It must just be the way he held the last syllable of my name that made it sound like Bella.

'I'm easy,' I said, linking fingers with David on his leg. 'Venice.'

'Mum – you're so predictable.' Jess groaned.

'But I love it there.' I laughed.

'Mum and Dad went there on their honeymoon,' Kit explained.

'And to celebrate some of the big anniversaries since,' Jess said.

'It's just beautiful, what can I say?' I shrugged.

'And it's our place,' said David, backing me up.

'But you've been there,' Kit said. 'Don't you want to go somewhere else? Somewhere new?'

'Anywhere in the world,' Ivo encouraged. 'Anywhere at all.'

Everyone was looking at me. I shrugged, smiled, embarrassed that I couldn't think of anywhere else quick enough.

'Anywhere I've got my family with me, that will do,' I said and then could have kicked myself black and blue. What the hell was I saying? Ivo sitting there without a family and I say something crass like that. I flashed him a glance, but he wasn't looking at me. He was looking at Kit.

'What about you, Ivo?' I said, desperately trying to gloss over what I'd just said.

He caught his bottom lip under his teeth, thinking about it, or perhaps trying to contain the number of possibilities.

'Somewhere in Asia probably,' he said, 'Maybe Bangkok to start with…'

'I've never been to Asia,' David said, 'but I have to say it does appeal. I love Thai food.'

Kit rolled her eyes, as though he were ridiculous. 'The version of Thai food we get here is probably nothing like the local dishes. That's why you have to go to these places, to get the *authentic* experience.'

I wondered briefly when both of our daughters had started thinking they knew everything.

'And then down to Koh Samui, to see the islands, although it might get a bit tacky down there.' Ivo was looking upwards, as though picturing a route. 'Maybe Chiang Mai, more in the mountains, the jungle, for trekking…' he added.

'It's good for seeing elephants there, in a sanctuary, not a zoo,' Kit chipped in, to us. 'You can go with them to their watering holes, even go in the water with them!'

'Is that safe?' I asked, but nobody answered.

'And from there, maybe across into Vietnam…' Ivo continued.

'Didn't we say Cambodia first?' Kit said, tugging his arm.

Aha. So they'd had this conversation already. Shared dreams.

'Yes, you're right, to see Angkor and the temples,' he agreed.

'And trek the Cardamom Mountains.' She nodded.

'Been planning, you guys?' David asked, laughing.

Kit stopped, blushed, glanced at Ivo.

'Not really…' she stammered.

'Oh, you know, we started talking,' Ivo muttered, 'about my year out – for the travel photography.'

'You know, just if it was going to happen,' Kit added quickly, but she wasn't meeting my eye. I glanced at David. We definitely had to have another conversation about her plans. Even if it wasn't going to be university, I didn't want her going travelling for a year with him. It would be better for her to go with a girlfriend, or a charity – just not him.

'Well I know where Gran's going,' Jess said with a giggle, pointing at Morag, who had dozed off in the warmth of the fire. Her mouth had dropped open and now she let out a muffled snore. 'Bed!'

'You're right. I'll take her down,' said David, as I knew he would. He woke her gently. She suddenly looked older, not her usual sprightly self, as he led her from the room. We heard him wrapping her coat round her in the hall, and then the front door open.

'You stay there, love,' Morag's voice came, with more of her normal gusto. 'It's bitter out. See you tomorrow.'

I pushed myself off the sofa to get a start on the kitchen. As I left the room, Kit and Ivo had their heads together over his phone. From this angle I could see a glimpse of pink scalp on the top of his head. Poor kid, he was pretty young to be thinning. Maybe that's why he kept it longer, to wear it up. Something in the way they leaned towards each other, the identical tilt of their chins, made me pause. Their determined chins. Excited chatter. As I passed behind the sofa I saw they were looking at a map.

The kitchen, away from the heat of the fire, was cool. Dodge followed me out and wagged at the back door. I let him out, told him to hurry up and watched him trot off up the garden to relieve himself before bed.

I'd stacked the dishwasher and was wiping the wooden table when Ivo came in, carrying a couple of glasses and a mug.

'Thought you might want these,' he said, placing them in the open dishwasher.

'Thanks,' I said, still feeling awkward about what I'd said. I couldn't leave it without apologising. I didn't want him to think badly of me. 'Ivo, I'm sorry I was so insensitive in there.'

He shut the dishwasher door and turned it on.

'About what?' he said and I cringed.

'That stuff I said about being anywhere with my family. It was thoughtless.' I grimaced.

'That's okay. I'm used to it.' He shrugged. 'I guess some people are luckier than others.'

Even though it was a subject that felt dangerous, I stepped into it, wanting to know more about Felix's death.

'It must have been tough, losing your dad so young.'

He was looking at me hard, considering his answer, and I couldn't bear the silence so I blurted out something to get him to say something, anything.

'Was he ill for a long time?'

I wanted to know for me, I realised. I didn't like to think of Felix withering, being bedridden, eaten up. He'd been such a force, so vibrant. But he'd smoked and lived in pubs with the band, so maybe it was cancer. It was the most obvious answer. I shook the crumbs from the table into the bin, flapped the cloth, turned to find Ivo staring.

'Ill?' he asked, dark eyebrows raised. 'Oh, no, didn't I tell you?'

I shook my head, waiting.

'He wasn't ill,' he said, blankly. 'He killed himself.'

I stepped back and banged my hip against the corner of the table. Felt the air rush out of my mouth like I'd just stepped into the ocean. Ivo watched me, squinting.

'God, how awful,' I breathed, holding my hand to my chest.

'He had an affair that went wrong, according to Mum,' Ivo said. 'Killed himself with a broken heart.'

Blackness was at the edge of my vision, worse than any cold-water shock. I reached a hand out to the back of a chair for support.

'He gassed himself with exhaust fumes in our garage,' he explained, although I hadn't asked the question, in fact I didn't want to know. 'I found him there, in his car.' He shut his eyes briefly, shook his head as if to clear it and then took a deep breath. I let my own breath out slowly, quietly, so that he didn't hear.

'Anyway, goodnight,' he said as he passed me again.

I held the chair in front of me, clutched at it until Dodge barked at the back door.

I found that it was surprisingly simple to be an adulteress for those few weeks. It illuminated my days. Broke up the grey of the beach, the horizon and the fog in my head. Felix burned brightly and I was like a moth to the flame.

David was easy to deceive, not just as he was out at work, but also because he trusted me completely. He knew nothing of my days, whether I gave him true or false accounts. If I said I'd gone to Snape Maltings, then he asked me how it was. If I said I'd had a difficult client, he rubbed my back and said better luck tomorrow. He had no reason to doubt me. As far as he knew, I was worthy of his trust. We'd been together for twelve years, married for three. No longer newly-weds; the honeymoon period had morphed into real life. It wasn't that I didn't love him. I did. But I'd lost myself somewhere along the way. Felix brought something to life in me that I hadn't realised had been hibernating.

Morag was easy to avoid, for once. She'd just begun a community class on exploring your family tree, and spent hours poring over records in the library for information about births and deaths. It gave me the space I needed to become someone else. Someone who could lie to your face. Someone who would plan ahead to deceive you. The liar. The cheat. The lover. But I lived for it. The excitement maybe, the risk. I craved it.

We had one weekend together where it was perfect.

David presented the opportunity on a plate when he told me he had to go away for a training weekend, a course he needed to undertake if he wanted to be promoted to Head of Juniors. I could hardly believe my luck. I reassured him I'd be fine, in fact I'd take the opportunity to go on a writing retreat, and pretended to book myself into one immediately. When he kissed me goodbye and swung his rucksack onto the back seat of the car, I was already mentally counting minutes until I could leave too without him *seeing me on the road behind him as we both drove the one route out of town.*

Felix was sitting on the wall outside the hotel I'd booked in Bury St Edmunds when I got there. My car headlights picked him out as I pulled into the car park, kicking his heels, battered old holdall crumpled on the ground beside him. He was pale in the illumination, dark-eyed, waiting.

I shook inside as we checked in as Mr and Mrs Jagger, a private joke. A girl showed us to the room and left, eyes on the floor as though she could feel the tension between us. Once the door was shut, we turned and held each other demurely, until the trembling stopped.

We didn't fall on each other. We didn't strip each other's clothes off. It was too much. Instead, I opened the minibar and mixed vodka with Coke in two glasses. Felix stood at the window and took in the moonlit view across rooftops and attics, and I noticed the tremor still in the muscles of his back.

We sipped, and talked, and let the facts sink in. We were alone. We had time together. We had a whole room to ourselves instead of a public beach, a family forest, a busy café. He put a CD into the player, I poured us another drink. We ordered room service and ate chips with our fingers, fed each other ice cream like teenagers, shed our normal lives like wet coats.

I felt free in a way I hadn't for a long time. No marriage. No responsibilities. No deadlines.

I placed the food tray outside the door to be collected and turned to come back in. He met me halfway across the room and put his hand under my chin, encircling my throat between thumb and fingers. I felt my breath catch. David would never hold me like that. It felt dangerous, exciting. He pressed, not hard, but enough to make me drop my head back, exposing more of my neck to him. He shook me once. I gasped. My head rattled. Then he kissed me and I was lost. He pulled my clothes off me without any thought of zippers or seams. He moved me to wherever he wanted me without request or niceties. He ripped condom packets with his teeth as he laughed. He played the line between pleasure and pain to the millimetre.

We stayed in the room for two days. Room service trays came and went. I had to get the minibar restocked several times. Eventually Felix left the room to buy a bottle of vodka at the local shop, pointing out that it was cheaper than to keep raiding the miniatures.

I slept, when I needed to, wearing his Hush T-shirt or naked and numb, a deep exhausted blackness. Whenever I woke, Felix would be sitting writing lyrics on scraps of the hotel jotter from beside the bed, piles of them around him, some screwed into little balls, others laid out flat for future use. Or he'd be drumming on the tabletop with the forefingers of both hands, humming a tune to himself, eyes shut. When he noticed I was awake again, he'd crawl up the bed, long arms, long legs, black curly hair loose of its ponytail, licking his lips. Smiling.

Another time, I woke to find his hands either side of my face, cupping my cheeks. His eyes were shining in the lamplight and his face was very close.

'What is it?' I asked, worried.

'The beauty of you,' he whispered. 'The sheer fucking beauty of you.'

I ran the bath and we faced each other, sinking into bubbles, my legs over his thighs. He rubbed my hair dry afterwards, and then his own.

I texted David, just once, on the Saturday night. Guilty, not because I was in a hotel room with my lover, but because I didn't want to text him at all. I didn't want to burst the bubble. I felt like an alternate me. I felt like Bella.

We talked about travelling the world as we lay in tangled bed-sheets on the last afternoon. The places we wanted to go, to experience, to see. I dreamed of driving the wild coast on the Garden Route in South Africa, the weirdness of floating in the Dead Sea in Israel. He talked about how he wanted to watch the sun rise on a beach in Ibiza and another one set from Rick's Café in Negril, Jamaica. For a brief moment I fantasised about seeing all of those places together, daytimes in the sunshine, night-times under starry skies, but I knew deep down we never would. I held him very tight as the room started to darken. It was time to go. Felix leaned at the window, watching lights go on across the town, as I scooped my belongings into my bag and tried not to think about what I was doing, what I'd done.

I got back home before David. In plenty of time to have a bath, scrub my body and feel the aftershock of the weekend. The flashbacks that made me close my eyes momentarily. The ache that I felt for Felix. The creeping guilt that was catching up with me. The nag in my conscience every time I absent-mindedly twisted my wedding ring on my finger.

It was later, when David came up to bed, that he found it. A white scrap of paper, rolled into a ball, that must have got scooped up with my stuff in the hotel room and fallen out as I unpacked. It lay on the carpet next to our bed. He picked it up, straightened it out and read it.

'Prompt from your writing weekend?' he asked, showing it to me.

It was Felix's writing. A lyric he'd been working on.

I swallowed, nodded.

'Your spark lights the way.'

Wednesday 20 December

Sea temperature: 8.8 degrees.
Air temperature: 6 degrees.

Ivo's words rang in my head. I'd heard nothing else since last night. I plunged myself into the sea, timed my breath wrong and swallowed a mouthful of freezing salty water. I stopped, stood, choked, spat. Wiped my mouth and waited for my breath to calm. Not caring that Nancy wasn't there again, still in bed with her cold. I just needed this, for myself. I submerged again.

An affair that went wrong.

Was he talking about me? He had to be. All the timings added up. Twenty years ago was just before I got pregnant with the girls. The timing was spot on. But still, I couldn't believe he had taken his own life. Even knowing him as I did. Even after the last time we saw each other.

'Gassed himself.'

I struck out towards the pier, wanting to be alone, wanting to thrash the water and try to clear the image in my head.

Exhaust fumes.

As soon as he'd said the words, all I could think of was Patricia Monroe on the town council. She was the contact listed on the local directory, the person to notify about fly-tipping. She usually reported the dumped mattresses or builders' ballast at our monthly meetings – until a few summers ago, when she had received a call about an abandoned car on a patch of common land towards Easton Bavents. When she went to check it out, all on her own, a 68-year-old widow, she found a body in the car. A hosepipe connecting the exhaust to the driver's window. A suicide. It made the local paper. A student from Colchester, laden with debt and a failed module, who had driven out to the beach to leave his life behind. When Patricia told us about it at the council meeting the following week, she'd cried at the memory, the image of the man's face she couldn't forget. Everyone thinks that if you gas yourself you just go to sleep, but it's not as gentle as that on your body. Patricia dabbed her eyes as she recalled the fact that all the capillaries in his face had burst, bringing blood to the surface of the skin, turning him red, almost ruddy. His tongue was so swollen that it held his jaws apart. She sobbed as she whispered that his eyeballs had popped. He was so disfigured that his family weren't allowed to see him for identification. I put my arm around her at the council table, but she still shook. She resigned from fly-tipping duty soon afterwards. Said she couldn't take the risk of seeing something like that ever again.

Last night I'd seen Felix like that. Every dream, he was there. Pale cheeks reddened with blood. His eyeballs gone. Nothing there any more to see the sun rise in Ibiza or set at Rick's Café. I swallowed another mouthful of water as I gulped, tried to hold in a sob. Trod water for a moment, spat. Checking my watch, I knew it was time to turn, back towards home. Back towards Ivo.

I found him there, in his car.

The way Ivo said it had made me flinch. Imagine one of the girls coming home to that. It didn't bear thinking about. But something about Ivo didn't make me warm to him. There was something underlying. The way he'd told me how it happened without me asking. Something about the way he'd looked at me, studied me. It unnerved me. Made me feel clumsy. Made me feel guilty.

I could hardly wait the week out for him to go. I needed some space, and Kit did too. She hung on his every word, clung to him physically like a limpet. I'd heard them last night when I was pretending to sleep, the muffled climax of sex across the landing, the creaking bed, a bang on the wall. It was too close, too intense. I was thankful David was asleep; I didn't want him to have to hear. When Ivo was gone, Kit could get some perspective back about university – and life in general – and perhaps leave him behind. I just needed to get through the next few days. Then perhaps we could all move on.

The current had picked up and pulled me towards the dunes. I slackened off on my kick, not needing to drive myself so hard. I used my arms for direction only, let the water carry me. When I reached my marker, I turned to the beach until I could stand, grabbed hulking great breaths of air and forced all bad thoughts out of my head. It was time to go in. To David and the girls. Ivo I would just have to put up with until the end of the week. However shocked or sad I'd felt hearing about Felix's death, I didn't want Ivo in my life.

At waist level as I approached the shore, I saw a bodily mass of grey turning in the waves ahead. At first I thought it was a live seal, but then I realised the water was too shallow and the animal too still. Whatever it was, it was dead, moving only with the motion of the waves, the pull of the current. It must be heavy, grounded, too, as it leaned in towards the beach and then tilted back towards the horizon with each ebb and flow. I edged round it, thigh-deep, to approach from the side, stopped horrified, gasped.

It was a baby whale. Or the remains of one. Badly decomposed, skin turned soggy and blubber hanging off. Tail half gone, leaving just the open chest, the fleshy head. I gagged, thinking about how I'd had my head in the water ten feet away; the same water had been in my mouth as had washed the flesh off this body, that carried tiny bits of its innards with it. The corpse shifted minutely towards the beach again, on its way to being washed up on the beach. Poor, poor thing. There was something so sad about it, a wasted body delivered to shore by the sea.

I turned away, sickened. I'd ring the beach warden and they'd instruct a clean-up crew. I pitied them, trying to scoop this up. I was sure they'd prefer the odd packets we got washed up, a message in a bottle, once a lost cargo of plastic toys. I could only remember one other dead whale in my lifetime. But these things happen. The sea was a harsh environment. It was precisely that danger and risk that drew me back every time.

As I walked up the shingle to the beach hut I shook the water off my gloves, wiped my hand across my mouth. Spat. For once I didn't feel clean, or born again, coming out of the sea. I felt dirty. Bad.

David was out with Jess when I got home. He'd left a note for me on the kitchen table, old-school style, instead of texting as the kids would have done. The note told me they'd gone to Snape Maltings as Jess wanted to buy some Christmas presents. He'd signed it with a D and a kiss, as always. It would be nice for him to get some time with Jess on her own. I hoped she'd find what she was looking for among the craft stalls; there was always plenty of choice.

Kit was slumped over a coffee at the kitchen table, flicking through her phone. Dodge sat beside her adoringly with his head resting on her knee. I heard the shower running upstairs and relaxed slightly. Ivo wasn't there. I smiled. I could get five minutes on my own with Kit.

'There's a dead baby whale on the beach,' I said and she lifted her head from the phone.

'Yuk,' she said.

'Yup,' I said. 'I've notified the beach warden.'

'Wonder why it died?' she said.

'Maybe it got separated from its mum.' I shrugged. 'Their mums protect them from predators.'

'Is that what you do, Mum? Protect me from predators?'

I was about to answer, yes, when she yawned and stretched, arms above her head, and I felt the usual swell of pride for her lithe young body. She was beautiful, Kit, elfin-featured. She rolled her head side to side, shook out her shoulders, and her hair fell away from her neck, exposing a plum-purple love bite, on the soft hollow just above her clavicle. It reminded me of the noises of the night before. I filled the kettle and put it on the hot plate of the Aga.

'You'd better wear a polo neck today,' I said and she blinked at me, nonplussed. I pointed to the spot on my own neck and she switched her phone to camera mode and turned it to face herself. Her eyes widened slightly when she spotted it, but her lips curled up into a satisfied smile.

'Oops,' she said.

Her dressing gown gaped at the front and I saw the writing on the front of the T-shirt. The Hush. I turned away.

'Dad's not going to like that, Kit,' I warned. I didn't either, to be truthful. It looked cheap, obvious.

'I'll put some make-up on it,' she said, not at all bothered, almost proud.

The shower turned off upstairs, the pipes creaking to a stop. Footsteps padded across the ceiling above. My chest tightened. Time to put my happy face on and get through another day.

'More coffee?' I asked as the kettle whistled, and she nodded a yes, rubbing Dodge's head until he squinted his eyes shut with pleasure. It was as I had my back turned that she said: 'Mum, can you talk to Dad about this university thing?'

I didn't react, just spooned coffee into cups and filled them with hot water.

'What do you mean, this *university thing*?'

'I just think there are other ways to learn things,' she said, 'rather than just in uni.'

Topping the cups up with milk, I stirred them.

'I think I might be better out in the world,' she said. 'You know – the university of life.'

I frowned then. That didn't even sound like Kit. It sounded like a load of twaddle.

'Is this about the travelling?' I asked, tinging the spoon on the top of one of the cups. Might as well get to the heart of it.

'It's just that January is the best time to be in South Africa...' she said and then flushed.

'January?' For a moment I was confused, then her blush made me realise what she was actually saying. 'I thought you were talking about going in your second year, not now?'

'Ivo wants to go earlier,' she said with a shrug. 'No biggie.'

'But your course—' I said, and then kicked myself. That was the wrong tack.

'I'm not enjoying it,' she said, blankly.

'But just because you're not enjoying one part of university, you don't want to throw the whole experience away,' I said. 'Don't throw the baby out with the bath water.'

She sighed, dramatically. 'And there we are, back on babies again, just like the baby whale. Maybe it's time for this baby to make her own decisions.'

I forced a smile, knowing the best way forward was to keep the conversation open.

'Absolutely, Kit,' I agreed. 'It has to be your decision. All that we want, Dad and I, is to help you think through all the options so that you make the right one.'

She softened slightly, scratched Dodge's ear absently. 'I know it's not what you'd choose for me, Mum. But I really want us to talk about it properly. Like adults. It's really important.' Her glance was conciliatory, hopeful, and I relented.

'So let's talk later,' I said, 'When Dad's here too.'

I held a coffee out towards her, a peace offering, and she grinned as she extended her hand to take it. A shadow caught my eye, a smudge dark around the pale of her wrist. Was it a bruise? Before I could ask, Ivo walked in and at the sight of him she tucked her hands into her sleeves as though hugging herself. His hair, still wet from the shower, curled around his face and reminded me of Felix coming offstage, sweating. Sensing he'd walked into something, Ivo stopped halfway across the floor, glanced from Kit to me and back again.

'Sorry...' he said. 'Am I interrupting?'

Kit laughed nervously. 'No,' she started and then I saw herself pull herself up, change her mind about keeping quiet. She obviously thought it was better to side with him. She chose him over me.

'Mum's a bit shocked at *this* though.' She pointed to the love bite on her neck.

Something crossed his face, a tiny tremor, and then he coloured, bit his lip.

'Oops,' he said, just like she had earlier, and it made me think they'd done this before. That they'd laughed before about his marks on her. She wore it like a badge of ownership. A brand she was proud of. My stomach turned.

'Perhaps we should try to contain ourselves, Ivo.' Kit giggled as she moved away from Dodge and over to him. 'While we're in my parents' house,' she went on.

He looked at me, half-smiling.

'Sorry Bell-e,' he said again and my teeth clenched.

'It's not like you'd hurt me, is it?' Kit simpered, rubbing herself against his side, trying to get him to put his arms round her, which he did, tightly. She buried her face into his chest, all but disappeared.

'What do *you* think?' he asked, over her shoulder. But he wasn't looking at her, he was looking at me. I tried a smile, but it slid away. Something felt wrong here; the atmosphere was off.

'Right, sex talk over,' Kit said, wriggling out of his hold. 'I'm off for a shower.' She picked up her coffee and squeezed Ivo's hand on her way out the door. I found myself trying to see her wrist again, but she moved too fast. We could both hear her run up the stairs, humming to herself. Ivo waited until she was in the room above us and we heard the pipes groan and the water start again. Then he bent to stroke Dodge, who had settled on the floor, rubbing his ears gently for a moment before turning his face up to me.

'I don't think you're in any position to question anyone's sex life,' he said and his eyes had a flatness to them, a blankness that reminded me of the dead whale.

'What?' I stammered, blindsided.

His tone, his expression; everything was wrong.

'Bell-a,' he whispered.

David and Jess arrived half an hour later with a blast of cold air and arms full of paper bags. Morag came in with them, making me feel guilty that I hadn't even thought of where she was that morning. I'd presumed she was downstairs, but obviously she'd enjoyed a trip to the craft market too.

David smelled of lemon aftershave when he rubbed a stubbly cheek on mine for a kiss. I gripped the front of his jacket, pulled him in. I wanted to bury my face in his chest as Kit had done with Ivo. I wanted to hold on to all that I had that was good in my life. Suddenly it all felt like it was going to come crashing down around me. He lifted my chin with his thumb and forefinger.

'You okay?' he asked quietly.

'I'm fine,' I said, giving him a reassuring squeeze, and then, quietly so that Jess wouldn't hear, 'We need to talk about Kit.'

He held my eye for a moment, and I managed a smile. 'Going travelling,' I said as a reassurance that everything was okay, and he grimaced and then nodded.

Morag plonked herself down in the chair nearest the Aga, the warmest one but also the one that was always in the way. She looked at the kettle from there, as though it might magically boil itself. I put it on the hot plate.

'A few different stalls, Mum,' Jess was saying, 'some nice new stuff.'

'Get everything you needed?' I asked, nodding at the assortment of bags around her chair. She opened a few and showed me bead necklaces for friends at university, a beanie hat for Kit.

'Found a Christmas present for Naomi,' she said, showing me a silver necklace in a box with half an old-fashioned sixpence coin hanging as a pendant. 'I'll give her this one to wear,' she said, 'and I'll wear the other half.' She pulled at the neck of her jumper to show me the other half of the coin, already secured on a chain round her neck. It was lovely. A real token of affection. Or more? I tried to catch her eye, but Jess was looking in the next bag. She shut the top theatrically. 'And I got a certain someone a very nice birthday present!' She grinned.

'Ha!' I said, trying to keep the mood light. 'Don't tell me! Is it a bus pass? Or a Zimmer frame?'

'You're not old, Mum. Fifty is the new forty, apparently!'

'Thank God for that!'

Kit and Ivo came in and sat on my side of the table and my stomach turned over. I glanced at Kit, but she smiled back at me as normal. He looked at me blankly. So, if he did know, he hadn't told her my secret. I let my breath out slowly. I didn't feel like I'd been able to breathe properly since his comment earlier. I'd blustered a laugh at the time.

'I don't know what you're talking about,' I'd said.

'Oh, I think you do,' he'd replied with narrow eyes, before leaving me there clutching the sink.

'My gorgeous wife, half a century!' David said now, pouring tea for everyone.

Chat started about what we were doing for my actual birthday on Saturday. David told them about the table booked at the Sutherland House Hotel. There were oohs and ahhhs. We only went there for special occasions; the last one had been the girls' eighteenth birthday.

'So is it a big deal? Being fifty?' Kit asked. 'Is it making you question the meaning of life?'

Morag snorted. 'She's nowhere near the age of wisdom, that comes nearer seventy…'

'Lucky we've got you then, the wise old owl,' Kit said and nudged her, much to Morag's delight.

'Less of the old, thank you very much,' she said.

'But seriously, are you where you wanted to be at this age?' Jess turned towards me, sipping her tea. 'Is it what you expected?' Everyone was looking at me. I tried to say something, but knew that whatever I said would be wrong.

'It's better than I expected,' I said, hoping they'd drop the subject.

'How could it not be?' David said, throwing his arm round the back of my chair. 'With us in your life?' Everyone laughed, except Ivo. I felt him looking at me and my face burned. I had everything in my life. He had nothing. Because of me, he thought.

'Shall we do a fifty at fifty list, Mum?' Jess suggested. 'Fifty things you want to do in the next year?' She picked up her phone to start typing notes. 'Can be anything, big or small.'

Everyone started bandying suggestions around the table, from the sublime to the ridiculous. Dye my hair pink, suggested Kit. Swim the Channel, from Morag. Go to the Grand Prix, said David, with a hopeful grin. Volunteer at a homeless shelter, prompted Jess. They carried on: ring a radio station, go on a TV quiz show. Jess wrote them all down, 'so that you can pick later'. Everyone laughed when David said 'Be together' as a suggestion. It was the one thing I toasted to every Christmas – 'Being together' – the one thing I treasured above everything.

Now, I couldn't think about anything but Ivo, sitting there potentially knowing what I did. My dirtiest secret that could smash my marriage apart. I looked at David, passing round home-made cakes he'd bought at the Maltings, enjoying the full table of his family. A huge lump of despair lodged itself in my throat and I couldn't swallow. I tried again but my mouth was dry as sand.

I reached for the cup in front of me to take a sip, an attempt to calm myself down. Ivo's hand shot out and caught mine, tight round my wrist, and circled it with his thumb and forefinger. I gasped. It was the same grip, I thought, that he would have used on Kit's wrists to hold her to the bed, or the wall, or wherever he wanted, if that was a bruise on her wrist. It hurt.

'That's my one,' he said with a smile, nodding at the tea, and letting my wrist drop before anyone saw how hard he'd held it.

'Sorry,' I stammered, confused and realising I'd gone for the wrong cup. Just like maybe I was jumping to the wrong conclusion about the bruise.

'Careful, Belle,' he joked, too loudly and confirming my worst fears, 'you don't want a reputation for taking things that don't belong to you.'

David raised his eyebrows in our direction.

'What's that?' he said.

'Just our little joke,' Ivo said. 'Eh, Belle.'

David questioned me with his eyes.

'Yes, I mistakenly ate his toast this morning too.'

'Can't trust her with anything!' Ivo said, raising his hands in the air.

Everyone laughed.

Jess decided it was way past time to put up the Christmas decorations, and dragged me to the landing.

'Less than a week to go. We'd normally have them up by now,' she said, pulling the loft hatch open to hook out the ladder. I held the bottom steady for her and up she went, singing, 'Deck the halls with boughs of holly,' as she went.

It was true. Some years, when the girls were small, we'd put them up in early December, but if not, then always after school on the last day of term. David had been broken up for half a week already but we still hadn't got to it.

In Kit's room opposite, Ivo coughed. It sounded like a reminder that he was still there. I stared at the closed door, wondering what they were doing on the other side. Was he going to tell her his suspicions? Whisper what he knew, on the pillow one night? Was he going to tell everyone that I'd had an affair, was the one his dad killed himself over? I couldn't live the rest of the week like this, with him taunting me – because that's what he was doing. I definitely couldn't live the rest of my life like this, with him holding it over me.

Jess started passing boxes down to me, boxes that had been in the family for years. I stacked them around my legs until she climbed back down with a 'Tralalala la, la la la laaaaaaaaa,' and we carried them to the lounge.

I opened the box nearest to me and unwrapped the first of the twin angels. They must be almost fifteen years old now. The five-year-old girls had come home from school with their Christmas art projects, a pair of wooden spoons decorated with doily wings, white hanky dresses and yellow string hair. They drew eyes and lips onto the spoon faces and hung a hook of string behind them to attach them to the branch. The two were almost identical, except that Kit had added red to her angel's cheeks and rouged her mouth, like an Aunt Sally doll, and used a black felt-tip pen to draw on eyelashes. After they'd gone to bed, David and I had laughed at our rather overly made-up tree angel. It was especially funny that Jess's one was more angelic-looking because she was naughty as hell at that age. A true demon.

The angels still hung on the tree every year, and the girls always remarked on them. In their early teens with embarrassment: 'Oh, you're not putting that on again are you,' or 'Look how dumb my one looks.' But more recently with sentimentality: 'Oh do you remember these?' or 'I can't believe you've still got these, Mum!' I'd always have them, that was the thing. They'd always take pride of place. They were one of my favourite things about Christmas. I unwrapped the other one and held them both in my hands for a moment.

Jess put candles on windowsills and arranged the terrible Santa sled and reindeer set on the coffee table, the one with real reindeer hair on the animals. They had been a gift from Morag one year after she'd visited a Christmas market. Another thing David and I had laughed at in the evening, on the sofa with a glass of wine. Sitting in the middle of the boxes, I was suddenly scared that I would cry, and busied myself taking baubles out of tissue paper and placing them in rows on the hearth, ready for the tree.

Ivo and Kit came in behind me. Jess trilled a 'Fa La la la la' at them and I heard them settle on the sofa. I kept unpacking. I couldn't bring myself to look at him, but I could feel his stare on my back.

'Where's the old tart, then?' asked Kit.

I froze, not wanting to see the expression on her face. If it was condemnation, accusation, then he'd told her. I couldn't bear to see her disappointment, or disgust. I'd lose her. I'd lose them all. I clenched my fists and looked over my shoulder.

'Aha! Here she is,' Kit said, lifting the made-up angel and showing it to Ivo. 'This is my one.'

He held it up beside her face as though looking for a similarity, and they both laughed.

Jess held hers out for inspection too, the markedly more virtuous version.

I let out a jagged breath and my shoulders dropped an inch. He hadn't said anything. Yet. But my gut told me he would. I needed to talk to him first, to try to stop my two worlds colliding. But in that second I recognised that if Ivo told Kit, I also had to be prepared to confess to David. It was the only way I stood a chance of keeping him. Of telling him how sorry I was. To beg for forgiveness.

Morag and David joined us as I unwrapped the last bauble and laid it on the hearth. The decorations rested in rows, reds and whites, candy-striped, glass, fabric, tin. Love hearts and balls, robins and bells, collected over decades, all ready for another year. I leaned against David's legs, glad of his presence but also terrified of him being in the room with Ivo. I kept my gaze low, watched the fire.

'So I was thinking,' Kit said, and I sensed trouble by the tone of her voice. It was the one she had always used when she was going to ask if she could stay out later, or buy a new jumper, when you'd already given her a curfew or her allowance. I felt David shift slightly behind me. He'd heard it too. We knew our girls well.

'Yeeeeesss?' David said, playfully.

'Seeing as your birthday is on Saturday and we're all going out to dinner...' The fire hissed and spat with a damp log. I jabbed at it with the poker.

'...and Christmas Eve is the Sunday...' she said in that sing-song way. I stiffened, realising where this was going.

'Instead of Ivo going home on Christmas Eve, which would be a bit sad...' She paused as though she wanted us to jump in, to suggest what she herself wanted to say. I pressed my mouth shut, stared into the flames. There was no way in hell I was proposing it. I wanted him gone.

'...perhaps he could stay for Christmas?' she said.

Jess tilted her head towards David to gauge his response, and out of the corner of my eye I saw Morag smile, like it was her decision to make.

The last thing I wanted was Ivo in the house a minute longer than was necessary.

'Where would you be going otherwise?' David asked, a question to buy himself time and a tactic we often used to give ourselves thinking space. I glanced at Ivo as he shrugged.

'Back to my digs, I guess.'

'On your own?' Morag said, and got a nod in return. There was a split second of silence. He'd played it well.

'Well, we can't have that, can we?' David said, and I heard my own breath rush between my dry lips.

'Of course you should stay,' said Morag. 'I know Belle's cooking's not the best but she doesn't do a bad turkey.' She grinned at me as though I should appreciate the compliment, and I gritted my teeth around a smile in return.

'Yay,' Kit said, but Ivo wasn't celebrating yet. He was looking at me.

'Yes, stay with us if you'd like,' David said. 'Christmas is not a time to be on your own.'

'Is that all right with you, Belle? I'd hate to think I was overstaying my welcome.'

'Of course,' I managed. 'Not at all.'

Kit squeezed Ivo with pleasure, and I turned away.

Dodge chose that moment to come in and wag a fart about with his tail. The girls shrieked and fanned the air.

'Dodge is the stinkiest member of the family,' Kit said, holding her nose. I jumped at the distraction, pulling Dodge towards me despite the smell. I buried my face in his neck.

'I don't know,' said Jess. 'What about Gran after Brussels sprouts on Christmas afternoon!'

Morag flapped her hands at them, chuckling.

'Ignore them, Dodge,' I said to him, ruffling his ears, keeping my eyes on his trusting ones. 'You're still Mummy's best boy.'

David stood.

'Right, let's get this Christmas started then. Who's coming with me to get the tree?' It was a rhetorical question really; it was tradition that he went with the girls. They always drove out to a farm on the outskirts of town to pick the right shape and height and then cut it down together. Morag and I usually waited at home, her sipping a whisky, picking tinsel off the carpet and tutting about my housekeeping skills. Me, drinking a glass of wine and wishing they'd hurry up. But this year, with Ivo in the mix, it was a different scenario.

'Me!' Jess jumped up, as I'd known she would.

'Us,' said Kit and my stomach clenched.

'Not me, if you don't mind,' said Ivo. Kit's face fell.

'Why not?' she demanded, lip out.

'I want to go and photograph the whale, if it's still there. I've never seen one.'

'I'll come with you then,' Kit said, and I was pleased to hear Jess tut.

'No, you go,' he said. 'It's what you always do, didn't you say?' He shrugged, stood up from the sofa. I felt a momentary relief.

We all stood up to go our separate ways. I went to get the whisky and wine. Jess and David went to the garage to find the stand for the tree. Kit and Ivo went upstairs. As I passed, heading to the bathroom, I heard them in her room. Drawers opening and closing, the sound of a bag being unzipped. Kit was not happy. I knew from her tone of voice that her jaw would be set.

'But you could come with us,' she was saying. 'And then I could come with you later.'

There was silence, which I knew would not go down well with Kit.

'Don't you want me to come?' she tried then, and I knew her face would now have changed to a wide-eyed pout.

'I just want to go and take photos, Kit,' he said and it was low and final.

'It's not like it's a tradition that stops anyone else joining in,' she lied. I didn't ever offer to go; nor did Morag. We knew it was their time. It was worth it to see the looks on their faces when they carried the tree back into the lounge and stood it in the window. Their choice. Their effort. Their Christmas tree.

'I don't want to,' he said then. 'I'm going to the beach. I need to make plans.'

'Well, I should definitely come then, shouldn't I?' God, she was determined. This was next level, even for Kit. Silently I willed her to let him go. 'Unless I'm not part of your plans?'

There was a silence and then the sound of a kiss.

'You're most definitely part of my plans, babe,' he said. 'You have a starring role.'

My heart sank as I'm sure Kit's swelled.

Two minutes later, Jess and David jumped in the front seats of the car, hats and gloves in their hands. Kit climbed in the back and waved out the window to Ivo as he pulled his jacket over his shoulders on the doorstep.

I watched David carefully check his mirror before pulling away, and my heart hurt at the thought of breaking his when he got home. But there was nothing else for it, I had to tell him. I couldn't let Ivo hold it over me.

'Any cake left?' Morag called out hopefully.

Ivo turned to me, fingering Dodge's lead on the hook.

'Can I take Dodge with me, for the walk?' he asked. Dodge heard the magic word and danced around his feet at the prospect and I couldn't say no. In fact, I couldn't bring myself to say anything at all. I nodded. Wanting Ivo out of my house, even if it was just for an hour. It was an hour for which I knew my family was intact. Ivo, seemingly oblivious, smiled over his shoulder at me, and the tilt of his head, the lift of his chin, reminded me of a smile I'd seen many times before. I shut the door behind him.

Ten minutes later, full of carrot cake and nursing a whisky, Morag turned her attention to her iPad and an online game of Scrabble. Seemed she'd rather play a stranger than have a game with me in real life, even though she knew I loved word games. Always had. I sipped my wine and picked at my nails. The alcohol warmed my insides, but didn't numb the nag of worry. They wouldn't be long, and when they got back I would have to find a time to talk to David. I couldn't run away from my secret anymore and I couldn't let someone else use it against me. But in the meantime, I couldn't just sit there, waiting for him to come back. I had to do something.

Wandering aimlessly room to room, I eventually found myself in my bedroom. I knelt on the floor beside the bed with an array of wrapping paper and presents before me. I'd only hidden them under there out of habit; it wasn't like the girls would go hunting for their presents anymore. There were quite a few to be wrapped and I might as well get on with it; after tonight, I had no idea what might happen. Would I even be here for Christmas if I told David about the affair? Or would he want me to leave? The thought stopped me dead. *Was this the last day I had with my family?* I pushed it away, clinging to the hope that David would see past it, forgive the transgression. It was so long ago. Almost twenty years. Surely he wouldn't throw away all of that for such a stupid mistake?

But if he did forgive me and I was still here for Christmas, would Ivo be too? Surely we couldn't coexist in this house? Things could be really awkward. In fact, I didn't think they could ever be normal. Even if David was able to move on with me, would he ever welcome Ivo, knowing he was the son of my lover? Knowing he held it against me? Even open-minded David, who was so laid-back he was horizontal, had limits. He had boundaries. And I didn't know if he could get around any of this. I spread out paper and pre-cut strips of Sellotape, relieved to have something to do with my hands.

I wrapped underwear sets for each of the girls, writing the gift tags with care, with all our love, M&D. I put them on the bed, ready to go under the tree when it was in position, for the girls to examine, sniff, shake and guess at.

There wouldn't be so many presents this year. We'd had Christmases when the pile was obscene and Morag would reminisce about stockings stuffed with a satsuma and a piece of coal. It was strange now the girls were eighteen; they no longer wanted the silly gifts, the jokes that made you laugh for five minutes. For the last few years, they'd wanted make-up and clothes and money, and that brought the pile down hugely. I'd been thoughtful this year in trying to get some things made that I thought people would love.

I picked up the family-tree picture I'd had designed and framed for Morag, and gave it a polish with my sleeve before starting to wrap it in paper. It was based on a flowering cherry, her favourite, and her name hung on a little wooden plaque from the top branch. David and I hung beneath her in the boughs and Jess and Kit's names hung from below like fruit. It was hand-painted and pretty and I hoped she'd love it and not think it tacky compared to the hard work she put into real family trees. As I put the last bit of tape on the paper, I wondered if David would tell her about my affair, after I told him. However badly she thought of me now, it was nothing to what she'd think if she knew. I wondered if she'd ever talk to me again. It felt like my whole family would shake on its foundations. I placed the gift on the bed with the others.

I made quick work of getting through the pile, trying to keep my mind on the job at hand. Peeling off price tags, neatening edges with the scissors before folding the paper.

Eventually I got to the photo books I'd created for Jess and Kit, the last things to wrap. I was so pleased with them when they arrived; they'd turned out exactly as I'd hoped. David and I had already pored over them, exclaiming over baby teeth and chubby knees, plaits and bunches. Now, holding them, it made my heart ache. It had taken me hours to sort through our old family photo albums and scan in the photos to include. Each girl's book was personal to her, although a lot of the photos were shared, as we had so many great pictures of the two of them together I knew they would both want a copy: blowing the candles out on their joint birthday cakes, or their first day at school standing on the front step with their arms round each other. But then there were others that were particular to them. Jess's period of wearing only purple. Kit's determination to learn to tap-dance after watching an old film. All of those were included too. The books covered the first eighteen years of their lives and were meant as a keepsake. Something they could take back to university with them, keep close, to remind them who they were and what they had around them if they ever needed it. All that love.

I picked up Jess's book and opened it carefully, not wanting to bend the spine. I flicked to the photo I loved the most. I knew exactly where it was and I'd given it a whole page to itself. It was a side-profile shot. She was about four years old, watching a Punch and Judy show, unaware of the camera, eyes wide in delight. Her tongue just peeped through her baby teeth and I could almost hear her squeal.

I closed the book, pressed it back together gently, and picked up Kit's. I knew the image I wanted to see of her too and coincidentally it was also taken on the beach. It had been such a big part of their growing up, the dunes, the sea. I found the picture and smoothed the page out as though rubbing Kit's skin. She stood facing me on the sand, barefoot and tanned, about seven. She held a crab out towards me, between her thumb and forefinger as we'd taught her, so that the pincers couldn't reach her. It wasn't a big crab, murky green, one leg missing, but she held it towards me like treasure and we had caught her smile perfectly just as it dimpled.

Now, though, looking at it, I saw something else. Something that made the hair on the nape of my neck prickle.

In my mind's eye I saw Ivo.

The dimples. The tilt of the chin.

The smile was the same.

I flicked forward a few pages, finding a different angle. Kit, aged nine, looked up at me from under her fringe as I called her name. Now all I saw was Ivo looking at me from the kitchen table when I offered him tea. I could hear my own breath as I frantically turned to another page. Kit laughed at a party, head back, eyes shut. The mirror image of Ivo laughing at something on his phone the day before.

I slammed the book shut.

They looked the same.

They looked like they could be related.

They looked like brother and sister.

My brain was racing, trying to make a coherent thought. It couldn't be true.

I banged my forehead with my own palm, once, twice, trying to quieten the buzzing in my head. My blood roared in my ears, louder than the surf in the mornings.

I had fallen pregnant with the twins the same month I ended the affair with Felix. I'd thought about it before but had dismissed it. David and I had never used protection and Felix and I always had. We'd only had sex a handful of times, in that hotel room. It couldn't be true. But then, an image of Felix grinning, laughing – tearing at the condom foil with his teeth – made me shudder. What if? My mouth went dry as dust. What if? A tiny tear, the slightest rip was all it took.

I pushed the book away, stumbled to my feet. My legs were numb from kneeling, the blood restricted. I fumbled with the window catch and pushed it wide, stared out into the dusk, gulping in breaths of icy air.

Minutes later, when my breathing had returned to normal and I pulled the window closed again, I caught my own reflection against the sky outside. The arch of my eyebrows just like Jess's. The shape of my jaw, like Kit's. The girls looked like me. And David too. Jess had his eye colour, Kit had his hair. Morag, not wanting to give me any credit for them at all, always said the girls, especially Jessie, were 'true Walker'.

They were an equal mix of us, which we'd always been thankful for. So pleased they weren't identical. So pleased they both had their own looks, their own styles, but equally happy to spot our traits in them, and to claim them as ours. They were their own people, but they were ours.

But what if they weren't ours? Or not David's, anyway. What if they were Felix's girls?

That would change everything. If I told David about the affair and the girls, he lost everything, through no fault of his own. I shut my eyes to think about the total devastation he would feel.

Car headlights shone down South Green and a moment later they pulled up outside, Christmas tree on the roof. As soon as the handbrake went on the doors opened and the girls piled out. David got out of the driving seat and stretched his arms above his head. Spotting me at the bedroom window, he waved at me and pointed at the tree, grinning. I caught a sob in my throat, smiled and gave him a thumbs-up.

I couldn't tell him now.

I had to find out the truth first, reassure myself the girls were his.

Then I'd decide what to do next.

'You feeling okay, love?' David asked, once the tree was settled on its stand in front of the window. Jess and Kit had disappeared into the house to get drinks and charge phones. Morag was off to the loo. He studied my face and I hoped he couldn't read anything in my eyes. 'You're a bit pale.'

The weight of anxiety on my chest threatened to block my throat. I cleared it quietly and nodded.

'Just a bit tired, that's all.'

'Sure?' His eyes asked questions of mine and I forced myself to smile.

He put his arm round me and tucked me in to his side, so that we could stand together and admire the tree. I smelled the fabric conditioner on his jumper and the lemon of his aftershave and wanted to cry.

'Well, you are knocking on I suppose,' he said, with a squeeze, and a nod at the tree before us. 'What do you think?'

'Tailor-made,' I said. It fitted snugly in the alcove and once lit would be visible to anyone walking past. They'd chosen well, as always. It was the perfect shape, full and bushy at the bottom and narrowing towards its tip, although still with plenty of branches to hang decorations from.

'Girls have a good time?' I asked David, still leaning into him.

'Hmm,' he said and wrinkled his nose. 'Think they might be a bit fed up with each other about something.' So he'd felt it too. The same thing I'd felt the night before. Something festering between them.

'Did they say anything?' God, don't let them know about me. Please, don't let them know about me.

'No. They were on their own for a bit as we walked around choosing the tree, and then it was more the silence between them afterwards.' So, something had been said. Or done. Unusual. They were normally so close.

'I'll pop up and see if they need anything,' I said, and slipped quietly out of the room. I padded up the stairs and opened the door to Jess's room. I thought it was empty until

I heard the spit of her voice through the door of the Jack and Jill bathroom.

'I mean it, Kit. You should tell them.'

'Oh shut up, Jess. For God's sake. They don't *need* to know.' They were hissing at each other. Something banged on the sink.

'Well I think it's something they'd *want* to know,' Jess snapped back. 'And if you don't tell them, then I will.'

The electric overhead light buzzed in the stunned silence.

'Two can play that game, Jess,' Kit said and I knew her eyes would be narrowed to slits. 'You tell them about him. I'll tell them about you.'

'You wouldn't.' It wasn't a question but it didn't sound convincing.

'I would, Jess,' Kit said again. 'Now fuck off.'

I stumbled backward out of the room before the bathroom door could open.

Jess came back into the living room five minutes later, took the string of white fairy lights from the box and began winding them around the tree's lower branches. Kit slunk in soon after, and slouched on the sofa.

'Where's Ivo?' she asked.

'Out with the whale still, I guess,' I said.

'He's not back yet?' She frowned. 'That's weird. It's not like he's going to get great photos now – it's dark.' I glanced out past the tree, to the houses illuminated on the other side of the road. She was right; all daylight had gone.

She checked her watch and tutted. 'I thought he'd be back by now,' she said as if it was a great inconvenience.

'Have you got withdrawal symptoms?' Jess said slyly. Kit checked Morag wasn't looking and then flicked her fingers up at her in a V-sign.

Jess smirked. 'No worries, you can stay and help me with this,' she said, reaching the lights to the top of the tree.

Kit tapped her fingers on the table, thinking.

'He took Dodge with him too,' I said. 'Maybe they're just having a nice walk.'

'I could go out and meet them,' Kit said, picking up her phone to ring him. Jess snorted and said 'bunny boiler' under her breath. Kit glared.

'Why don't you just wait for him to come back?' David said. 'You don't need to be rambling around in the dark.'

She shrugged but dialled Ivo anyway, listening for a few moments before sniffing and hanging up.

'Didn't pick up,' she said, looking at her watch again.

'Maybe he just wants a bit of time to himself,' I said, trying to encourage her to stay with us. I felt it was more likely Ivo might tell her if they were out on their own. I felt safer when we were all together.

'He's not used to being part of a family, remember,' David said. 'Just relax. He'll be back soon.'

David rummaged in the cupboard and put on the Christmas CD, immediately starting to sing along and pretend to play the bells. I lit the candle on the coffee table and soon the room smelled of cinnamon. Kit half-heartedly twirled some tinsel around the fir, and hung a few of the big baubles on high branches, which Jess quickly rearranged, putting the larger ones at the base with the smaller balls at the top.

Soon we were all gathered round the tree, passing tiny china doves and robins, hanging bells. Kit made sure she was standing near the window so she could sneak a quick look outside at the steps whenever she got the chance. The twin angels were the last things to be attached, side by side at the top.

We stood back, in a semicircle, and David turned off the main overhead lights, leaving us in the cosy glow from the dying fire. He gave Jess the nod and she flicked the plug switch with a 'Ta-Da!' and the tree lit up in all its white, twinkling beauty, reflecting in the window behind. Everyone cheered. The tree was picture-perfect, but more meaningful to me was the look on their faces. David proud and happy, his arm round Morag's shoulders as she clutched her hands in front of her chest like a prayer. Jess's eyes, above her rosy cheeks, caught the lights from the heat of the room. Even Kit stopped agitating for a moment and grinned. I saw the shadow of her dimple in her cheek. It felt like a precious moment of time, even more special because everything might be about to fall apart.

None of us heard the front door open or Ivo come in. But I felt the draught and when I turned round he was there, behind us. I gasped.

'I'm sorry,' he said as everyone else spun round.

'That's okay,' said David with a laugh. 'You made us jump!'

'No, I mean – I'm sorry,' he said and shook his head. It was then I saw the lead hanging from his hand.

'Where's Dodge?' I asked, suddenly worried.

'He spooked on the beach and ran off,' Ivo said, wringing his hands together with the lead between them. 'I've been looking for him for hours.'

'Oh no,' David said. 'You should have come and got us. We could have helped.' We were already moving to get coats and hats, to go out and look, bring him home.

'What spooked him?' Kit asked, sidling over to Ivo, more worried about him than the dog. I felt my skin bristle.

'A motorbike backfired,' he said, 'and he just went.' He pushed his hands through his hair, looking distraught. Kit rubbed his arm.

'Come on, girls,' David said pointedly. 'Ivo, perhaps you can show us where and which direction he went.'

'He's never been worried by motorbikes before.' Jess was already stuffing her feet into her trainers.

'Maybe it was because he was with me, a stranger?' Ivo shook his head. 'I'm so sorry. It's all my fault.'

'Just one of those things,' David said kindly. 'I'm sure Dodge will come back when he hears our voices.' Ivo blew out between his lips, looking like the weight of the world was on his shoulders.

We headed for the door, Christmas tree forgotten. Coats were zipped, gloves pulled on. David took torches off the hook in the hall cupboard and passed them out, along with spare leads.

'We'll split up when you show us where, Ivo,' he said, taking charge. 'Mum, you stay here in case he turns up at the door.'

Morag patted his shoulder. 'He'll be fine, love,' she said and David gave her a hopeful smile before pulling the door open to the night and heading down the steps.

'Try not to worry, hen,' she said then to me and I did a double-take at the softness in her voice as she patted my sleeve. Jess and Kit put their heads down into the wind and followed him. Ivo held the door for me and pulled it closed behind us.

'God, I do hope nothing's happened to him,' he said as he paused next to me on the step. 'I know he's Mummy's favourite boy.'

The tide was fully in, the water reaching halfway up the beach. A small square was cordoned off with tape, marking the body of the whale. It had not been moved and was almost submerged, but the water wasn't strong enough to dislodge it from the sand or drag it back out to sea. The wind buffeted us from the north, cold enough to make my eyes stream.

'Belle, I think we should split up,' David said, 'he's more likely to come to either you or me.'

'I'll come with you, Dad,' Jess said, not looking at Kit and Ivo, putting her hood up.

'We'll go with Mum,' Kit said and my heart sank. But then I realised that if Ivo was with me, I could keep an eye on him and at least he wasn't on his own with David.

Ivo set us off in the direction of the dunes and we split into our two groups. Jess and David set off towards Ferry Road, with the aim of taking in Salt Creek on the way back. Kit and Ivo and I stayed the beach side of the dunes heading straight to the river mouth, where the Blyth met the sea.

Dodge knew this place like the back of his hand. He knew every rabbit warren, every grassy track. In eight years, the only time he'd ever spooked was when a stunt kite had flown fast and low overhead, whirring in the air above him. Then he'd bolted. Run like a dog possessed along the sand, deaf to my shouts. I'd caught up with him eventually, almost at the foot ferry, and he'd still been trembling, terrified. But he'd only been about six months old at the time; it was totally under-standable. Since then, he'd been pretty much bulletproof.

'You mustn't blame yourself,' Kit was saying to Ivo. 'We'll find him.'

We walked and called until my throat hurt, trying to make myself heard over the surf. I didn't talk to the others. I had nothing to say. We made it to the river and back again, continued to the pier in case he'd doubled back. As we stood there under the lights, David rang my phone.

'Anything?' he asked and I knew he hadn't found Dodge either. We agreed to circle back with the hope that he may have found his way home, but as we approached the house I saw Morag at the front window, with her hands pressed around her eyes at the glass, peering into the darkness outside, and my heart sank. He wasn't there.

We all met on the doorstep. David shook his head. I bit my lip.

'You go in,' he said to the girls. 'Mum and I will carry on looking.'

'I'll come with you,' Ivo said, pulling his scarf tight round his neck. 'It's the least I can do.' Kit looked at him like he was her hero and I wanted to vomit. It was his fault Dodge was lost.

'Probably best for you to stay here, not knowing the area so well,' David said.

'I'm kicking myself, David. I should have told you earlier,' Ivo said. 'It's never good to keep bad things to yourself.' He fixed me with his dark eyes, looking sorrowful.

'Text me, Mum,' Jess said as David and I turned back down the steps. 'I'll ring the police and the coastguard and ask them to keep an eye out.'

Kit reached out and squeezed Jess's arm, their argument seemingly forgotten for the time being. 'And I'll list him on the local lost dogs' websites too.'

'I'll put something on the Southwold and Aldeburgh Facebook pages,' Morag said, already reaching for her iPad. The door shut behind them and we set off.

David and I stayed out until the tide turned again, the backward suck of the water losing its power on the shingle, the incoming surge throwing driftwood onto the stones. The Christmas streetlights stayed on behind us in the town, but house Christmas lights clicked off to darkness as their residents went to bed. The stars brightened their hold on the sky. We hardly talked to each other, just took turns to call Dodge's name. We walked well-trodden tracks, silver with moonlight across the marshes. We held gloved hands as we walked.

The set of David's jaw reminded me of his face when he was revising for his finals at university. A quiet determination on his usually genial face. When something was important to him, he had a focus, an intensity that you wouldn't expect. To everyone else he was a friendly, cheerful chap. Affable. Thoroughly nice. But I knew how deeply he felt things. How at his heart he was passionate, loyal and true. How he would do anything for those he loved. I'd seen it the first time I ever visited his home, the patience and humour, love and respect he showed to Morag, alongside the fierce protection he showed me.

It was why I chose him to begin with.

It was what had made me stay with him all these years.

I couldn't lose him now. I'd almost done that once already.

And I wouldn't lose Dodge either.

On the Monday after my weekend with Felix, David went to bed with the flu. I'd never known him to be so ill, so weak; he was always the one who held me up, the one who supported me. He was in bed for five days straight, sweating, tossing and turning with fever and chills. Moaning with the aches in his bones. He must have caught it from someone on his course. I took to the spare room to stop from getting it myself, and warned Morag to stay away for a while.

He slept for the first twelve hours and I hoped that might clear it, but he woke sunken-eyed and exhausted. I couldn't get him to eat anything, and he'd only sip at water if I held it to his lips. I did so, feeling like a traitor, a cheat. Looking at his mouth and thinking about Felix. Feeling the heat in David's back as I sponged him down with a damp cloth and remembering the burn of Felix's skin against mine. My phone beeped with a message, but I couldn't bring myself to look at it.

I tried to work at my desk in the office downstairs, close enough to hear if David needed me. I tried to write the copy needed by the Health Trust, but every creak of the bed above made me stop, listen. I felt like I was being punished. I knew it was ridiculous, but I'd been bad and now David was ill. My penance was to look after him as best I could. It was up to me to make him better. I missed my copy deadline for the first time ever. I ignored the ring of my phone. I focused everything I could on David.

I cooked soups and stews. I stripped and changed the bed to give him the pleasure of fresh sheets. I smoothed his fringe away from his wet forehead. But he just got worse.

By the Wednesday afternoon he was mildly delirious, calling and muttering to himself, thrashing at things that weren't there. It was enough to scare me and I called a work colleague, Doctor Sue, one of my copywriting support group, who always answered our medical enquiries or checked biological facts before we submitted work.

'It's just the fever breaking,' she said, calmly. 'Keep him cool. Keep him hydrated. Keep a check on his temperature.'

She was reassuring but it was terrifying. David thrashed and moaned as his body burned. Cried and vomited with the pain of it. I sat with him for the night. I took off layers of his bedding even though he shivered. I opened the window and let in the autumn air, damp as it was. I laid cold compresses on his neck and head until slowly, slowly, he cooled down.

I talked to him through the hours, to reassure myself as much as to calm him. In the dimly lit room I reminded him of nights out when we were at uni, or drunken parties and mutual friends. Of our first romantic meal out, when I'd got myself accidentally locked in the toilet between starter and mains and he thought I'd done a runner. As I wrung out the flannel, I recalled our first holiday, island-hopping in Greece, ferries and hostels and white sand. I told him he had to get better soon so we could plan for Christmas, and asked him whether he wanted turkey or beef. I ran my fingers over his temples, trying to ease the frown there, and told him to stop worrying so much about his career. That it would all work out. That whether or not he got the promotion, it wouldn't change the way I felt about him. The job wasn't the most important thing. I held his hand and talked about how much I loved it when we decorated together, choosing the colour for the room and then painting side by side. The dark midnight blue of our lounge. The sunshine yellow of the kitchen. I ran my fingertips along his eyebrows as he slept and told him I was sorry that I'd lost sight of him. That I loved him. I loved him. I always would. I'd just lost myself some-where along the line.

The clatter of the letter box woke me. I was leaning against the bed, holding on to David's hand. His breathing was regular and his skin had the faintest tint of colour to it. I put my hand on his cheek and it was cool to touch. The fever was over. It was gone.

I pulled the window shut and tucked him under the covers, conscious now of the temperature in the room. My phone tinged and I saw it light up on the bedside table. I picked it up and left the room so I wouldn't disturb him, pulling the door shut behind me.

The message icon was flashing and I clicked on it.

There was a stream of messages, one after the other after the other. All from the same number. Felix. I scrolled to the bottom, shocked. I knew I should have let him know that I couldn't talk, but it hadn't felt right. In fact it would have felt really wrong.

I scrolled to the first message and clicked on it. Monday, 9.15 a.m. One of our normal times for a message exchange, as David would normally have left for work.

'To live is the rarest thing in the world,' it said. 'When can I see you?'

I scrolled on, to Monday night,

'Dreaming of you at night is better than real life without you in my day,' it said. 'Where are you?'

The number of messages had increased on Tuesday, and there were even more on Wednesday, almost one an hour. Some of them were simply a question mark. Others were quotes, or some lyrics, or questions about when we would get together. The intensity of them made me nervous, the words made me uncomfortable.

The postbox clattered again, bringing me back to the present, and I padded downstairs, pushing a hand through my hair, stretching out my back. I could smell my own body, tired and musty. I longed for a shower. I could just tap out a reply now, a quick explanation about why I'd been so absent. But something stopped me.

I turned to the front door to collect the post but there was nothing on the mat. As I approached, the letter box lifted again and someone looked through the slit at me.

Felix.

'There you are,' he said through the door.

My stomach dropped as my worlds smashed together and I felt the panic of David asleep upstairs and Morag probably just waking, below in her flat.

'Let me in, then,' he said, and I hurried forward, thinking it better to at least get him off the doorstep should anyone be passing. David was asleep; him inside with the door shut had to be the better option.

There was electricity around him when he came in, like a static buzz. His eyes darted around the hall and behind me into the lounge, taking it all in. His eyebrows shot up at our wedding photograph on the wall. He ran his fingers along my coat on the rack, and rubbed the material between his fingers.

'What are you doing here?' I whispered, glancing at the stairs. 'David's home. He's ill.'

He considered that then, and nodded.

'I was worried about you,' he said, as though that excused everything.

'Sorry,' I said. 'Emergency.'

'Couldn't find the time to text back?' he asked. 'Too busy playing Florence Nightingale?'

I shook my head, annoyed. It had been the longest night of my life and now I was getting a hard time for doing the right thing.

'Sorry,' I said again, just wanting him to go.

'It's okay now I've seen you,' he said then and wrapped his arms round me, holding me tight against his chest beside our wedding photo. He was trembling. I allowed it for a few seconds and then wriggled away, feeling mussed, dirty, wrong.

'I'll text you,' I said. 'But you've got to go.'

He licked his lips and I noticed one of them had been bleeding.

'Promise me we'll be together soon,' he said as he opened the front door.

'I'll text you,' I said and he took that as a yes.

The door shut behind him and I couldn't help but bolt it. Hurrying to the bay window in the lounge, I could see him loping up towards the Red Lion on the Green. It was only then that I wondered how he even knew where I lived. I sank into the armchair and realised I was still holding my phone.

I clicked back to the messages list, with the thought of deleting them. I had to open and read each one before it would let me erase it. The last one, sent at six thirty-five that morning, when I was sleeping on the floor beside my husband, said,

'You might call it madness. But I call it love.'

Thursday 21 December

Sea temperature: 8.7 degrees.
Air temperature: 7 degrees.

I was later than normal but there was only a lone man on the beach, nobody I recognised, swinging his metal detector left to right in front of him as he trawled for treasure. He was intent on his task and paid no attention to me, which suited me fine. I wanted to lose myself in the sea.

The water was the only thing that might help to clear my head and I was going in without Nancy, whether it was safe or not. I'd slept for only a scrambled few hours, when I had tossed and turned and had once woken up with a gasp, thinking I'd heard Dodge barking. I sat up in bed and searched the silence, testing out its depth. Nothing. David mumbled and put his arm over me, and I tucked into him for comfort. After that, I dozed, in and out of consciousness, tormented with impossible dreams of Felix and David meeting and then of the girls crying in rooms I couldn't access, doors I couldn't open.

David had woken early too, and we lay face to face on the pillow making a search plan for Dodge. We dressed quietly, pulling on jumpers and jeans, treading gently on the stairs. I didn't want the others to wake, I didn't want them to come. I checked the back door, clinging on to hope that

Dodge might have found his way home, but the step was empty.

'He would have barked to be let in,' David said when he saw me, and I nodded, acknowledging the fact that he was right, however much I wanted him to be proved wrong. I checked the websites we'd listed Dodge on, but apart from a lot of messages from well-wishers, there was no news.

We searched for another couple of hours, calling above the gulls' cries, shaking the dog-biscuit tin, hoping at any moment to see him running towards us from the dunes, tail wagging. There was no sign. It was a bad omen. If Dodge had just spooked, we would have expected him to find his way home. He knew the beach as well as he knew his back garden.

We headed home.

'What if he's hurt somewhere?' I said, feeling desperate.

'I'll go make some posters to put up,' David said. 'You go for your swim.'

'I'll walk the dunes again first,' I said, not being able to bear giving up.

We couldn't say more than that. It was too worrying to speak about. Even voicing my concerns felt like I might conjure it to happen. I didn't want to jinx anything. And yet I knew too that I had other worries, and was distracting myself from them, almost, with thoughts of Dodge. It gave me extra time to be with David. It gave me a moment to think.

The water took away all thought as I submerged myself. Aiming for the pier, I let my strokes build until I was powering through the waves. I needed to calm the thoughts in my head. I needed to exhaust myself.

Yesterday felt like a bad dream. Images flashed through my head as I swam. The dead whale. The bruise I had thought I'd seen on Kit's wrist. Ivo's teeth marks on her neck. His expression when he told me he knew I was his dad's lover. The photographs of the girls where they looked like Ivo. The identical dimples. The tilt of a chin. Dodge wagging his tail as he went off down the step with Ivo. I lifted my head for a breath stroke. It was too much to think about all at once.

I had to break this down. One thing at a time. Start with the easiest.

I struck out again in a crawl, focusing on a plan to find Dodge. David was already working on the computer creating a poster when I left. By the time I got home, he would have printed it out. If I got him to walk the dunes and pin it to lamp posts and telegraph poles, I could walk into town and put it on community noticeboards. Loads of people in town knew Dodge; they'd keep a lookout if they knew he was missing. And maybe I'd get the girls to walk down to the fish shacks and shops along the Blyth and ask around. Dodge loved sniffing round there – tourists often dropped fishing bait or the odd chip. That would do it, surely? Between that and the forums, we'd hear something. It wasn't like he could just disappear into thin air, was it? By teatime he'd be home, sitting by his bowl. We'd all be moaning at him for farting in the kitchen. I'd find him.

Right. Next problem.

Ivo knows his dad's lover was me. Panic made my breathing catch and I spluttered on a few drops of seawater, spat it away. I gritted my teeth and made myself face into the facts as objectively as possible, however much it turned my stomach. Ivo knows I am the woman his dad had an affair with and he blames his dad's suicide on that affair. My chest ached and I gulped another lungful of air. So my secret wasn't a secret anymore. After twenty years, it was out, like Felix was back to haunt me. My arms were feeling heavy, tiring already, but I kept going.

But maybe nobody else had to know. A lot depended on Ivo. It felt like he wanted something from me, but I didn't know what. I had to talk to him, quietly, calmly, adult to adult. I would find a time today to ask him what he wanted out of this situation. And hope that wasn't a dangerous question.

I had to accept, that if it came to it, I would have to tell David about Felix. The thought of hurting him was horrific. The act of breaking his trust would wound him deeply. But I would have to just tell him the truth. That it was a mistake. That I regretted it immediately in the cold light of day. That all I could ever hope for would be his forgiveness. I just had to hope that after everything we'd been through, he would be able to move past it. We'd had almost thirty years together, built a family and a home. Surely, he would see the value in that. The love. I would do anything to keep us together. Anything.

I turned. Time to head back.

Last problem. The one I didn't even want to think about.

What if the girls were not David's children? I sobbed through the water at the thought. This would kill him. More than anything else, more than me being unfaithful. This would be the thing that would break his heart. And mine. Our girls. We'd built our lives around them.

I had to know this before doing anything else. But how? Where to start? I'd seen all kinds of ancestry investigation kits in Morag's family-tree magazines. Countless adverts that told you how to trace your forefathers and how to use DNA testing services. There were pages and pages of them at the back of each month's edition; it was obviously big business. They were affordable, cheap even for getting such an important answer, but they all seemed to involve sending off samples of hair or blood or a swab test, and how on earth was I meant to do that without arousing suspicion? Anyway, I didn't have the luxury of time. The results could take weeks to come back and with Ivo breathing down my neck I needed to know now – today if possible. Then I'd know which battle to fight next. I dragged myself the last few yards to my marker and checked my watch. Just in time. I swam to standing and stood for a moment, facing the beach, bracing myself against the tug and sway of the waves. What I needed was advice. Someone who knew medicine.

Doctor Sue.

Sue could help. Why hadn't I thought of her yesterday? She'd been my go-to person for any medical content for so long, I could ring her and ask her about the causes of bad breath one day and the benefits of hormone replacement therapy the next without her batting an eye. I could ask her anything. I could pretend it was for a job or an article, or any old excuse really, and she'd be happy to help. I pulled my goggles off my face, letting them hang off my hand in the water. Now I was clear on what I needed to do.

Find Dodge.

Talk to Ivo.

Ring Doctor Sue.

I cut through the water and headed into the hut. I had a busy day ahead.

I called through to David as I went in the front door. He was in my office, obviously still working on the posters for Dodge. I stuck my head round the door and saw him hunched at my desk. I offered him a coffee and he nodded a thanks. I could hear the printer whirring into action as I left.

I was unpacking my bag in the utility room, hanging the wetsuit on the rack, shoving my towels and costume in the dryer, when I heard Kit and Ivo talking in the kitchen next door.

'Do you think you should try to talk to them about it today?' Ivo asked.

I froze, hand in the tumble dryer, not even daring to take a breath. Someone picked up mugs; they clinked together.

'I don't know,' Kit said. 'Maybe I should try to get Mum on her own first?'

I stood up slowly, straightened my back. Maybe my plans for today were already too late. The cupboard door banged open and shut and I couldn't hear Ivo's answer.

'Not sure it's the best day for it,' Kit said. A chair scraped on the floor as someone sat down at the table.

'Let's face it, babe,' Ivo said. 'There's never going to be a good time.'

The tap ran and there was a metallic and hollow sound as they filled the kettle.

'Yep, but with Dodge missing…' Kit said.

'Well, she's not going to like it whenever you tell her.'

I shut my eyes. Did Kit know too? Had he told her?

'They'll get used to it, babe,' Ivo continued. 'Not everyone likes university. It'll be okay. I'm sure they'll understand. They seem like good people.'

It wasn't what I'd expected him to say. I cocked my head, waiting for more. What was his game?

Her reply was muffled, like she had her head pressed against him. And I let my breath out slowly, so as not to make a sound. She didn't know. Yet. The kettle started to whistle.

I opened the external utility door and closed it again, pretending I was just coming in from the side of the house. I made a pretence of stuffing things in the tumble dryer, and then went through to the kitchen. As I'd expected, Ivo sat at the table. Kit stood at the stove pouring tea. They glanced at each other quickly on the back of their conversation. Then Kit got out another cup for me and said, 'No sign of Dodge still?'

I shook my head.

'Oh, Mum. What are we going to do?'

'We're going to find him, that's what we're going to do,' I said with a determined nod, trying to be optimistic. 'Dad will have one too, I'm sure,' I went on, indicating the kettle, and she put another mug in the row. I noticed she chose his one. 'World's best dad'. My eyes got hot and wet and I blinked, quickly but not quickly enough. Kit saw.

'I'm sure you're right, Mum,' she said, leaving the tea-making station and closing the gap between us. She put her arms round me and pulled me against her. She was slightly taller than me these days, lithe, strong. She smelled of shampoo and musk and another smell, something alien. I breathed it in deeply, trying to identify it, until I realised it was him. Ivo. She smelled of him. I pulled away, without being obvious, and patted her arm.

Ivo was pouring the hot water, having taken over Kit's spot. His phone rang, vibrating at the same time, buzzing a little dance on the wooden tabletop next to us. Ivo reached his hand out towards it, but Kit got there first, picked it up and answered with a customer-service smile.

'Ivo's answering service,' she chirped.

Ivo glowered at her and threw both hands in the air. Her grin faltered as she realised she'd done the wrong thing.

'Who should I say is calling?' Kit continued, trying to make light of the situation.

There was a pause while we all looked at her and she frowned in concentration, obviously trying to work out the next right move.

'Let me see if he's available,' she said, then pressed mute and whispered to Ivo: 'It's your flatmate, Mack.'

He shook his head fiercely and turned away, back to the tea.

'What shall I tell him?' Kit said.

'Tell him I'm not here,' he replied, with his back to her. Kit bit her lip, before pressing the button to return to the call.

'I'm terribly sorry, he's not around at the moment, Mack.'

Ivo leaned on the sink and stirred sugar into his tea, not four feet away.

'Yes, he must have stepped out.'

Ivo tinged his spoon on the side of the cup and put it on the draining board. David came in with a handful of A4 posters.

'Of course, I'll tell him,' Kit said with a nod. Ivo raised one eyebrow, only half interested.

'Leave it with me,' Kit said, very professionally. 'Thanks for phoning.' She pressed red to end the call. Ivo held his hand out and she put the phone in it. He shoved it roughly into his pocket.

'He wants you to ring back,' Kit said, flushing. 'Says he's left you lots of messages.'

'Why do you think I didn't want to answer it?' He shrugged. 'He's always moaning about something.'

'Some flatmates are like that,' said David. 'I had one that didn't want me to eat curry in my own bedroom because of the smell.'

'Anyway, he said he needs to know your plans immediately about Cleverly House, so can you call back.'

Ivo's eyes glinted and Kit looked crestfallen.

'Probably just wants to know about your travel plans? So he can plan to get a new roomie in the summer?' David suggested. I saw the glance Kit shot Ivo. It reminded me of when the girls were younger and had been naughty together. It was a warning to say nothing, a look of collusion. A flash of agreement.

'Don't worry, David,' Ivo said. 'I'll sort it out.' He looked at me. 'I don't leave things undone.'

'Hang on a second, isn't your house on Beverly Way?' Kit asked. Ivo nodded. 'So you live in Cleverly on Beverly!' she said, delighted with herself. David snorted and the moment was gone.

Half an hour later, the teacups were in the sink and the house was empty. Kit and Ivo had taken a bundle of posters into town, and Jess and David were doing the rural sites out towards the marsh and the river. Even Morag had taken a bundle and was walking the promenade, chatting to all her acquaintances and raising the alarm. David had done a great job of the poster. He'd scanned in a picture of Dodge, under a big banner in capitals: LOST DOG. It gave yesterday's date and listed both my and David's mobile numbers, just in case one of us was busy. I said I'd stay home, in case Dodge turned up. David squeezed my hand then, meeting my eye. I couldn't help but make a silent wish. *Find him, please*. He nodded as though he'd heard me.

As soon as the front door slammed, I padded to the office. I needed medical information about the girls. Anything I could find that might help Doctor Sue tell me what I needed to know. The more information I had in front of me when I rang her, the better.

My filing system was pretty organised and I knew I had a file for the girls' medical histories somewhere, but couldn't remember what I'd listed it under. I pulled out the first drawer, A–G. The files ranged from Apple ID passwords at the front to Guarantees at the back. I pulled out the second drawer, and there it was: 'Medical – Jess and Kit'. The one behind it was 'Medical – David and Belle.'

Their file felt disappointingly slim as I lifted it out of the drawer, but I knelt on the floor and rifled through the contents to see what might be of use. There wasn't a lot. An X-ray of when Jess broke her wrist roller-skating. Some leaflets from the doctors about the use of the contraceptive pill. A repeat prescription for Kit when she had an outbreak of eczema during her GCSEs. Vaccination cards, ticked and fully up to date. I sat back on my heels. This wasn't going to help.

I looked round the room, searching for a clue, something else I could use, and my eyes came to rest on the family picture I kept on my desk. David with slightly thicker hair, holding a chubby Kit, and me with a rather severe bob, holding an even chubbier Jess. It was a friend's wedding and we had dressed the girls in matching outfits, one of the rare occasions that we ever did. Their grins showed about eight teeth between them and still managed to tug at my womb almost twenty years later. Such cute babies.

That was it – their baby books. The little red books we used to record their every detail in – height, weight, growth charts. Everything about them was in those pages. The baby clinic marked x's on graphs, the health visitor wrote notes in margins. I'd pored over those charts to make sure Jess wasn't too heavy and Kit was hitting her weaning milestones. Those books had been my bible that my girls were healthy and well. Now they might hold the information that I needed. Where were they? I stood, glanced left to right, knowing they weren't in this filing system, trying to remember where I might have put them.

I would never have thrown them away. I'd kept everything sentimental about the girls from when they were babies. I flicked through the filing drawer, looking for inspiration. House insurance. Illness cover. Loft insulation. Of course – the loft, that was where they'd be.

I ran up the stairs and pulled the ladder down, tugging it twice to check it was fully extended. I went up into the darkness and, when my head and shoulders were fully through, tentatively patted the floor to the right of the hatch to find the light switch. A bare bulb flickered into life and I clambered up.

I shuffled, crablike, onto the boarded area, and shivered. It was freezing up here. A strand of cobweb hung from the light bulb, moving with the draft. I flapped it away from my face and it clung to my fingers until I wiped it on my thigh. If my filing system was organised, the loft was not. This was more David's domain.

Boxes were packed along the side under the eaves, each of them luckily marked with a felt-tip pen to give a clue as to contents. Ski wear. Granny's crockery. Summer curtains. Other items stood alone: spare radiators for the year our heating failed, old deckchairs, a chest of drawers and a decon-structed exercise bike. None of that was what I wanted. I crawled more towards the back of the house, where the older stuff looked to be. Fancy-dress costumes, one box said. I was getting closer. I moved it to the side and a spider skittered across the floorboards, dashing for the shadows.

'Baby clothes', the box behind said and I felt my breathing quicken. The one next to it simply said, 'Baby bits', and I pulled it towards me hopefully. It was full of memories, but nothing useful. A couple of harnesses we used to carry the girls in, strapped to our fronts. A few baby picture books, one chewed at the corner. A cube that made noises if you poked it or turned a handle. But nothing medical. I moved on. Two boxes later I found them, right at the bottom, probably to keep them flat. Two plastic-coated, red baby books.

I opened up the first one – Kit's – and went through page by page. Details of her weight and length at birth. Details of her vaccinations. Notes written by a health visitor about weaning experiments. But no blood type. I scanned Jess's too, but it was the same. Dammit.

My phone beeped in my back pocket. My heart leapt with hope, but the text from David read: 'No joy yet. All posters up. Home soon. xx'. I slapped my phone against my thigh in frustration. No sign of Dodge, and I was running out of time to find something here. Where else to look? Wondering if my phone could have the answer, I googled, 'where to find my child's blood group' and pressed enter. Immediately a list of results came up, the top one being a mums' forum where the exact same question had been asked. I clicked on it and watched the answers load.

Lots of mums had replied. Most of them with the same news: 'It's not normally tested on babies in the UK unless there is a specific issue.' Jess and Kit had been born two weeks early but were healthy weights with no concerns, which probably meant they wouldn't have been tested. I groaned and scrolled. Came across another reply: 'it's quite often done as part of the heel-prick test in the baby's first twenty-four hours, but not recorded in the red book.'

I could have clapped my hands. It had jogged my memory. The twins were indeed not yet a day old and David had gone home to bring Morag for a visit. I'd been alone in the ward when the nurse came to do the heel-prick test. I was nervous, exhausted and wishing he was there with me. It was my first time trying to juggle the two babies on my own and I felt like I didn't have enough hands. The nurse took Jess from me first, leaving me with an armful of air. When she pricked her with a needle and drew out the tiny bead of blood, I felt the sting as much as Jess, who shut her eyes and wailed, flailing her little hands in the air. The nurse passed Jess back and deposited the drops onto various test strips, talking to herself as she did. I asked her what she was testing for specifically, so that I could tell David when he came back. Sickle cell, she said, cystic fibrosis. Other terrible diseases that made me say a silent prayer. But also, she noted down their blood types. And I asked her to jot them down on their cot name tags, meaning to tell David later. Although I don't think I ever did; things were chaotic in the first few weeks until we found our groove.

So I needed their cot tags. I knew I had them and I knew exactly where they were, sentimental idiot that I was. I backed out of the loft, clicking the light off as I went. I pushed the ladder back up into the hatch and slid the cover across. You'd never know I'd been up there. I went to my bedroom and pulled open the cupboard. Reaching up, I carried the girls' baby boxes to the bed. Basically they were 'expensive shoeboxes', or so David thought. I'd bought them in a baby shop when the twins were still in a double pram, loving the thought of keeping them as a memento. Their baby photos on the lids told me which was whose, and inside they held everything from the first tooth left for the tooth fairy to the first lock of hair. It also included their wristbands from the hospital – and their cot tags.

Jess's was first and there it was: 'Twin One. Born 12.16 p.m. 5/9/2001.' And there in the corner, in a hurried scribble, it said 'AB'. Kit's tag showed a similar set of information: 'Twin Two. Born 12:49 p.m. 5/9/2001.' With a single letter in the corner of the card. 'O.'

'Definitely not identical then,' the nurse had said. 'Only identical twins have the same blood group.' I remembered her words so clearly.

So I had their blood groups. And I knew where I could get David's and mine. I shoved everything else back into the boxes, more roughly than usual, and slid them back into the cupboard. From the front window of the bedroom, I checked the road both ways, but couldn't see the family walking home. I checked my watch. They'd be back soon.

Back in the office I delved into our medical file this time, looking for our blood donation cards. We'd donated a few times when the girls were younger, but I was slightly anaemic and sometimes they'd turn me away after the finger-prick test and eventually we stopped going. But I'd kept our cards, in case we got back to it, and as a mark of trying to do the right thing. I found them, slightly tatty-looking and old, but intact. Then the front door opened and voices filled the hall. I rammed the cards into my jeans pocket and shut the drawer. I had as much information as I could get, but the call would have to wait.

David opened a beer at lunchtime. I couldn't blame him. I felt desperate too, about everything.

'Anyone else?' he asked as he prised the lid off. There was a general round of 'no thanks', so he raised the bottle to everyone in a half-hearted toast and then put it to his lips. I set out French bread and a plate of ham and cheese and soon everyone was filling baguettes and eating. David picked at his plate. I rubbed his thigh under the table.

'You've got to eat something,' I whispered. He tried a smile but it was weak. When David brought Dodge home as a young rescue dog, the girls had just started secondary school. David babied the dog just as much as he had babied the girls when they were tiny. All the advice told us to leave the dog at night if it cried. That it would soon get used to its surroundings. That it would soon learn that it got no atten- tion after bedtime, and that it would have to hold its bladder until we got up in the morning. I was happy to try it but David couldn't lie there and listen to Dodge's whining. 'He's had such a rough start already,' he'd whisper across the pillow. 'He just needs a bit of reassurance.' For the first two nights he got up and went downstairs and lay beside Dodge's bed on the kitchen floor on a camping mattress. Both mornings when I came down, Dodge would be on the mattress with David, and they'd be asleep together. The third night he didn't sleep down there, but still went down to check on Dodge when he cried. It reminded me of when I did the night feeds with the girls, leaving David to sleep. It was the other way round with Dodge. David had shadows under his eyes for the first few weeks of having Dodge in the family, the same shadows he had now.

'I'll just check the websites and then I'm walking up to see Naomi this afternoon, if that's okay?' Jess said, wiping coleslaw from her mouth. 'She's back today and she said she'd come and look for Dodge with me.'

'Urghh, Naomi,' said Kit, rolling her eyes at Ivo. 'Don't know what you see in her.'

Jess flinched.

'That's so nice of her,' I said, frowning at Kit. She usually liked Nem. They'd known each other for ever. Why was she starting now?

'What's wrong with Naomi now?' Jess asked, sharply. The twins faced each other and Jess set her jaw.

'It's just she's so...' Kit screwed up her face as she searched for a word, 'provincial.'

'If she's provincial, then so are we,' Jess said shortly. 'We all grew up round here.'

'I don't mean it geographically,' Kit said as though talking to a small child. 'I mean in terms of her mindset.'

'I like Naomi,' David said, trying to diffuse the situation. 'She's a great girl.'

'But she's not very *sophisticated*, is she?' Kit snapped.

'Sophisticated?' Jess laughed, but not because she found it funny. I saw the glint in her eye. She was not going to have anything bad said about Naomi. She nodded at Kit. 'And you are, in your joggers and hoodie?'

Everyone's tempers were frayed. The girls were worried about Dodge too, maybe that was it.

'Narrow-minded then,' Kit shot back. 'She's just a simple person with simple likes. I couldn't see her wanting to go further than Sheringham for a holiday.'

Ah, so we were back on the travel theme.

'You're wrong. I told you, we want to go to Mexico,' Jess said, pushing her chair back and ending the conversation. 'Anyway, I don't care where she goes on holiday. Why should you? I like her just as she is.' She dropped a kiss on the top of my head as she went past. 'Back in time for tea,' she said. 'Let me know if you hear anything?'

'Say hi to Naomi for me,' I said and Kit couldn't help herself,

'And from me,' she snorted.

I sighed, exasperated, and started to clear plates, dropping crumbs in the bin and piling crockery by the sink. There wasn't enough for the dishwasher; I might as well wash it up by hand. It would keep me occupied.

David took his position next to me with a tea towel. I ran the bowl full of hot soapy water and we began, side by side, as we had done for decades. The simple act almost undid me and I wanted to put my head on his chest and hold on tight. Instead I plunged my hands into the too-hot water and blinked my hot eyes clear. When I glanced at the table a minute later to see if I had everything to wash in my pile, I saw Ivo nudge Kit, nodding. As I turned away again, Kit took a deep breath as though psyching herself up.

'Dad, can we talk?' David turned to face her as he dried a plate and she murmured, 'I know it's not the best timing…'

'Sure,' he said. 'What's up?'

'I've been having a look at other courses,' she started.

'And? What did you find?' he asked.

'Nothing really,' Kit said and I felt him bristle.

'What do you mean, nothing?' he asked. I paused and turned too, presenting us as an alliance. She glanced from him to me and back again. Ivo put his hand on the back of her chair, clearly supporting her.

'There are no others that I like the look of,' Kit stammered. 'Well, not any more than I like Public Relations.'

David placed his dry plate on the worktop and picked up another.

'What sort of thing did you look at?' he asked, and his tone was steady. Kit glanced at Ivo and shrugged,

'All sorts, actually,' she said. 'Media Studies to American Studies.'

David nodded.

'Creative Writing maybe.' I cocked my head to that one. She'd never expressed an interest in writing before, although I'd tried to encourage the girls in English as I loved words so much. 'Because you can write a book from anywhere. Or Entrepreneurship,' she went on, 'So I could start my own business, wherever I was.'

My warning signals were all going off. This wasn't about a course. This was about a lifestyle. Ivo's lifestyle.

'But I just don't think any of them are me. Not at the moment.'

David had almost polished the pattern off the plate with the tea towel by the time he put it down.

'So what do you want to do?' he asked.

Kit pressed her lips together and then licked them, her tongue quickly slicking them so as to get her words out. Ivo gave her the faintest glimmer of a smile, an encouragement if ever I'd seen one. I *knew* he was behind this. I could feel it. Kit had never mentioned being unhappy with her course before he came along. A hard knot of something lodged itself in my gut. I wished she'd never met him. I wished we didn't even know he existed.

'I think I might take a year out,' Kit said in a rush, the words running into one. I passed David a soapy mug, to give him time to respond rather than react.

'At the end of the year?' he asked, but Kit shook her head.

'Probably now,' she said. David frowned and stopped drying up. A sud of soapy water slid off the bottom of the mug onto the tiled floor.

'You mean drop out?' he said.

Kit shrugged and dropped her eyes, giving Ivo a glance under her eyelashes.

'Maybe,' she said, 'although that makes it sound bad.'

'And then will you go back to a different course next year – when you *do* know what you want to do?' Bless David, I could tell he was trying.

'Maybe,' Kit said again and I wanted to shake her.

'What do *you* think, Ivo?' I asked, suddenly wanting to put him on the spot. To punish him for putting the idea in her head. He sat back, surprised, and then fixed me with his eyes. He considered his words before opening his mouth.

'I think Kit's really bright and really creative,' he said. 'I think she could be whatever she wanted to be.' She smiled at him, delighted. Ah, clever. Him giving her free rein meant that we would look like the ones trying to pen her in, tie her down.

'But sometimes, it's just sticking at something that really counts, even when the going gets tough,' I said, and then bit my tongue as I saw his eyes harden.

'Like marriage?' he said and my stomach hollowed.

'I guess so, yes,' David said, putting his arm round me. 'Like marriage.'

'But sometimes things aren't worth hanging on to,' Ivo said, and I held my breath.

'Exactly,' Kit chimed in. 'If the course isn't right, there's no point hanging on and finishing the year. I might as well stop now. Then I can go to South Africa with Ivo in the new year,' she said.

David looked confused and Kit carried on, 'I told Mum about it.'

David raised an eyebrow at me and I realised we'd never had the conversation about Kit going travelling.

'Sorry, love, I haven't had a chance to fill Dad in, what with—' I started.

'Everything that's going on,' Ivo finished for me with a slight smile. 'Your mum's got quite a lot on her plate, Kit.' Making himself out to be so understanding. My back teeth ground together.

'And how are you going to pay for that?' David said.

Kit fidgeted with her fingers under the table before answering.

'I have Gran's nest-egg money.'

David stopped drying the plate and put it to one side.

'But that was for university.'

'Not really.' Kit shook her head. 'Granny just said it was for our futures when she gave it to us.'

She was right, and I felt my chest deflate with the knowledge of it. Morag had given each of the twins ten thousand pounds when they turned eighteen, for university or a car, or a deposit on a house when the time came. She was 'canny with her money', as she put it, and would do anything to avoid us paying inheritance tax. Having only done her first term of university, Kit had barely touched her money.

'So I have the money to do it.' Kit's chin was firm. I'd never seen her this single-minded. She was relentless.

David's phone rang and we all looked at each other, almost relieved to halt the conversation and hopeful it could be news of Dodge.

David picked up the phone and then shook his head at me as he answered.

'Everything okay, Mum?'

Morag. For once I was pleased about her interrupting. This conversation was getting much too heavy. What we needed was to have a chat with Kit on her own. Perhaps I'd suggest it to David. We could orchestrate something to separate them for a while. Preferably for ever.

'So what do you think, Dad?' Kit said as David hung up.

'I think we'll have to talk later,' he said. 'Gran's flooded the bathroom.' He picked Morag's keys off the hook and headed for the door. 'As if we don't have enough to worry about. Call me if you hear anything,' he said and was gone. Leaving me with Kit. And Him.

'Hello?' Sue said over the background beeping of a checkout. 'Belle?'

'Hi Sue,' I said. 'Is it a bad time?' I glanced over my shoulder but the hall was empty. Kit and Ivo had gone upstairs, 'to chill' after lunch, and I could hear the low beat of music, the occasional creak of a floorboard.

'Depends if you're ringing to remind me to pick up eggs?' She laughed. She was obviously in her local supermarket. Funny how we talked every few days, we Skyped now and then, she was someone I would class more a friend than a colleague, and yet I'd never been to her house, or had a drink with her. I knew she lived somewhere near Cambridge, but nothing more than that.

'No, it's a work thing,' I said and then corrected myself to stick to my concocted story. 'Well, kind of!'

'I can listen,' she said and I could picture her the other end, phone trapped between ear and shoulder as she piled loaves of bread and packs of sausages onto the conveyor belt.

'Well, I think I told you my mother-in-law is mad about family trees,' I started, sticking to the script now.

'The infamous Morag, mother-in-law of dreams?' Sue laughed and I made myself laugh too. 'Yes, you've mentioned it before.'

'Well, she's doing a family tree for a client and there's a bit of a concern about a sensitive issue,' I said, wondering if she'd buy it.

'Go on,' Sue said. Beep, beep, beep.

'The woman who's getting the tree done thinks that her husband might not be the father of their twins, and she's asked Morag to find out if possible, as part of the research.'

'Blimey,' said Sue. 'Not you, is it?' She laughed at her own joke.

I made myself laugh along.

'As if!' I managed.

'Only joking,' she said quickly, maybe realising she may have overstepped our professional relationship.

'No worries,' I said. 'Anyway, the client has told Morag she doesn't want to do anything about it, she just wants to know. It's not going to change anything, if you know what I mean.'

'Sometimes these things do change things though, just by someone having the knowledge,' Sue said. 'I've seen it happen.' A tannoy announcement crackled into life and we waited until it was over to resume our conversation.

'Well, I hope you don't mind, but I mentioned to Morag you might be able to help. You're the only person we know who might be able to tell us something from the information she's given – blood types, for example…'

'Happy to look for you, but blood groups can be inconclusive too.'

'That will be eighty-five pounds and ninety-three pence please,' someone said, somewhere near Cambridge.

'Look I've got to go, I haven't got enough hands here,' Sue said. 'Email me what you know and I'll see if it tells us anything.'

'Thanks Sue. I'll do it now,' I said as I put the phone down. The floorboards creaked as Ivo walked about above my head and I watched the ceiling until it stopped.

I checked my email for the hundredth time, for anything from Sue, but there was nothing. Maybe I should have told her it was urgent. I couldn't exactly email her again after just a few hours and demand her results. For all I knew she wasn't even home from her shopping trip yet. Perhaps she'd gone to the gym on the way home, or popped in for a coffee with a friend. She might not have even read my email.

I hadn't been able to sit down since I sent it. I'd walked to Gun Hill and then along the promenade again looking for Dodge, ending up at the dunes, his favourite of all places. All my fellow dog-walkers stopped me to talk, to ask for news of him, to promise me they'd keep their eyes open. I thanked them, kept walking. Kept calling. At every corner hoping to see him bounding towards me, relieved and happy to see me. All the time a horrible nagging sickness in my gut. Dodge wasn't coming back. The girls were so antagonistic with each other, secrets seemed to be ready to spill in all directions. Everything was falling apart.

Since I got home, I'd stayed in the kitchen. David was downstairs with Morag, resealing the shower door. Jess was at Naomi's. Kit and Ivo were still upstairs, the low murmur of their voices rumbled, subdued, the ongoing beat of music. The day had gone, grey clouds having given way to dark, overcast skies. The stars would be well hidden. I stared out, spotted Dodge's bone on the patio, his water bowl by the step. It didn't make sense.

Footsteps on the stairs behind me.

'Want to watch a film, Mum?' Kit said, grabbing a family bag of crisps from the cupboard. Ivo leaned in the doorway. 'Take our minds off things?'

'What you watching?' I asked, out of habit rather than interest.

'An old classic apparently.' She took a couple of bottles of beer from the fridge. 'Ivo suggested it.'

'*Fatal Attraction*,' Ivo said. 'It's about an affair.'

I gritted my teeth and shook my head slightly at him. He smiled. Something burned in my guts and I could taste it bitter in my mouth. Kit didn't notice that I didn't answer.

'You wanna?' she asked again, but seemed happy enough when I shook my head and turned away. I noticed Ivo was trailing a blanket from her room so they could snuggle on the sofa. I put my head in my hands and wished David was there to give me a hug too.

'You okay?' she said suddenly, looking back at me sitting alone at the kitchen table, no activity in sight. No recipe book. No iPad. Just me.

'Just worried,' I said and managed a smile. She faltered and I knew if Ivo hadn't been there she would have come back and hugged me.

'It's okay,' I said. 'Go on.'

She held me with a look, considering. I needed her to go. Because then he'd go too, and I couldn't bear him looking at me.

'Actually, if you guys are out of your room for a bit, I might go up and do the beds and towels.' Anything to distract myself and stop the thoughts in my head.

Kit smiled then, much happier with active, practical Mum than anxious, lethargic Mum.

'Sorry, it's a bit of a state up there,' she said as they went. I let my breath out as they closed the lounge door. The TV clicked on and the film began.

She was right about the room. It smelled different in there as I opened the door, damp and woody. Not Kit's usual mix of perfume and apple shampoo. I opened a window, wanting to clean the air, blow any trace of Ivo away. She had a good view of our walled back garden from her room, the nicest probably, but tonight it was black, empty, and I drew the curtains of both windows against it.

The bedside lamp was the only light and it threw shadows on the walls and on her posters of old films, *Ferris Bueller's Day Off*, *The Godfather*. The bed was not made, the sheet had come free of its corner and the pillows were piled against the headboard. It looked, and smelled, like a student hovel. I stared at it for a moment, not wanting to touch the sheets he was sleeping in, then forced myself to step forward and take the duvet in my hands. Trying to remove the cover, I pulled at the buttons too quickly and one popped onto the carpet. I put the duvet cover on the floor and yanked the sheet from the mattress to add to the pile. The pillowcases came off easily – I knew which one was Kit's; it smelled of her hair – and soon the bed was stripped naked and I felt better. I fetched clean bedding from the airing cupboard on the landing and remade the bed, tucking the fitted sheet tight under the corners to fix it in place and shaking the duvet in its white cover before letting it settle smoothly on top.

The rest of the room was a tip. They hadn't unpacked their bags and they sat open on the floor against the wall, clothes half in, half out, like a fabric puddle. I thought Kit at least would have put her things away. She was here for the whole of the holidays. I wanted it to be like she was home again. But I didn't want to go through her bag and do it for her; that felt wrong. I pushed her bag towards the cupboard with my toe, as a nudge towards her doing it when she came back in.

Other random garments lay on the floor where they'd been taken off. Kit's joggers. Ivo's T-shirt. A pair of black knickers. I scooped up anything that belonged to Kit and threw it on the dirty pile of bedding. One sock. A vest top. A hoodie with a smear of ketchup on the front. A pair of jeans I'd never seen before. A top she must have bought since she'd been away. I realised how little time I'd spent with Kit over the week she'd been home. How difficult it was with Ivo there. I bit my lip; he was taking her away from us, just by being around.

The light had been left on in the bathroom that connected Kit's room to Jess's. I could see it through the crack in the door, and hear the quiet buzz of the fan it operated. With no window, this was the only ventilation, and if towels were not hung back on the radiator they didn't dry very well. I pushed the door open. As suspected, there were at least four towels on the floor, and one hanging lopsided off the edge of the bath. I stooped to pick them up, cold and damp, and threw them en masse onto the pile on the bedroom floor.

The light above the mirror illuminated my face and I stopped to stare, shocked. It was a pale imitation of me. My eyes seemed to have sunk slightly into my skull. My cheeks seemed to be dropping year by year into jowls. It was the fifty-year-old version of me. But it was more than that. The expression in my eyes. The tightness around my mouth. I looked worried. Scared.

I pulled my shoulders back, and shook my hair away from my neck. Standing up straight, I looked better. I pinched my cheeks to give them colour and bit my lips gently to make them pink. I had to look normal. I couldn't let David suspect anything. And I couldn't let Ivo think he bothered me. As yet, I still didn't even know what he wanted. Until I did, I had to keep everything as it usually was, a normal routine. I blinked at myself at the mirror and nodded.

Using a flannel, I cleaned the mirror, wiping away flecks of toothpaste and water. I picked up the toothbrushes lying around the sink and stood them in the pot. I swilled water around the sink and threw some used make-up wipes in the bin. Honestly, Kit was slovenly. Ivo's electric shaver was charging, resting on the cistern. Seeing the green light flashing, I unplugged it and tidied the cord, then opened his toiletry bag it to slide it in.

There was a multipack of condoms inside, and one of the empty foils stuck to my fingers with static. I recoiled and shook my hand, wanting it off, but it just moved to my next finger and then the next as I shook it about. I stopped still and peeled it off with my other hand, sticking it to the inside of the bin and wiping my fingers on my hip.

Grabbing the towel that hung limply off the bath, I pushed open the door to the bedroom.

Ivo stood in the middle of the room, his shadow looming large behind him on the wall. I jumped, clutched at my own chest. He smiled.

'Guilty conscience?' he said and I wanted to punch him. Suddenly I just wanted to bang my hands hard on his chest; I felt so helpless and he just thought it was all fun.

'Just getting the washing,' I stammered and threw the towel I was holding on the pile. 'Where's Kit?'

'Fell asleep watching the film,' he said. 'I obviously keep her up too much at night.' He smirked and again I felt the surge of anger towards him. How dare he think he could talk about my daughter like that? He wouldn't dare say something like that in front of David. He thought he had one over on me and he could say whatever he wanted. I had to end this. I had to be the adult here.

'Look, maybe we should talk,' I said.

He tilted his head to one side.

'I'm listening,' he said. I took a deep breath.

'We need to talk about your dad. About what happened,' I said.

'Your *affair*, you mean?' he said, sitting on the end of Kit's bed. I felt off-sided being a different height to him, so I pulled the chair away from the wall and sat too.

'Yes,' I admitted. He raised an eyebrow, waiting. 'I was so sorry to hear that Felix had died,' I started, trying to empathise with him, get him aligned. It was such a shock. 'I couldn't believe it when you told me.'

'I bet it was, seeing as it was your fault,' he said.

'I don't mean that, Ivo,' I said quietly, 'I mean, he was one of the most alive people I ever met. He literally buzzed with life. To think of him dead is awful.'

Despite himself, Ivo leaned forward, interested in what I was saying. I carried on. 'When he sang – the audience felt every word. And he'd dance like a wild thing, throw himself around the stage in a primal way, just feeling the music. It was amazing to watch. The crowd couldn't get enough of him.' I smiled at him to show I meant it. The memory was real. I could still see him.

A smile passed over Ivo's face and showed me the boy he'd once been.

'So you loved him then?' he said. It would be easy to say yes, to try to appease him. I paused, but then shook my head.

'No,' I said. 'I was infatuated. But not in love. I loved David.'

His eyes darkened.

'What was it then?' he spat. 'Just a bit of fun?'

I breathed out slowly, trying to find a way to explain it fairly and honestly.

'It was an escape, from boredom, from adulthood, to be honest,' I said. 'And a mistake. That's why I couldn't believe it when you told me he'd killed himself. There must have been someone else. It couldn't be over our fling.'

He flinched at the word and I hurried on.

'It's just such a tragic waste. Such a shame and why ever he did it, I couldn't be more sorry.'

He blinked quickly as though holding back tears.

'It's so long ago though, Ivo,' I murmured. 'Can't we just leave it in the past?'

'Forget about it, you mean?' he said.

I nodded.

'As if it was nothing?' He stood and I realised they were tears of anger as he punched his own palm. 'As if *he* was nothing?' he said, looking at me incredulously.

'There's nothing I can do to change the past,' I said quietly to talk him back down. 'And there's nothing to gain from telling anyone,' I added, and even I heard the pleading note to my voice. He looked at me then and I felt the power shift again.

'For me there is,' he said, and smiled. 'There's justice.' He tapped the side of his forehead with a finger. 'And peace and quiet, knowing I've done right by him.'

I stared at him and made one last-ditch attempt. I wasn't too proud to beg.

'But Ivo, you can guess what will happen if you tell Kit, or David, or anyone. You'll break up my family. You'll destroy it.'

He shrugged and walked towards the door.

'Just like you did mine,' he said and closed the door behind him.

In the silence of the room after the door shut, my phone tinged and my heart stopped, but it was from David, not Sue. 'Sorted out the leak. Going to walk to the dunes again to look for Dodge. Xx'

I sent back a quick message telling him I'd check online again, with a fingers-crossed sign and three kisses, wanting to be with him but also wanting to have the space to talk to Sue if she called. I felt like I was waiting for something to happen and I couldn't bear it. Waiting for Ivo to say something. Waiting for Dodge to come home – but with every hour that passed, that felt less likely to happen. Waiting to hear about the girls. My guts churned and I realised couldn't remember having eaten all day. I picked up the pile of washing at my feet and left the room. It was better to keep busy.

The television played in the lounge and I could hear the spit and crackle of the fire. I went the other way, to the utility room to sort the laundry, not wanting to see them.

I was just programming the machine when they came into the kitchen. Kit yawned and stretched after her snooze.

'Want a coffee, Mum?' she called, seeing me through the open door.

'I'm fine thanks, love,' I replied, amazed my voice didn't tremble or break. I shut the machine door and the water began to flood into the drum. I went in. They had their heads together at the kitchen table, both of them looking at Ivo's phone. The slant of their cheekbones mirrored each other, high and beautiful. I turned away, started to clear up the random clutter left around, half-drunk juice, empty biscuit packets.

'That one's amazing,' Kit murmured, 'and this one.' She was scrolling through his photos, probably admiring pictures of herself. He pointed out things, 'perspectives', 'aesthetics' and 'colour pop'.

'I could never take pictures like these,' she said, turning her eyes up to him. I wiped the table down and looked away from her fawning.

'If you turned on the gridlines on your camera it would help immediately with your composition,' he said. 'And try to remember the rule of thirds – I told you about that.'

She nodded, scrolled.

'Where are the whale ones from yesterday?' she asked. He took the camera back, found them and held the screen towards her, flicking through them in front of her face.

'Oh my God, they're disgusting,' she gasped and I remembered the slack skin, the blind eye of the baby whale, the water dragging at its innards. 'Disgusting – but brilliant!' she corrected herself and he flicked to another one.

'Yuk,' she said. 'They're like a study of death.'

I wished David would come home as a wave of tiredness washed over me. This pretence, this worry was weighing me down. I wanted to rest against his chest and shut my eyes.

'Have you seen these, Mum?' Kit asked and I shook my head, feigned interest.

'You're the first person I've shown, babe,' Ivo said.

'I should think so too,' Kit cooed.

He lifted his eyes to me.

'Would you like to see?' he said.

'They're amaaaaaaazing, Mum,' Kit gushed.

He came round to my side of the table and clicked on an image before handing me the phone. It was a close-up of the torn skin, the blubber below cracking through, pink and raw. I flinched.

'Awful, aren't they.' Kit grimaced. 'But so good.'

'Flick through,' Ivo said, nodding at me, and I moved to the next image, a blind eyeball, so close as to reflect Ivo's own image in the black. He definitely had not observed the cordon around the carcass. He must have been within touching distance to take these. The dead eye was sightless, soulless. I flicked on again.

This time it was the body against the sand, the tide lapping against it, like a wall. The skin was pitted, rotted almost from its time in the water.

'My favourite is the eyeball,' Kit announced. 'I think you should enter it into a competition.'

'Keep going,' Ivo said and I scrolled again. 'Right to the end.'

The last image was a selfie of Ivo, close up to the camera. He wore Dodge's lead round his own neck, pulled high and tight above his head, like a noose. His eyes were shut and he was letting his tongue loll out of his mouth like he was dead. It was hideous.

I clamped my hand to my mouth.

'God, Mum, they're not that bad,' Kit said. 'Talk about overexaggerating. It's only a dead whale.' Clearly, she hadn't seen the last shot.

Ivo took the phone out of my shaking hands and looked at the image himself, careful to angle it away from Kit.

'Not to everyone's taste, maybe,' he said and clicked it off. 'But good composition.'

I couldn't get enough air. My chest was heaving and I could hear my breath but it felt like I was breathing through a wet towel. I clutched the back of the chair beside me. What kind of sick picture was that? And what did it mean that we hadn't seen Dodge since?

'You okay, Mum?' Kit asked. I pushed myself off towards the door, floating on legs I couldn't feel, grabbed my coat off the hook.

'Fine…' I said but it came out gravelly, rough. 'Going out,' I muttered, aiming for the front door, my only wish to get out, into the fresh air, feel the wind on my face. I had to get away.

'Going to look for Dodge?' Kit asked behind me and I managed to get out the door before the noise came out of my mouth. A sob. A moan. It ripped through me as I ran down the steps. All my worst thoughts were obviously true, but not only had Ivo had something to do with Dodge's disappearance – it looked like he'd actually hurt him.

I couldn't bear the thought of it. Dodge was the most trusting dog. It was almost as though he knew we'd rescued him all those years ago. He'd lean against you when you sat on the sand. He'd lay his head in your lap as you watched a film. He'd nudge you gently with his nose to get attention and raise a paw to encourage you if he liked your strokes. To think that someone might hurt him was appalling. 'Mummy's best boy' rang in my ears. Eyes blinded with tears, I blinked, stumbled on the pavement. I turned towards the beach as someone called me, their voice high and excited.

'Belle!'

It was Nancy.

'Belle! Look!'

She was being pulled towards me at full speed by Dodge, on a makeshift rope lead. He strained, leapt up at me, almost knocking me off my feet in his excitement.

'Dodge!!' I shouted and dropped to my knees on the pathway. He jumped up, licked my face, beside himself with happiness and relief. My shout must have been audible from the house; the front door opened and then there was Kit next to me, hugging us both. I realised I was crying and laughing all at once.

Ten minutes later David was home, and we'd rung Jess to let her know, and Morag had come up, and we all sat round the table making a fuss of Dodge as he went one person to the next, making the most of the attention. He'd already eaten a huge bowlful of dog food and now Morag was picking bits of roast chicken off a carcass in the fridge to treat him with. Ivo ruffled the dog's ears every time he went past, seemingly as delighted to see him as the rest of us.

'So weird though,' David said. 'I mean how on earth did he get into your beach hut?'

That was where Nancy had found him when she visited the hut for the first time that week. Finally feeling recovered from her cold, she'd suddenly realised she hadn't been back to the hut after the hypothermia episode and had gone to secure it. She had found a frantic Dodge inside. I shut my eyes, bowed my head with guilt as I realised I hadn't texted her to remind her to lock up. It was my fault.

'Maybe he ran in there for a hiding place after he took off on the beach?' Kit suggested.

'That would make sense, I mean he does know it,' Nancy said.

'But if he went in, how come he couldn't get out?' Morag said, pulling off a sliver of wing meat for a salivating Dodge.

'Maybe the wind blew the door shut?' David said. 'It was pretty wild that night.'

'A whole day and a night, trapped!' Nancy said, shaking her head.

'He must have been terrified,' Ivo said.

'I'm blaming myself, I should have checked the hut sooner,' Nancy replied. 'I knew he was missing.' She looked devastated. I reached across the table to her.

'How were you to know?' I said. 'And we've got him back now, thanks to you.'

'I just don't understand it,' Nancy said. 'You'd think we would have heard him barking.'

Dodge looked up quizzically as though he knew we were talking about him.

'He can't bark though, can he?' Ivo said.

I looked at him.

'What?' Nancy said.

David explained, 'Dodge had an operation when he was a puppy – before we rescued him. His first owners got his vocal cords cut to stop him barking. Must have thought he was too noisy. Then they abandoned him anyway. Bastards. He's never been able to bark since, have you, boy?'

Dodge tilted his head as if in agreement. Everyone laughed.

I kept my eyes on Ivo.

'Have you heard him try, Ivo?' I said.

'It's hilarious!' Kit chipped in. 'Like a little squeak.'

'No, I think Kit must have told me.' He shrugged.

Kit glanced in his direction with a smile, and then buried her face in Dodge's furry neck as he passed her on his way to me. His eyes were soft and warm and I felt a surge of happiness, despite everything. Dodge was home. One of my worries had come to nothing. Maybe they all would. I crossed my fingers.

It was later, as I showed Nancy out, that I felt someone's eyes burning into me. Turning, I saw Ivo leaning against the bannister, a small smile on his lips as he stared at me, and I knew I was wrong.

I decided to walk Dodge as the lights came on in the houses opposite, turning onto Gun Hill and walking between the looming shapes of the cannons.

I had to think, to consider how and what I was going to say to David. I had to tell him what worried me about Ivo. He was odd. He was threatening. I couldn't allow him to be part of our family.

I was scared. I closed my eyes, blew out, once, twice, taking control again. I knew that meant I would have to tell David everything; but I had to. I was sure Ivo was out to hurt me, and he was doing it through what I loved. We might have Dodge back but what was he planning next? I wanted him gone, away from Jess and Kit, away from all of us.

I turned towards the dark dunes. Dodge bounded ahead, completely unscathed by his adventure, happy to be on the beach again. My stomach lurched at the thought of speaking to David. I swiped at the tears on my face, wiped my nose on the back of my hand. But it was not the time for self-pity, and I turned for home, pulling my collar up against the cold.

I'd reached the dune path when my phone rang in my pocket and, when I pulled it out, Sue's name illuminated the screen.

'Belle,' she said, 'Not too late, is it?'

I cupped the phone close to my ear and hunched my shoulders to hear her over the wind and tide. I had no idea what time it was, and I didn't care. I just needed to know what she was going to say.

'No, it's fine,' I said. 'Just out with the dog.' I checked I could see Dodge on the sand ahead.

'Wow,' she said. 'Sounds windy where you are! It's just I'm tied up in the morning with meetings, so I thought I should get Morag her results tonight.'

'Thanks, Sue,' I said, turning my back to the sea to hear better. 'Really.'

'It's interesting stuff, actually,' she said. 'Morag might need to have a sit-down and a cup of tea before she talks to her client. Or maybe even a whisky.'

From the darkness of the beach, the town twinkled. Christmas trees shone their coloured lights from windows and the festive lights in town flickered and swung with the wind. I couldn't say anything. I could only wait.

'You know I told you I might not be able to be sure from blood types if the dad *was* the dad? Well, in this case I can be sure of my findings.'

My mouth dried and I licked my lips. Was that good?

'Go on,' I said.

'I didn't think I'd be able to be conclusive because several blood groups when put together can create offspring with the same blood groups,' she said. 'For example, the mum might have blood type A and the dad might have blood type

A, and their child could be blood type O. But this is also possible if the dad has blood type B or O. Do you see what I mean? So, sometimes it is impossible to prove that someone *is* the father. Are you with me?' she checked again and I murmured a yes. This was exactly why I used her for work questions. She was careful in her explanations, keen to ensure I understood.

'So for a while I wasn't sure what I was looking at with the blood groups you gave me,' she said. 'It really is remarkable.'

I moved to the side of a dune to find more shelter, and the wind dropped away.

'Are you there?' Sue asked.

'Sorry, just getting out of the weather,' I said, 'so that I can hear.'

'Well, the first thing I noticed is that the twins are non-identical. They are fraternal twins as they have different blood groups. That's the obvious assumption to make. Anyone would say the same.'

I knew that already.

'But then I looked at the parents' blood groups and that's when things got interesting. The mum is type A and the dad is type AB. That got me sitting up. AB is the rarest of the four blood groups, so that could help me narrow things down.'

I knew that too, about the rarity. David had always been so proud of his blood type when we went to the blood donation clinic, because everyone said his blood was in demand. They used to treat him like a prince, joke about 'draining his whole arm if we could.'

'The thing about blood type AB is that whatever blood type the other parent is, the children will always have a blood type that has an A or a B in it. So any child will be A, B or AB.' Sue paused, caught her breath. 'So, looking at the results for the twins, I was then suddenly thrown. Never seen it before.'

I moved closer to the sandbank, wanting something to support me. I could feel the world changing under my feet, my reality shifting. I could see in my mind's eye the cot tags, the spindly writing in their corners.

'Basically, one of the twins *could* be the child of the father whose blood group you gave me. And the other one *definitely is not.*'

I sank to the bank, sitting down in the brush, remembering those tiny letters. All those years ago. The answer was there in black and white. Jess was AB. Kit was O.

'So, the twin with AB blood group *could* well be the father's. The twin with blood group O *is definitely not.*'

The shock was too much. I buried my free hand in the sand beside me but still felt as though I was caught in a current, being dragged out to sea. I saw Jess's gentle smile and brown eyes, just like David's. I saw the quickness of Kit's grin, the angle of her cheek, like Felix.

'So that really is interesting, because it also means the twins are not even necessarily twins. They are potentially what are known as heteropaternal twins. Sharing a womb but born of different fathers,' Sue exclaimed, excitement in her voice.

'My God,' I said. It ripped out of me, a cry, as I took in everything it meant.

'I know. Crazy, right? It's really rare but it does happen, if two different eggs get fertilised by two different people in the same menstrual cycle. Two dads. Two children.'

I heard Sue take a mouthful of whatever she was drinking, and felt the dryness of my own mouth.

'So basically, the twins are not even twins,' she concluded. 'Well, I guess they are as they shared a womb, but they are really half-sisters.'

My girls. My beautiful girls.

'Anyway, I'll leave you to your evening. You must be mad, being out on a night like this. Let me know what Morag says when you tell her. With any luck, she might choke on her teeth!' She cackled and I managed to say something, a thank-you, a goodbye, and then she hung up and I looked at the blank screen for a long time.

And then the hammer really hit home.

Kit was in a relationship with her half-brother.

I shut my eyes at the horror.

Two days after Felix had turned up at the house, I agreed to see him. The texts were constant and every ping of my phone put me more on edge. They didn't even slow down much at night; there was only a few hours, between about 2 a.m. and dawn, when there was silence. He must hardly sleep. I remembered him in the hotel room, perched at the end of the bed, writing words as I slept. David was now well enough to sit downstairs and watch TV, and was already talking about going back to work on the Monday, but I put off leaving the house, wanting to stay in the security of it with him. I tucked blankets around his knees, brought him supplies of water and painkillers, before forcing myself to go, shut the front door. I didn't want to face up to the situation. What I'd done.

I met Felix at Amelie's, a tiny bar outside Aldeburgh. He was already there when I arrived, tapping his index fingers against the tabletop in the corner, drumming a tune in his head. He was beautiful to look at, lost in his own world, but I felt strangely detached. Something inside me had shifted — or rather, was back to where it should be. He saw me and raised his hand, the concentration falling from his face, leaving it open, expressive. The table in front of him was empty, so I bought myself time by ordering two drinks, and took them over. As I sat down, his hand found my thigh under the tabletop and squeezed, proprietary, hard. I fought the urge to push it away.

'Got a new idea for some lyrics,' he said. 'Think this could be the one, Bella. The song that makes it big.' He wrapped his hand round the bottle and took a big slug of his beer, swallowed two, three mouthfuls before lowering the bottle. His fingernails were dirty and there was an ink stain on his thumb.

'So, I've planned the tour,' he went on, still without a hello, as though he'd seen me yesterday, or I'd just come back from the loo. 'We'll start in London, work our way round the UK's big cities — Manchester, Leeds, Brighton — and then finish again in London. It

will give time for word to spread in the capital and all those that missed out the first time can book the end dates.'

He showed me a scrap of lined paper, well wrinkled by his hands, which listed ten or twelve locations.

'I've starred the ones where I think we might need extra capacity,' he said, pointing at Leeds and Southampton, 'got quite a following there.'

He showed me the underline beneath London. 'And that means extra security,' he said with a nod.

'I didn't know you'd been asked to tour,' I said, happy to small-talk for a bit, put off what I had really come to say.

He shook his head, then nodded it.

'It's coming, I can feel it.' He took another gulp of his drink. 'The guy who owns the record shop in Sheringham said he's mates with someone at Decca Records and he's told him all about me.'

He sniffed hard enough to dislodge something at the back of his nose.

'This time next year, I'll be number one. Platinum-selling records.' He swigged again. Almost half of the bottle was gone already.

'You never know,' I said, glad when he lifted his hand from my thigh to push his hair back off his face. I resisted the urge to wipe my leg. The lack of sleep was showing on his face. A slick of sweat sat on his brow.

'How's the patient?' Felix asked suddenly and I opened my mouth to reply, but he started beating the table again with his fingers, shutting his eyes to concentrate on the beat.

I took a sip of my wine. He wasn't interested in the reply.

'What have you been up to?' I asked, and it sounded like a polite question I might ask someone in the post office that I hadn't seen for a while. I sipped again, wondering at the weirdness. Why it felt so strange to see him. The only thing that had changed was me. He opened his eyes and found me.

'Went to the park with my boy yesterday,' he said.

'Your boy?' I asked, confused. He nodded. And that was how I found out that he was a dad. That he had a son at home, a child he'd never mentioned to me all the times we'd been together. A small human being that he'd created and now didn't even warrant being introduced with a name.

'I'd rather have been with you though.'

All those texts the day before, he'd been playing with his son and he'd been texting me. I felt something inside me deflating. Everything about this felt wrong. It didn't feel sexy or exciting. It felt sordid. Sad. It made it worse. This thing that we'd done.

There was a vibration coming off him. I felt it as surely as I felt the turn of the tide. It felt unpredictable, strong.

'You'll be there with me, Bella, next year when I'm famous. We'll be drinking champagne and popping pills in the afternoons.'

I rubbed the stem of my wine glass between my thumb and fore-finger, thinking.

He started singing again.

'The clocks all stopped, the bells don't ring,

Until I have my everything.'

He sang, husky, low. I recognised that it didn't tug at my gut like it had.

'What do you think?' he asked, bringing his face close to mine. I smelled a staleness on his breath, like he'd just woken up.

'Sounds great,' I said and he was off again. Before, I'd always loved his excitement, his enthusiasm, but this felt more random. Disjointed thoughts, manic movements.

'I really think this could be it,' he said. 'I wrote it thinking of you. You're my inspiration.'

He finished his drink and put his hand in his pocket, took it out and shook a few coins into his palm.

'Want another?' he asked, but there was obviously not enough money to cover mine as well as his and I shook my head. Anyway, I didn't want to stay that long. 'Driving,' I excused and he made his way to the bar, rubbing his hands together. I watched as he talked to the barman, heard him mention a tour and a record deal. I turned away.

'So when we gonna get together again — properly?' he asked as he sat down again, and grinned at me in what he thought was a sexy way, and in response I pressed my lips together. His teeth were ingrained with brown stains, coffee or nicotine. The thought of putting my mouth on his disgusted me and I knew then, in that instant, that I would never have sex with him again. That I should never have done so in the first place. I'd just lost sight of myself somewhere along the way, lost sight of what was important to me; my husband, my marriage. But I wouldn't lose sight of it again. It was my only focus. He reached for my hand and squeezed it.

'The days don't pass, the birds don't sing,

Until I have my everything.'

I stood up, pushing the chair back with my legs. It screeched on the flagstone floor.

'I have to go,' I said. 'I'm not feeling well, sorry. Must have caught it from David.'

He looked surprised and then stood too, put his arms round me. He smelled musty, like washing that hadn't dried properly. I held my breath until he let me go.

'Feel better,' he said. 'See you soon.'

Friday 22 December

Sea temperature: 8.6 degrees.
Air temperature: 6 degrees.

The first drops of icy rain hit me as I walked down the deserted beach for my swim. By the time I submerged and the salt water stung my face, it was pouring, making the surface water dance and smudging the horizon into a grey smur. Charcoal clouds brooded in the north, promising a dark, wet day. The pier lights twinkled through the spray and I headed towards them.

My arms were heavy already and my legs felt weak. I'd not slept for long, maybe a few tortured hours. I'd listened to David's breathing and watched the dawn creep in before dragging myself out of bed, whispering to David that I was going for an early swim. He'd stirred, asked me if Nancy was going too, and I'd checked my phone to see her message. No – although she felt better than she had, she still wasn't right. He stared at me until I reassured him – 'I'll be fine, don't worry' – then he put a hand out to hold mine momentarily and went back to sleep.

I struck out, past the nearest groyne as my first marker. I forced myself to focus on my breathing, and my stroke, to stop the images in my head. A kaleidoscope of pictures, all jumbled up together, flitting one to the next. Dodge's tail wagging. Kit's smile. The whale's dead eye. Jess's hand holding mine as we walked to school. Doctor Sue in the supermarket. David, laughing. David, rubbing his eyes when he was tired. David, David, David. I knew I had to be calmer to be able to think straight. I had to work out what to do.

The news from Doctor Sue was the worst it could have been. The impact of it had hollowed me out. Not only did it change David's life if it came out, it changed the girls' lives too. Everything they'd grown up believing was a lie. The very foundation of their existence – that they were twins – was untrue.

As I kicked forward, I remembered all the times people had exclaimed about them, told me how lucky I was to have twins. I'd agreed. The special bond they had, choosing to sleep in the same bed, sharing a room even when we offered them each their own. The secret language David and I believed they'd spoken to each other before they learned proper words to talk to us. The similarities they shared – they both hated asparagus, loved the colour purple, couldn't whistle, loved to dance. We'd believed these all to be the result of them being twins.

The girls talked about it too. How they were closer than their friends were with their brothers or sisters. How they relied on each other more. How they intrinsically knew when the other one needed them, without being told. They'd be devastated to find out it wasn't true. That it was all a fallacy. An illusion. It would rock their worlds. They couldn't know.

I spotted my second groyne on a breath stroke. My lungs were bursting and I made the decision to turn and head back. The current would be against me on the return and I was tired already.

Tired of thinking what would happen if David knew. If it had just been an affair, I had thought he might be able to forgive me. But this? How would he cope with knowing that Jess was his child and Kit was not? How could he ever accept it?

Although Doctor Sue had only said that Jess *might* be David's, that it wasn't conclusive, I knew without a shadow of a doubt that she was his child. For a start, their colouring was the same. They were both left-handed. And they could both roll their tongues. We'd discovered that on a lazy Sunday once when the girls were little – David and Jess could curl their tongues into little tubes, but Kit and I could not. It had been one of those funny games, sticking our tongues out and screwing up our faces with the effort, which meant nothing at the time but came out later as important, after the eye-colour incident in the other teacher's class. When they discussed it in the staffroom and he'd explained about other traits that kids inherited from their parents. Tongue rolling was one of them. David could do it. So could Jess. She was his, I'd swear to it.

But Kit was not.

David loved both of his girls, deeply and well. He was the one who used to take Kit to theatre club at the weekends, sitting through dress rehearsals and helping her learn her lines, tie her ballet shoes, practise tap-dancing steps. He learned the moves to 'Gangnam Style' and the Macarena so that they could do them together in the sitting room, not caring how funny he looked, arms and legs everywhere. He was the one that took Jess to her rugby practice every Wednesday, standing on the freezing sidelines every weekend and buying her hot chocolate on the way home, whether her team won or lost.

It wouldn't be fair to tell him, to change the way he might look at Kit, how he felt about Jess. Or to make him pick them apart by their differences instead of celebrating them for who they were as we had always done.

Then another thought hit me. What if I told him and he thought the girls should know too? It would literally split our family down the middle. David and Jess on one side. Kit and me on the other. I slammed my arms though the water. I was almost home.

And what of Kit? I cringed every time I thought about it. She was the most badly impacted. The one whose father was not her dad. The one who was sleeping with her half-brother. I choked on a mouthful of freezing salt water and had to stop, tread water, cough until my eyes streamed and I didn't know if it was seawater or tears running down my cheeks.

As I got my breath back, I thought that I hardly cared what happened to me in the face of this. But I would save them from knowing, at all costs. I'd keep David in the dark if it kept his heart and his family intact. I'd protect Jess and Kit from finding out that they were less than they'd thought they were to each other. I'd have to deal with Ivo on my own.

To do that, I had to know whom I was dealing with. And what he was capable of.

I had to find out who Ivo really was.

The rain was lashing, icy cold, as I came off the beach. I was almost at the steps to the house when someone called my name and there was Naomi, under a huge red umbrella, coming down the Green. I waved, waited, and she put the umbrella over my head as she got close enough, even though I was drenched already.

'Hi Belle, I'm on my way to yours,' she said with the grin I'd known for years. Her cheeks had hollowed out, and she'd lined her eyes with mascara, but otherwise she still looked as she had when she was ten. 'Meeting Jess,' she explained as we turned together and ran up the steps.

'Gosh, I don't know if she'll be up yet, love.'

'She should be. We planned it yesterday. We're off to Ipswich for a bit of shopping. Want to make a day of it.'

I opened the front door and she shook her umbrella outside and leaned it against the wall before coming in.

'That'll be nice,' I said, thinking it would also be good to have Jess out of the way; it would mean I had one less person to worry about, even if only for a few hours. 'Come on through.'

Sure enough, Jess was in the kitchen when we got there, eating a slice of toast. I could smell the Marmite and peanut butter she loved to mix together. When she saw us her face lit up and she waved her toast at Naomi. With her mouth full, she pointed at the kettle, one eyebrow up.

'I'll make it,' I said. 'One sugar, Naomi?'

'No sugar thanks, I'm on a diet.' So that explained the new leaner face. Shame, I'd always loved the curves on her. She plonked herself down at the end of the table, back to the door, as comfortable in our house as she was in hers.

'Almost ready,' Jess said through her toast, then swallowed. 'We're going shopping, Mum. I told Dad last night but I didn't see you.'

'Sounds good,' I said, pouring Naomi some tea.

'Such good news about Dodge, Belle!' Naomi said.

'I know,' I said, nodding. I slipped with the kettle, fingers still clumsy with the cold from my swim, and the steaming water splashed off the rim of the cup, spattering my hand. I gasped, swore and put the kettle down with a clang. Turning quickly to the sink, I put my hand under the cold tap, turning it on as far as it would go. Soon my hand was numb, but I kept it there for longer, wanting to chill it completely.

As I turned the tap off I heard footsteps on the stairs, two pairs. Five seconds later, Kit and Ivo came in. I focused on Kit, quickly taking a reading of her face. She smiled at me, relaxed, happy. Wet-haired, make-up-free. Straight from the shower. Blissfully unaware.

'Hi Nem,' Kit said to the girl she was calling 'provincial' yesterday, and Naomi turned with a smile already forming – then stopped when she saw Ivo, a flicker of confusion on her face.

'Hi Kit!' she said and then to Ivo, 'Uh, hello?'

'This is Ivo,' Kit explained, and he nodded at Naomi and moved to the kettle, testing its weight to see if it had enough water in it.

'Do I know you from somewhere?' Naomi asked, frowning. He glanced at her, took out two cups.

'Don't think so,' he said. I watched him moving about in our kitchen and could only think about how I'd like to never see him again.

'You look really familiar…' Naomi said, screwing her face up, and I could see her doing maths homework or a science project with Jess at the table.

'You making a pass at my boyfriend, Nem?' Kit laughed and Naomi coloured, a flush starting at her neck and creeping up her cheeks.

'No,' she flustered. 'Of course not. He just looks like someone…' Ivo shrugged and Naomi laughed at herself.

'Sorry,' she said. 'Ignore me.' She sipped her tea self-consciously and I thought that Kit could have been a bit kinder. Ivo stirred their tea and clinked the spoon against the rim.

'Shall we?' he said to Kit, indicating the ceiling with his head, wanting to go back upstairs.

'Yep,' said Kit. 'We're watching something on YouTube. About a place called Wilderness in South Africa. Looks amazing. We're thinking of going travelling, you see,' she said to Naomi in a patronising way.

Ivo passed her carrying both mugs, and Kit grabbed a packet of biscuits to take up with them.

'Nice to see you, Nem,' she said over her shoulder, and they were gone.

Naomi looked pleased to see them leave. Jess was chattering about what shops she wanted to go to and where they might have lunch. Soon, they were putting on coats and moaning about the rain.

'What time does the bus go?' I asked.

Jess checked her watch. 'Ten minutes, we'd better scoot.'

'Takes ages to get anywhere from here,' said Naomi, doing up her zip. 'Wish we had a train station.'

I pulled my purse from my bag, took out a twenty-pound note and tucked it into Jess's hand.

'Buy yourself something nice,' I said, wanting to hug her, breathe in the smell of her hair. She grinned and gave me a quick kiss on the cheek, butterfly soft.

'That's who he looks like!' Naomi suddenly said as they moved down the hall. 'There was a guy in the summer, rented a room from my Aunty Eileen.' Her aunt ran a B&B on the promenade and Nem worked there in the holidays. They were a close family. 'I swear it was him I saw him there one day, either that or he has a double! Do you remember Jess, it was when we made that TikTok on the beach with Dodge and it went viral?'

Jess laughed and nodded. 'Over a hundred thousand likes!' she said, pushing her glass up her nose, proud.

We reached the door and they both stuffed feet into trainers without untying the laces. 'Aunty Eileen told me afterwards he was asking questions about where the young people of Southwold were going to university. Part of a study on travel networks, apparently.' She clapped her hands together, delighted she'd remembered. 'He was really interested in how far people travelled for education. Aunty Eileen told him about me going to Nottingham Trent, Jess going to Exeter and Kit going to Bristol.'

My breath halted in my throat.

'It wouldn't be him though,' she said. 'Aunty Eileen was fuming. He disappeared without paying and left the room in a right old state.'

Jess opened the door, her mind already in Urban Outfitters, and she and Naomi stepped together into the rain.

The door closed behind them and I stared at it. Had he been here, in Southwold, in the summer? Ivo *was* distinctive-looking and if Naomi thought she'd seen him before, she most probably had.

I didn't like what I'd heard. It was no happy coincidence that Ivo had just bumped into Kit when he got a job at the student bar in Bristol.

It was all premeditated. He'd found out where the girls were going to university. And then he'd waited to get one of them on their own, away from the family, to worm his way in.

It was orchestrated. It was patient. My breath caught.

I flicked through my phone to Jess's TikTok account and scrolled backward in time, through clips of her doing dance routines and photomontages, to the summer before. The film of Dodge was easy to spot by the number of likes. The bluest of skies and white-crested waves on the beach. Dodge sitting picture-perfect on the sand, head tilted to one side.

'Speak, Dodge,' Jess said, off camera, and there it was. A squeak. Once, twice, three times as Dodge opened his mouth as if to emit the loudest bark. A squeak.

My skin went cold. It was out there for everyone to see.

I opened the comments on the clip. There were hundreds of them: laughing faces, 'so sweet' notes, love-heart emojis, on and on for pages.

But the one that caught my eye was the one from a sub-scriber called Karmarama. An image of a rope knot next to the name, just like Ivo's tattoo. The words, 'I wish I'd been lucky enough to have a pet like this.'

Footsteps on the stairs made me slam the phone down on the table, terrified.

Was it him? It felt like it was.

How long had he been watching us?

Planning?

Kit appeared with an empty biscuit wrapper.

'Gonna take some toast up,' she said, putting two slices in the toaster.

Looking at her, I wondered if Ivo had any feelings for her at all. Or was he simply faking it, to get to us, to get to me? He certainly made a good show of liking Kit, but it was she who was hanging off him, touching him all the time, clearly smitten.

My heart hurt at the thought of Kit's heart breaking if she found out he was just using her. And at the idea that it just as easily could have been Jess he came home with this holiday. Either one would have served his purpose.

'It's just the most amazing place, Mum,' Kit was saying. 'And just along from Knysna, where the cliffs are called The Heads.'

The toast popped up and she took both slices out and wafted them a few times to cool them down.

'And you can see whales at Plettenberg Bay,' she said. 'Live ones!' She laughed, as though she'd forgotten all about the dead whale and its eyeball.

'Maybe you should watch the video, Mum,' she blathered on. 'Then you'll see why we want to go there.'

Clearly she was set on going travelling. She put her head on one side and looked at me. 'Can we sit down at lunchtime – perhaps go to The Sole Bay? You and Dad, and Ivo and me? And talk about the university thing?'

This was obviously a conversation that would lead to the one about her going away with Ivo.

Time was against me. I had to find out more about him.

'Of course we can.' I chose my words carefully. 'But before we all sit down together, I need to ask a few questions while Ivo's not here.' Kit's eyes widened with suspicion. 'It's just that I know the conversation is going to include you going away with Ivo, and that's a big decision.'

She pursed her lips, considering.

'You'd be spending twenty-four hours a day, seven days a week together. Travelling, eating, sleeping, everything. That's intense, Kit. It can strain even the best friendships.'

She opened her mouth to speak, but I carried on.

'I know people who were friends when they went on a two-week holiday to the Mediterranean together and then never spoke again when they got back!' I was lying through my teeth now, fabricating stuff to make my point, but I kept going. 'You're talking about going to faraway locations, and you need to be really sure of who you're going with. So, love, how well do you really know Ivo?'

Immediately she was defensive. 'Really well. We talk about *everything*.'

I nodded, and her shoulders dropped an inch.

That's good,' I said, pulling out a chair and sitting. 'Tell me more about him.'

'Why?'

'It's just you've not said much. For example, I only know you met at a bar.'

'Yep, free shots all night.' She giggled.

'Did he give them to your friends too?

'Just me.'

So he had singled her out.

'And then what happened?'

'We were just kind of together after that first night.' She blushed and I guessed they'd spent that night together.

'Then, he was there when I came out of my lecture the next day, waiting for me. He'd bought us a sandwich and a coffee and we sat in the park.' Kit smiled at the memory. 'And after that, we just *were*. He'd come by after his lectures or shifts at the bar, or he'd be sitting on the bench outside campus if I was at a seminar. He didn't play games like other boys. He was all-in. It was amazing. Like he just wanted to be with me.'

She bit a corner off her toast.

'So where does he live? Do you go to his place as well?'

'No, he prefers to come to mine.'

I pricked my ears up.

'Why's that then?'

'His housemates. Ivo says they're grungy and leave the place in a mess. Says they're not the kind of people he wants me to be around.'

'So, it's been pretty full on?' I asked. 'Things have progressed quickly?' I smiled at her to reassure her I wasn't judging. '*I've* certainly never seen you like this before.'

She grinned. 'It's the real thing,' she said as though she couldn't quite believe it herself. 'I've talked to him about everything. Hopes for the future. Ambitions. Everything.'

'And does he tell you everything too?'

Kit shrugged.

'He's quite open, for a boy, but every now and then he'll be a bit quiet. I don't think boys and girls work the same, Mum,' she said. 'You must know that – they just don't talk like we do. They like to choose when they tell you things.'

Morag let herself in as usual.

'Thought I'd see what's on the agenda for today,' she said as though it were some sort of holiday club. I didn't have the energy for it.

'Not sure yet, Morag,' I said taking a deep breath. 'Jess is shopping with Naomi.'

'That's nice.'

'David's having a lie-in…'

'Well deserved.'

'Kit and Ivo are watching a travel programme upstairs.'

'Educational,' she said with a nod. 'What about you?'

'Me?' What could I say? I'm trying to save my reputation, my marriage and my girls from Ivo? I didn't say that. Instead I managed, 'I'm warming up and then I am going to have a shower.' My hair still hung wet on my shoulders from my dip.

'There's a Christmas carol concert at Walberswick later,' Morag said. 'I thought it would be nice for us all to go.'

'We're not all here though,' I said. 'Jess has gone to Nem's. She's staying the night.'

'The rest of us then. A family outing.'

When she said things like that, there was very little room for argument. David would agree, it would be a nice 'family' event. The girls would go along with it to please their gran. But this time, it wasn't just family.

'I'm not sure, Morag.'

'We could walk there,' she said. 'Take Dodge with us.'

'It's not that,' I said. 'It's just Ivo...'

'What about him?'

'I'm not sure it's his kind of thing,' I said, using him as an excuse.

'You don't like him, do you?' she said, suddenly. Her eyes were very blue, just like Kit's. And then I realised – that could only ever be a coincidence. They weren't even related. I didn't know who I suddenly felt sorrier for. All of us would be broken.

'I've seen the way you look at him,' she said. 'Like he's not good enough.'

'Nonsense,' I said, trying to laugh it off, but she shrugged.

'You'll learn,' she said, settling back in her chair and looking towards the kettle. 'Nobody ever feels good enough for your child. That's just the way it is.'

The Sole Bay was busy again. The last Friday before Christmas was always good business for Betty; there were two or three tables of office parties, celebrating the last day of work until after the holidays. Some of them looked like they'd started a bit early.

We nabbed the last table in the corner as David went to the bar; not the best, as it was next to the corridor to the toilets, but the only one available. I spied one of our posters about Dodge pinned to the noticeboard on the wall, along with taxi numbers and B&B adverts. David spotted us and wound his way over from the bar with a full tray of wines, beers, nuts and crisps.

'It's Christmas lunch menu only today,' he said, balancing the tray carefully on the edge of the table, 'so I thought we'd just have a drink and snack buffet.'

Kit was next to me, which I was pleased about. She was wearing Ivo's sweatshirt and a pair of jeans. The top, clearly too big for her, hung off one shoulder and made her look even smaller. She looked eager and nervous, like she had on her first day of school. Ivo lounged in the chair next to her, but kept his hand on her thigh in silent support.

I passed drinks around and we piled the packets in the middle. David quickly swiped some dry-roasted peanuts. Kit opened some crisps and placed the packet between her and Ivo, but didn't eat any.

'Cheers.' David raised his glass and took a good swallow of beer, smacking his lips afterwards. 'First today,' he said, as always. He was happy, oblivious to everything unravelling around him.

'So, tell us what's on your mind, Kit?' he said, not shying away from the conversation.

She glanced at Ivo and then went for it. It was a pretty compelling argument, to be fair to her. Some parts of it sounded rehearsed and some words she used didn't sound like her at all. But she made good grounds for 'pausing in her education' instead of 'pursuing something that would not benefit her later in life.' She was careful not to use words like 'dropping out' but instead said 're-evaluating' or 'taking time'. She didn't mention travelling at all. She just focused on why she wanted to 'reconsider her path'. The facts were that university was not what she'd hoped. She wasn't connecting with her course. She wanted to be sure she was focusing on the right things.

David listened and sipped, nodding occasionally. Eventually she stopped and took a large mouthful of her wine, letting out a shaky breath. It meant a lot to her, I could tell.

'So if you do "pause",' he said, playing her own words back to her, 'then what would you do instead?'

Here we go. I knew the answer to this already. She answered in a rush, the words running into each other.

'I'd go travelling with Ivo. See the world. Experience things I can never experience here, whether in Southwold or Bristol or anywhere else in the UK.'

Her face lit up.

'I think it would really broaden my horizons,' she went on. 'I could get to know myself and then know more about where to apply myself when I get back.'

Again, it sounded like she'd been practising her pitch. She looked at Ivo and he gave her a tiny nod. I imagined he was squeezing her thigh under the table in approval. David glanced at me, eyebrows up. What could I say? I had to try to keep her at university while Ivo went off travelling. If I could separate them, even for a few weeks, things might cool off. Kit might meet someone else. Ivo might disappear. If I could pave the way into the conversation, I knew David would pick up on it.

'I think Dad would agree with me, love, it just feels really quick,' I said. 'I'm worried you haven't really given university a chance. It's only been a term.'

She scowled and then quickly rearranged her face into a more pleasant expression.

'A term is quite a long time, Mum. It's been three months. I'd know by now if I was enjoying it.'

'I tend to agree with Mum, Kit,' David said. 'It might feel long to you, but in the grand scheme of things, it's really short.' He took a pull of his pint. 'I was thinking more about trying for another term.'

Something flashed across her face and her jaw jutted slightly forward. She wasn't going to take this lying down.

'Then we could reassess after Easter?' he said. I knew the way his mind was working. If he could get her to Easter, he would be thinking, he could encourage her to finish the year. Then maybe transfer her points to another course.

'I really don't want to do that,' she said, face flushing.

'Have you spoken to Jess about it?' I asked, to soften the conversation. She shook her head, dismissively.

'She doesn't understand. She's happy in Exeter.'

That made me think Jess probably wasn't as supportive of the idea as Kit would have liked. Otherwise she would have said so.

'What do you think, Ivo?' David asked and I bit my tongue. I wished he hadn't asked Ivo's opinion. I didn't want him to give her any ammunition.

Ivo tilted his head to one side, as though giving thought.

'I know Kit's not enjoying her course, we've talked about that a lot,' he said, starting well. 'And I believe there are loads of ways for people to gain experience, rather than just the traditional routes.'

Kit nodded emphatically. I had to admit it was clever; he was making our preferred option look more like the dull, old-fashioned way of doing things.

'I know you're planning on travelling for your course,' David said. 'But that's different to Kit just travelling without an end gain.'

'If you're worried about the travelling itself, David, I can assure you I'd take care of Kit.' He turned to me. 'Belle, you can trust me. I wouldn't let her out of my sight.'

David looked at me, paused a beat and then looked back at Kit.

'I really think you should try another term,' he said and a flush started at her neck. She took a mouthful of her wine, a large one. Dutch courage.

'I'm not going to do that,' she said, quietly, ruthlessly almost. The table behind us erupted into noisy laughter and clinking of glasses, and we had to wait for it to subside before we could continue.

'Look Kit, I can't force you to stay on. We all know that. I just don't want you to do something you'll regret,' David said when he could be heard.

Kit looked at Ivo and shook her head.

'I won't regret it,' she said. 'In fact, it's the thing I'm most sure of in my life at the moment.'

She pulled her phone from her coat pocket and scrolled.

'Which is why I emailed my tutor this morning, with-drawing from my course – "with immediate effect",' she read out loud, then held the screen towards us to see. I heard the intake of breath from David, the slight catch in his throat.

'So all this talking,' he said. 'What was the point in that?'

'I was hoping you'd see that it was what I wanted.'

'But you were going to do it anyway, whether we agreed or not,' I said, and she held my eye for a second before nodding.

'But I was hoping to get your blessing,' she said.

Never. Never could I give my blessing to her being with him. Some fluttering anxiety was making it hard to get a deep breath and instead I took a long careful swallow of my wine.

'Well, that's that then.' David found my hand on the table and laced his fingers through mine. Ivo watched.

'And, in the spirit of striking while the iron is hot,' Kit said, scrolling on her phone again to show us something else, 'we've booked the tickets to South Africa.'

She passed her phone to her dad. David scrolled, seeming to have trouble finding what he was looking for. I held my breath until he spoke.

'How have you paid for that? Gran's gift?'

She nodded.

'Does she know you've done that?' David asked.

'No, but I think she'll be happy for me. It's the experience of a lifetime.'

They faced each other for a silent few seconds.

'I paid for mine, obviously,' Ivo interjected. I doubted that he had; Kit was such a generous person that I was pretty certain that she would have paid for both tickets, which would have cost a fortune at this time of year.

'But this is a one-way ticket…' David stammered, and this time they both nodded.

'Open-ended,' Ivo said, 'it gives us more flexibility as we're not sure where we'll go next, or where we'll end up. Or when we'll be back.'

My wine tasted warm and sour in my mouth.

'And the departure date?' David said, scanning the phone screen again before looking up, stunned. 'You can't be serious?'

'Sunday,' Kit said, grimacing as though confessing to a crime. 'We leave the day after tomorrow.'

'You won't even be here for Christmas?' I cried.

'Sorry, Mum,' Kit said, reaching to squeeze my hand. 'It was the best ticket we could get. Please don't be upset.' I noticed she used the word best, and not cheapest.

Ivo smiled at me across the table as though he'd won, then threw a peanut in the air and caught it perfectly in his mouth. I hoped he'd choke.

It was one of those moments where we had to bend.

David and I both knew it.

Kit was old enough legally to make her own decisions. We couldn't force her to stay at university. She had to live her own life. And the last thing I wanted was her to leave on bad terms. I know all of those things would have run through David's mind, just as they did mine, but he didn't know what I knew.

So we accepted the situation for the sake of peace.

I knew David was fuming. But not half as much as I was.

I racked my brains for a solution as I sipped wine and listened to Kit chatter about the Garden Route. She was animated, relieved, clutching at Ivo's elbow to bring him into the conversation, holding on to him as she laughed, gazing at him with shining eyes.

Now Kit had told us what she wanted, she was on cloud nine, and so excited for the next part of her life, the great travelling adventure. It was almost as if she was already gone.

If only I could be happy for her. If she were going with anyone else, I probably would have been. University wasn't the be-all and end-all, and it was her life.

Morag was waiting in her front window as we walked down from South Green. She waved at us and put her hat on, obviously waiting for us so we could walk to the carol concert. As she opened the front door, I met her on the doorstep.

'Can I use your loo, Morag? Before we go?' I said, hopping foot to foot. She frowned but opened the door for me. 'I'll only be a mo. We won't miss anything.'

I dashed past her, towards the bathroom at the back, as I heard Kit tell her the news.

'Guess what your Granny Gift is going to enable me to do!' she gushed. 'The trip of a lifetime.' I didn't wait to hear the rest.

Morag's apartment was one of the reasons the house had been so perfect for us. She'd wanted to be self-contained from us – the feeling was mutual – and this two-bedroomed basement gave her space. We'd pooled our money. Morag's from downsizing after Andrew, David's dad, died. My inheritance from my parents. David's and my names on the small mortgage left to pay. Twenty-five years we'd been here. It meant something.

The bathroom smelled of the new sealant David had applied. Everything was in its place, neat and orderly. Morag's dressing gown hung on the back of the door. SPF face creams and body butters were stacked on the shelves. A small bottle of her favourite nude, no-nonsense nail varnish. I washed my hands, staring at myself in the mirror without recognition.

I spotted the framed newspaper clipping on the sitting room wall as I walked back through. Front page of the *Southwold Gazette*, slightly yellowed now with age. A photograph of Morag twenty years earlier, hair longer and loose, not even the age I was now. She had her arm firmly round a pigeon-chested boy whose knees were bigger than his thighs. They both stood, smiling awkwardly for the camera, the sea behind. Billy Graham. The little boy she'd saved. It had made all the local news, not just the papers. She'd been interviewed on the radio and the teatime television programme. People had stopped her in the street to congratulate her and she'd pretend to be embarrassed while she grinned ear to ear. Looking at Billy's little face, I wondered if he ever thought of Morag now. But he was probably just getting on with his life these days, not giving a thought to the woman who'd saved him. And that was the way it was meant to be. Children should not carry burdens from the past.

I glanced around the room. Framed photos lined the mantelpiece, the shelves of the bookcase. A black-and-white photo of David as a child in a school, in a uniform that looked as stiff as a board. A sepia wedding photo of Morag and Andrew. Technicolour close-ups of Kit at the beach, Jess on a bouncy castle, photos we'd taken and had copied for Morag. From every wall of her room she was surrounded by family, and I could imagine her polishing them every week, talking to each one. Just as I was about to leave the room, something struck me that never had before. There were none of me.

I scanned again along the lines of loved ones. And wait – there I was. It was a group shot of the four of us. I could remember the occasion perfectly. It was a party to celebrate Jess and Kit getting good grades for their GCSEs. David and I flanked them as they held up their certificates. The photo was just as I remembered the occasion, David beaming with pride, Jess and Kit grinning with relief; and there was my arm and shoulder. A glimpse of my hair. The rest of me had been cut out so the photo fitted the frame.

'Come on, Mum,' Kit called.

Maybe it wasn't what was in the picture that mattered, I thought, but what was going on outside the frame.

Not only did I need to know who Ivo was, I had to know where he'd come from.

Christmas lights hung around the harbour at Walberswick. Despite the cold there was a line of small children holding crab lines off the side of the jetty, buckets at the ready.

Kit and Ivo, not interested in joining in with the carols, bought a cheap line and bucket and cadged a bit of bacon from one of the locals Kit knew before joining the kids to try their luck.

Watching her face above her duffel coat, I saw the way she looked at Ivo, the light in her eyes as he spoke. She was in love, as clear as day. And in two days she would be gone.

My eyes scratched. They were hot, wet and tired.

David took my hand as we went with Morag to find the carol service.

'We'll have to FaceTime a lot,' he said quietly as he led me to the large Christmas tree that had been erected on the green.

A van was selling hot mince pies and coffees and the local pub was serving mulled wine. We cupped our hands round the warmth of the plastic glasses and looked at the small number of stalls selling home-made Christmas cards and locally made jewellery, sculpted from glass ground smooth by the sea.

Morag bought handmade coasters and put them in her ever-ready string bag, then followed us around, chatting to other women like she was visiting royalty, updating people about Dodge's return, wishing people Merry Christmas.

The local brass band started tuning up and we all turned towards the tree. Carol sheets were handed out. David, standing between Morag and me, held ours.

'Hope they don't go on too long,' said Morag before the carols had even started, even though it had been her idea to come. David couldn't help but laugh. The music started and we sang. Only when we got to the last one, 'Silent Night', and the local primary school sang the first verse on their own, did I allow myself to cry.

Kit and Ivo were still at the jetty, as I'd expected, and we wandered back to them. They had one crab in their bucket, red cheeks, blue fingers, big grins. She looked so young next to Ivo.

The Christmas lights blew in the sea wind; boat masts clanged in the harbour as Ivo went down to the jetty edge to return the crab to the water.

'Last ferry in five,' the vicar called, and we headed down to the tiny wooden pier to wait for Jake, the ferryboat man. We watched him row across from the other side, cutting an angle across the river to then slide in with the current to our stop. He'd decorated his rowing boat for the occasion, with tinsel on the oar handles, and wore a Santa hat over his bald head. Jake was Walberswick born and bred. In the high season he and his family rowed boats all day long, twelve passengers at a time, loaded with buckets and bait for the crabbing. He was burned to a deep conker-brown in the summer, and even though I knew he was older than us, his arms and shoulders were as wiry and strong as they had been when we first arrived.

He grinned at Kit and asked after Jess, nodding to Ivo when Kit introduced him as her boyfriend. Jake helped Morag down first, holding her hand carefully as she stepped onto the boat. He settled her in the middle seat and tucked a blanket around her knees against the cold. She'd have scoffed if I did that for her at home, but she accepted it grate-fully now. Ivo and Kit went in the two-man seat at the front, and David and I sat either side of Morag.

'We used to do this loads when we were kids,' Kit was saying. 'Days out crabbing. Ice creams on the quay.'

'Childhood of dreams,' Ivo said. I kept my eyes on the bank ahead, brain empty. Jake chatted to David from behind us.

Morag nudged me.

'Will you show me how to use FaceTime?' she said. She looked very small and surprisingly old, suddenly, under her blanket, and something tugged inside me. She loved those girls. Nothing would change that. She was going to miss Kit too. I nodded.

'Course I will,' I said, tucking her blanket more snugly around her knees, 'it's really easy.'

'I'm not stupid, you know,' she said and I patted her leg, not rising to it. Not this time.

Jake was pulling hard into the current, and I knew he'd hold his course until we were past halfway. I felt slightly untethered, and wished I could hold David's hand.

We drew into the wooden pier on the other side and Jake's niece pulled the boat until it bumped gently against the jetty, holding it tight with a rope.

'Ladies first,' said David and Kit moved past us and clambered out without help. She knew the routine, and was ready to reach for her gran to help her ashore. I watched them as they set off up the jetty.

As David went to climb out next so he could pull me up, Ivo slammed into me from behind, hitting me full-force on the shoulder,. I staggered forward, and the boat rocked wildly as Ivo fell forward past me and landed on the floor. I hit the side hard, wood into ribs, but managed to clutch at the boat and stop myself going into the water.

A cry made my stomach turn. Ivo was lying sprawled in the bottom of the boat, rubbing his head, dazed. But it wasn't him who was hurt but David, caught between the boat and the jetty, his face contorted. He was trapped. Crushed.

Jake's niece dropped to the wooden boards and held the boat away from the jetty with her feet, carefully protecting David from being hurt further. 'His leg is caught,' she said.

Ivo was now sitting on the bench of the rowing boat, looking confused. I could hear Kit running back towards us.

'Hold it steady,' Jake said, and then he hoisted David onto the jetty.

David shouted, eyes rolling.

I was transfixed with horror.

David's thighbone had ripped through his trousers. It stuck out the side of his leg, shining white in the moonlight, about three inches above his knee.

Behind me, Kit cried out.

'Phone the ambulance,' I said to her over my shoulder.

I knelt by David, murmuring to him, not sure if he could hear me through his pain. Morag stood on his other side, shaking her head, in shock.

Jake laid the blanket from the boat over David, leaving his injured leg clear. Then he took off his own coat and rolled it into a pillow.

I heard Kit giving directions, describing the injury. Her voice shook when she said about the bone.

'I'm so sorry, Belle,' Jake said as he made a tourniquet for David's thigh. 'Never had an accident in all my years on the river.'

'I know,' I said. It wasn't Jake I blamed.

'I'm so sorry,' Ivo said. 'It's all my fault.'

It was the second time I'd heard him say that. The first time was when Dodge disappeared. It was dangerous being around Ivo, and my skin prickled with fear.

'I got my foot caught up in this.' He held up Morag's string bag.

'If it's anyone's fault, it's mine,' Morag said and began to whimper and shiver.

'Ambulance will be here in ten minutes,' Kit said. 'I think I should take Gran home, Mum.'

David groaned and I knew I couldn't leave him. And although I didn't like the thought of Kit and Ivo leaving, it was obvious that Morag needed to be in the warm.

I had an idea. I said to Kit, 'I think you should stay with Gran tonight in the flat.'

Morag managed a wan smile, and Kit squeezed her tight. Good. I knew Kit wouldn't be allowed to have Ivo in with her at her gran's.

Kit and Morag would be tucked up downstairs. And Jess would be at Nem's until the morning.

I watched them leave, holding David's hand as we waited for the ambulance. He was moaning softly to himself, eyes shut. The river lapped against the jetty legs and the wind blew across the marsh grass. The thought of being on my own in the house with Ivo that night made my skin crawl, but at least I knew the others would be safe.

The ward was quiet. David was sleeping. After an operation he had been medicated up to the eyeballs, and hadn't moved since. His leg rested on the bed, reset, the broken bone held in place by metal pins that punctured his skin in three perfect holes either side, the leg protected by what looked like a Meccano frame. Every now and then he murmured and flinched, without waking.

I didn't want to leave him just yet, but I couldn't bear to look closely at his leg.

The other patients lay quietly. The teenager next to us watched something on his laptop using headphones, the screen illuminating his face. A nurse bustled in and out, closing curtains, talking in low tones and giving out painkillers. When she got to us, she lifted David's wrist, took his pulse and marked it on his chart.

'Nasty break,' she said. 'How's your house for wheelchair access?'

'Terrible,' I said, thinking about the steps from the Green up to the front door and the different levels we had on our upper-ground floor where the kitchen and living room were. I'd been racking my brains about how to make it work since the doctor had told me earlier that David would be in a wheelchair for at least six weeks, but more likely eight to ten. It was Morag who gave me the answer, when I rang home to let her know the operation had all gone well.

'The basement is easy access,' she said. 'He can be down-stairs with me.' Then as an afterthought, 'you can come too, of course.' It wasn't something I was looking forward to, but it was kind of her. She wanted to help.

David wouldn't be leaving here for the next few days. And before that I needed to persuade Kit not to get on that plane.

The nurse checked David's temperature.

'Bet you weren't expecting to spend your Friday night here, were you?' she said to me as she ran her finger down his chart. 'Do you fancy a cuppa?'

I nodded and felt my eyes brim at her kindness, my tears hot and salty. 'It's all right, love, don't worry. It's just the shock.' The nurse's shoes squeaked on the lino as she went to get me my tea.

I rubbed my eyes, suddenly exhausted. I looked at David, and my thoughts turned to Ivo. The only thing I knew about him was that he worked in the student bar at Kit's university. But the university would be shut for the holidays. There would be nobody there to tell me anything.

Then I realised: I could track down where he lived. Someone had rung, hadn't they? Kit had made a joke out of it. The name of his house rhymed with the name of the road… Beaver on Hever? Bleather on Heather? I racked my brains. No. It flashed back to me. Cleverly on Beverly. That was it. I went to the maps on my iPhone and typed in Beverly Road, Bristol, but nothing came up. I closed my eyes, seeing again Kit's face as she laughed about the name. I bit my lip in frustration. I tried Beverly Way – and there it was. I had it. I knew where Ivo lived and, unless David took a terrible turn for the worse before then, I was going to Bristol first thing in the morning.

Felix seemed to have aged a decade in the fortnight I'd avoided him for. He waved across the bar at me, stood, sat again, picked up his drink and took a long slug. It was a short, dark drink, maybe whisky or bourbon, next to three empties. I put my lime and soda on the table and sat opposite him, out of touching distance. His knee was jigging under the table, so fast it rattled the ice in his glass.

'Tour's off,' he said. I wasn't aware it had ever been on. I made a sympathetic noise, half heartedly.

'In fact, The Hush is dead,' he said, 'the boys found a new lead vocal. They've re-formed into some kind of indie band. Although let's face it, they're never going anywhere without me.' He stood suddenly and the chair screeched on the floorboards. He pretended to march alongside the table, lifting his knees one after the other in a jerky little dance, as he hummed a funeral dirge.

'Rest in Peace, The Hush.' He raised his hands to a pretend audience as if he was a vicar at the pulpit and then threw himself back down in his chair.

His eyes were bloodshot, like he hadn't slept for a week, and I could smell the plaque on his teeth from my seat.

'Maybe I'll never get my break.' A nerve pulsed in his cheek and he clenched his jaw as if to get a grip on it, then banged his fist hard on his thigh, growled in frustration. 'Maybe they'll never see what talent I've got.'

'Look on the bright side — if you're not touring, it's more time to spend with your son,' I said, trying to calm the situation, bring him back onto an even keel. Why hadn't I spotted the signs when we first met? The conversations that ran one to the next, I had just put down to excitement. The drumming, the singing, the random lyrics I had put down to artistic temperament. I'd seen the highest of his highs and been caught up in them myself. Because I wanted to escape the everyday, the safe, the adult life I'd grown into. Because of that, maybe I hadn't let myself see the lows, the unpredictability, the swings, the frenzy. Or maybe he was just worse now. I noticed the flesh around his thumbnails was bleeding, chewed and ragged-looking. He was definitely worse now.

'Nikki's kicked me out.' He dropped his head into his hands for a moment, put his fingers into his hair like he was going to pull it out from the roots. 'Doesn't matter though, eh?' He lifted his face and smiled fiercely at me, dimples piercing his cheeks, a ghost of the first time I saw him. 'It was always going to happen when I told her about us.'

My mouth went dry and I sipped at my soda.

'You told her?' I whispered, chest aching for this woman I didn't know.

'Course.' He shrugged. 'I had to if we're going to be together.' He put a hand on the table, palm up and open, waiting for me to put mine in it. Instead I put both my hands in my lap. He frowned at me, then tapped the side of the table, setting my teeth on edge. He shut his eyes and started singing some lyrics I half-recognised about 'the one I love'. Even his voice sounded tired, broken. Instead of its usual sexy husk, it was jagged, cracked. I glanced around and saw the quick looks and half-hidden laughs of the other customers. The nearest table frowned and tutted.

A waiter appeared, although I hadn't known it was table service. He stood at the table facing me, slightly angled away from Felix.

'More drinks?' he asked, fixing me with a look I didn't immediately understand.

Felix ordered another without hesitation. I shook my head, swilled my soda in the glass. As soon as I'd finished this, I wanted to be gone. For good. Not like last time, when I'd left before ending things. Ironic that I wanted to be gone back to my lovely, safe, everyday life with the man I loved, the life that I'd thought was so confining. Now I saw the rhythm of it, recognised the touchstones of its security, the foundation of it built on love and trust. When the waiter brought Felix's whisky back a moment later, he paused, made eye contact again, and asked me if I needed anything else. I frowned, shook my head, still missing his point. He licked his lower lip quickly and then said, 'So everything is okay?' He flicked his eyes towards Felix. I glanced at Felix myself and then I understood. I saw him as the waiter did. As the whole room did. Jittery. Drinking too much. Unpredictable. I nodded an embarrassed yes and muttered a 'thank you', and he gave me one last look before turning away.

'Call if you need anything,' he said kindly and headed back to the nearest end of the bar, where he picked up a tea towel and started drying stuff that was already dry. He was staying within shouting distance.

'Have you told the patient yet?' Felix asked, and I noticed the slight slur to his voice now, the whisky roughing his throat. 'Dav-eeeeed.'

'No.'

'I can come with you if you want?' he said. 'If you'd prefer me to be there. To meet him.'

'Meet him?' What the hell was he talking about? A panic was rising in me. I remembered his eyes squinting at me through the letter box as he knelt on my front doorstep.

'You know, I'm sure he'll want to know who I am. When he knows we're together.' He smiled again, like he'd won a prize. He really thought he was going to be celebrating.

I realised the time had come to end this. It had gone too far already. I could hardly bear to let my mind touch on his wife, his child, devastated by this — this mistake.

'Felix, we're not going to be together,' I said and my voice trembled. I cleared my throat. He blinked at me, once, twice, uncomprehending. I had to be clear. Be final.

'I'm not leaving David,' I said and this time my voice was stronger.

His lips parted slightly as though to say something, but I shook my head at him – no – and carried on.

'Whatever this was,' I said, pointing from him to me and back again, 'it's over.' I watched the words register and then the tic begin again in his cheek.

'But you love me,' he said, confusion fuddling his face.

I took a deep breath and then blew it out slowly.

'No,' I said. 'I don't. I love my husband.'

He slammed his glass down hard on the tabletop and someone behind me in the bar gasped.

'It's over,' I repeated. The look between us went on too long and I realised there was nothing else to be said. I pushed my chair back and stood.

'Good luck, Felix,' I said.

The waiter held the door open for me. My hands shook as I fished my car keys from my pocket.

Saturday 23 December

Sea temperature: 8.5 degrees.
Air temperature: 4 degrees.

The grass crunched white under my feet as I crossed South Green to the promenade, my footsteps leaving a trail behind me in the frost. The lock of the beach hut glistened with tiny ice crystals as I unclasped it. My breath plumed in the air ahead of me as I waved across to Nancy and jogged down the beach in my wetsuit. The shock of the cold water sluiced me clean of hospitals and the salt scrubbed me of all doubt as I struck out. I felt strong again, decisive even, as I cut through the water towards the pier. Today I was going to do something to take control of the situation. Today, on my fiftieth birthday, I felt more me than I ever had before. I knew what was important. It was love. It was family. That was all.

David had told me to go home from the hospital when he awoke from his drugged sleep at about midnight. I'd kissed his pallid cheek and readied myself to leave him in the weird half-light of the ward, the teenager in the next bed still watching his iPad. The nurse waved me off and told me to call in the morning if I wanted an update before I came in.

'She's not coming in the morning,' David had said, trying a smile. 'It's her birthday. A big one.'

I shook my head. 'Of course I'll be here,' I said.

'No, you won't,' he told me. 'Or the spa I've booked for you will be going to waste. The tickets are in my bedside drawer. I insist. It's your birthday. Please go, Belle.'

'You might as well,' the nurse said from the side of the bed. 'It's not like he's going anywhere!' She nudged me with her elbow as if we were friends.

'I can't do that—' I started to say, and then realised a made-up spa visit was the perfect cover I needed for going to Bristol.

David nodded. 'Yes you can. Have a massage for me.'

'I love you,' I said, bending to kiss him again.

'I love you more,' he said.

I made it home by 1 a.m. and found Morag at the kitchen table, with a mug of tea. Kit had already gone downstairs to bed, but Morag had decided to wait for me and had saved me some dinner, sausages and mash. I was hungry, but it was covered in sweaty cling film and the gravy was congealed-looking, and I couldn't face it. I told her all over again about David's operation and then I took her down the steps to her bedroom and turned on her bedside lamp. She looked shaky, older than I ever usually thought of her.

'Are *you* okay?' she said quietly, once she was in bed.

I blinked, surprised.

'You're worried about something,' she said. 'More than just David.'

'Oh, you know,' I said, trying to smile it off. 'Everything and nothing.'

'It always looks better after a sleep,' she said, settling back onto the pillows, and suddenly I thought about the next day.

I was leaving the girls and Morag alone with Ivo for the whole day. Was that a bad idea? I licked my lips, wondering. I told Morag about the spa day David had bought me, and his insistence that I should go.

'So you should,' she said. 'It might do you good.'

'Morag,' I said, voice low. 'I need you to keep an eye on the girls for me tomorrow. While I'm away. Can you do that?' Maybe it was my tone, or the way I was holding her gaze, but she didn't snap or argue. She just nodded.

'Of course, Belle.'

I gave her a rare hug before I shut the door, and she patted my back, as though comforting me too.

Back in our house, Kit's bedroom was quiet, although a lamp shone from under the door. The thought of Ivo in there reminded me of Felix sitting at the end of the bed, tapping, writing, waiting for me to wake. In my and David's room, I checked all around it to make sure I was on my own, and then I dragged my chair to the door as quietly as I could and wedged it under the handle.

Even then, it took me a long time to fall asleep, jumping myself back to consciousness several times before I finally let go. It was a scratchy slumber, fractured and grey to start with and then a deep velvet black. There were no dreams like the night before. No kaleidoscopes of faces, features merging into each other. Jess becoming Kit becoming Ivo. Just a complete darkness.

When I woke, I was clear and focused.

Today was the day I was fighting back.

I wouldn't let Ivo win.

The sea was alive around me, the current charging me, giving me energy for what lay ahead. I drew my strength from it, letting its force drive my blood, make me strong. It had always been my saviour, keeping my mind sane and my mood even.

Now I let it feed me, ready for the day ahead. My breath was rasping in my throat, I was swimming harder than normal, faster. I put my head down and turned, ready to head back. If I'd known, all those years ago, what that one stupid weekend would set in motion, I would never have spoken to Felix in the first place.

.I'd just made a mistake. A stupid, selfish mistake that I was ashamed of. But I would not let it wreck the lives of everyone I loved.

As I walked up the beach, Nancy was heading to her hut. She clapped her arms around herself in acknowledgment of the temperature and called over to me: 'How come so early today, Belle?'

I fumbled with my padlock with frozen fingers. Waited for the click before pushing the door open.

'The early bird catches the worm,' I replied with a jut of my chin.

The car ticked quietly as it cooled down. I leaned on the steering wheel to look at the house.

It was a ramshackle detached building, with steps leading up to it from the Bristol pavement. A wide door, dark-blue paint chipping off to show the grey beneath. The gutter under the eaves had clearly been broken for a long time; there was a green stain on the stone from water running constantly down the front wall. The windows were dirty, and I thought back to my old student houseshares. They had been scrappy terraces, or old Victorian places with cracked paving slabs. A student in every room, a shared bathroom and named shelves in the kitchen fridge. This looked worse.

I rolled my shoulders, stiff from holding the wheel too tight as I sped west on the motorway, and let my breathing steady. The satnav had brought me directly there, but it had been a long drive. I'd left a note for the girls explaining that their dad had begged me to go to the spa day he'd booked for my birthday, and have a break after the worry with Dodge and then his accident. I knew they'd believe it – David was always putting other people first – and it gave me the assurance that the girls wouldn't expect me to answer my phone. I'd also asked them to look after their gran, which I hoped would keep them all together. I'd called the hospital on the way down and they'd reassured me David was feeling no pain. I spoke to him briefly and he sang me the first few lines of 'Happy Birthday' and said he wished he were at home. I'd told him I loved him, as always. Since then I hadn't given a second thought to my birthday. I'd just concentrated on driving and lane changes and navigating the unfamiliar roads. Now I was here, actually in Bristol, I was very focused. I just needed a second to acclimatise, to gather my thoughts before I went in. I'd only get one chance to ask questions.

The door opened and a boy came out. He hesitated on the top step and lit a joint, his cheeks hollowing as he sucked it hard into his lungs. He zipped his coat up to the neck as he passed me in the parked car, then tucked his head down into the wind and was gone. I tapped the steering wheel, apprehensive, suddenly wishing I wasn't on my own.

I picked up my bag from the passenger footwell, checked my phone and got out. Took a moment to stretch out my spine, flex my neck, then walked, as quickly as possible, up the few steps to the door.

A name plate, 'Cleverly House', hung by one screw on the wall by the front door. There was no bell that I could see, so I knocked. It echoed inside the hall but nobody came. I banged harder. I hadn't come all this way to be faced with an empty house, surely?

A shuffle behind the door preceded the lock being drawn and a sallow face peering at me through the crack. A teenage lad, from what I could see, with suspicious eyes. Suddenly I realised I had no clue as to what I was going to say.

'Hi,' I started. He waited.

'I'm here about Ivo,' I said and he looked at me blankly. 'Ivo Carlyle?'

He blinked. I wondered if he was stoned. 'I've got some questions and I wondered if you could help,' I went on.

'Sorry,' he said and went to close the door, maybe panicked that I was an authority of some kind. I put my best middle-aged mum voice on and put my own hand on the door to hold it open, desperate.

'I'm looking for Ivo. He's my nephew. And he's missing.' The lie slid out easily. It's amazing what you can do when your family is at stake.

'I don't know an Ivo.'

I scrolled my phone to a picture I'd taken of Ivo and Kit and Jess when they first arrived, before I knew who he was. I showed the boy the screen.

'Oh,' he said, 'Ian?'

So he was even lying about his name.

'Oh, sorry, we all call him Ivo. It's a family thing.' I made myself smile affectionately at the screen. 'Can you help me

– just a couple of questions? It might help us track him down. We're worried sick.'

The door opened and he nodded back towards the dimly lit hall. I stepped into the smell of socks and damp and the sound of music somewhere in an attic bedroom.

'Thanks,' I said. 'Could I see his room? It might have some clues.'

'He might have locked it.' But he shrugged and led the way up the stairs. The carpet sucked at my trainers, holding them to every grimy step. The aroma changed to the sweet, cloying scent of marijuana.

He shuffled past three bedroom doors and knocked on the fourth. When nobody answered, he tried the door, and shrugged again when it opened. I went in first. It was tiny, a box room. 'Not much space in here, is there?' I said, light-heartedly.

'He pays the cheapest rent,' the boy said, leaning in the doorway.

I edged into the room. An unmade single bed under the window, the sheets grey where he would have lain. A bedside table with nothing on it except a half-drunk glass of water. I opened the wardrobe door. Inside was bare except for some cardboard packaging and a porn magazine, its lurid cover facing upwards. Metal hangers hung empty on the rail. It looked very much like Ivo – Ian – had left for good.

The boy sighed behind me. 'Fuck,' he said. 'I thought he must have just been out. He owes rent.'

A girl appeared next to him and leaned on his shoulder. 'Hi,' she said, curious. The boy explained Ian was missing and she gave a little gasp of excitement.

'Have you spoken to him recently?' I asked the boy and he shook his head, one lank strand of hair falling over his eye.

'But Mack did,' the girl chipped in. 'Or tried to, to find out when he was coming back – rent's due on the first – but some girl answered. Said he'd call back. He never did.'

'Are you friends with Ian or do you just live together?' I asked them both.

'I wouldn't say we're mates,' the boy said. 'Mack just offered him the spare room when it came up.'

'So you don't hang out together?'

The boy wrinkled his nose and shook his head. 'No. I mean, everyone knows him in Bristol. He's been around so long.'

I nodded, hoping for more. I was right to hold my breath.

'Wasn't it a music doctorate he studied?' the girl asked him, twiddling with her nose stud.

'Sociology?' he asked back.

'Thought he was with a band now?' She raised her eyebrows.

So he definitely wasn't a photography student then. That much was clear.

'So you don't see him socially? You don't know where he might hang out?'

They both laughed. 'You'll always find him at the freshers' balls.'

'Trying to impress the new blood.'

'Does shifts at one of the uni bars.'

I smiled and nodded.

'I feel a bit sorry for him really,' the girl said, and sniffed. 'I mean, it's a bit sad to be nearly thirty and still living in a room like this.'

I coughed to cover my surprise. Thirty? Kit had said twenty-four. I remembered the flash of his thinning scalp under his man-bun, the five o'clock shadow at the end of each day.

I scanned the room again. No clues to be found here.

He'd fed Kit a pack of lies. About his name, his age, his course. But I wasn't sure that even if she knew all that, it would be enough to get him out of our lives. She was in love – and love was blind.

'No girlfriend on the scene then?' I asked as a last resort. The look they gave each other was a definite no. I sighed, clean out of questions.

As I moved to leave the room, I kicked something that was lying just under the edge of the bed. A watch? I bent to pick it up.

'Aha, that's why you can't track him then,' the boy said. 'I wondered why you didn't know exactly where he was, or the police didn't at least.'

I looked at it again.

'His tag,' the girl said, seeing I had no idea what I was holding.

My stomach lurched. An electronic tag. What on earth had he done to deserve one of those? I'd never seen one before, let alone held one.

'He's done a runner for sure, then,' the boy said, and then, obviously thinking again about the rent, 'Fuck.'

'I'd heard there was a bit of trouble,' I stammered, bluffing.

The girl widened her eyes.

'You could say that,' she said. 'From what I know, he really hurt someone.'

I licked my lips. The bass upstairs was getting harder. The walls of the room felt smaller around me.

'But I thought the tag would be off by now,' I continued.

'He hasn't had the court case yet,' the girl said. 'Although it's pretty soon, I think.'

'He was talking about going home for it,' the boy said. 'Back to his mum's.'

My mouth was suddenly dry. The smell of marijuana, so thick in the air, was making my head swim.

'What? But I thought—' I said, before catching myself.

They both looked at me. I had been going to say, 'I thought his mum was dead – he told me she was dead.' Instead I gushed an excuse: 'Sorry, our families have fallen out a bit. I'm on his dad's side, you see. We live up in Southwold.'

'Oh wow, his dad the famous muso,' the girl said. 'I've heard all about him. He was in some band…'

'Southwold?' the boy said. 'Was it you he went to see in the summer?'

I thought back to what Naomi had said. Dread made the hairs on my arms stand up.

I nodded. 'Yes, that was the last time we saw him actually. So, the court case is in his mum's town?'

The girl scratched at a spot on her cheek as she nodded.

'Is she still in Bath?' I said, picking a town at random.

'London, I think,' she said.

'Have you got her new address?' I asked. 'We've lost touch and I really need to see if he's okay. Especially now!'

'We can't just be giving out people's addresses. Privacy and all that,' she said, tossing her head.

I lifted the discarded tag, as a reminder that this man was an absconded criminal. 'Okay, if you prefer the police,' I said, then sniffed the air loudly. 'I wouldn't have thought you'd want them at the door.'

The girl twisted her nose stud again and shared a look with the boy.

'I'll get it,' he said and disappeared. The girl watched me a little too closely as I waited, and I felt a flush of blood creeping up my neck. He reappeared with a form, paperwork for the rental agreement on the house. The names and addresses for the resident of each room, the name and address of their guarantor beside them. And there for room number six, Ian Carlyle. And next to it, Nicole Carlyle. Or Nikki, as Felix used to call her. I snapped a picture of the details on my phone.

Outside, I heaved in great lungfuls of sweet, cold air on the doorstep before I got into my car to begin the next long journey. As I pulled away, the electronic tag lay beside me on the seat.

Another strange door, very different to the last. A quiet backstreet in South London. A terrace of houses stretching from one end of the road to the other, brown-bricked, low garden walls. Front doors set in archways, every house the same apart from a few painted fronts.

I sat outside the house I'd identified as Nicole's, looking for signs of movement; and also plucking up my courage. Not used to driving so far in one day, I felt drained and wired at the same time. I still wasn't one hundred per cent sure what I was going to say to her, but I had to know what Ivo had done. Although how I'd face this woman whose marriage I'd destroyed, I didn't know. I swung myself out of the car resolutely and locked it over my shoulder with the fob as I took the four steps up the tiled garden path to the front doorstep. I rang the bell quickly, the point of no return. The chimes sounded inside.

The door opened a crack and a woman peered at me cautiously, then stared past me, over my shoulder, before unlocking a chain and opening the door. She was wearing slippers and she pulled her cardigan around her shoulders against the air. It hit me then, what I was about to do, the shock I was about to give her. The memories I would drag up. And her nice Saturday afternoon ruined and shattered with things she'd probably rather forget. For a split second, when I opened my mouth, nothing came out. She saw, and asked, impatiently,

'Yes?'

My head felt like I'd stood up too quickly, a lightness making my vision swim. She put a hand out towards me as though I might fall over. 'Blimey, you all right?'

I reached for the wall to steady myself as the blackness tunnelled my vision into a pinprick.

'Put your head down,' she said and I felt her hands on my shoulders, holding me steady as I put my head between my knees. The ground swelled and heaved under my feet like the tide moving pebbles and I took a deep breath – two, three – to bring everything back into focus.

'Don't rush,' she said as I straightened up again.

I blew out slowly, felt my body come back to me. White sparkles pricked and fizzed in my eyes.

'Happens to me all the time,' she said kindly, still holding my arm. 'Normally when I've skipped breakfast.'

'You might have a point there,' I managed, nodding. I'd eaten a banana after my morning swim as I got into the car, but nothing since. It hadn't crossed my mind. I felt the empty cavern of my stomach rumble.

'Better?' she asked, and smiled matter-of-factly when I nodded a yes. Her eyes were tired-looking, but soft. She looked like a caring person. A nice woman. I had to say something now or I never would.

'I came to talk to you about Ian,' I said and she took a step back, horrified.

'What's happened now?'

'Nothing's happened,' I said, quickly. I was getting this all wrong. 'He's fine.'

She quickly glanced left and right along the street. 'Come in. Let's not do this on the doorstep.'

I hesitated, not sure it was right for me to enter her house, this woman who still didn't know who I was or what I'd done to her, but she nodded again and opened the door wide, saying, 'Let me get you a glass of water or something.'

I followed her into a front room and sat where she pointed, on a sofa in the window, dressed with a blue crocheted throw. I took my coat off and laid it across my knees, held my hands towards the open fire that crackled and hissed in the hearth. It was a cosy room. A book lay open on the arm of the chair, a thriller judging by the black-and-white cover, the splash of red. The rug was cream and matched the curtains, the walls were painted duck-egg blue.

Nicole went out to the kitchen and I heard the run of the tap as she filled a glass of water for me. She wiped the base of it carefully before putting it on the side table, next to a photo of a boy as a teenager, awkward-looking, gangly. Ivo,

I realised with shock. Other pictures sat on shelves and cabinets, different ages, different fashions, but all Ivo, or the two of them together. The only other decoration was a miniature Christmas tree in the corner and a handful of cards.

'So, what is it about Ian, then?' she said. 'Do you know where he is?'

I nodded, took a long swallow of the water. It tasted of iron and ran cold into my empty belly.

'Thank God for that. I've been worried sick he might turn up back here. The police are looking for him, you know,' she said, blowing out loudly. 'He's jumped bail.'

So it was true. He'd been awaiting a court case. I shuffled forward to the edge of the chair.

'He's in Southwold,' I said.

'Southwold?' she said and then shook her head in frustration. 'What's he doing there?'

I put the glass back down, wondering where to start. Then I realised I just had to bite the bullet. I needed her help.

'I don't know, but I believe he went there on purpose.' I took a deep breath. 'To find me. To cause me trouble.'

She raised her eyebrows.

'I'm Annabelle Walker,' I said, knowing I had to tell her. 'But you might know me better as "Bella".'

'Bella?' she repeated as her eyes searched my face.

I nodded.

'*The* Bella?' she asked and I could only press my lips together tight in guilty confirmation.

A clock ticked on the mantelpiece. Some children skipped past on the pavement outside.

'Of course,' she said. 'I should have thought.' She closed her mouth tightly enough that I could see the clench of her teeth through her cheek, then shook herself visibly and asked, 'What's he done?'

I told her about Ivo coming home with Kit, seemingly the perfect boyfriend. How since then he'd begun to taunt me about my relationship with Felix, and how he seemed to be sinking deeper and deeper into a bad place. When I mentioned Felix's name, I felt the heat of my flush start at my neck and crawl over my cheeks.

'He just can't let it go,' Nicole said, between clenched teeth.

I waited, held my breath.

'It's always tied up with Felix,' she said, sounding defeated. 'When he died, I probably gave in a bit too much with Ian. Let the rules get broken too often. Looking back, I didn't set the boundaries he should have had. He was at a difficult age – just before secondary school. But I felt he'd been dealt a tough hand already, and I wanted to soften the blow, you know what I mean?' She looked at me and I nodded an encouragement. 'Turns out the gentle touch was the wrong way to go.' She sniffed.

'I didn't even know Felix had died,' I said. 'Until Ivo – sorry, Ian – told me. I'm really sorry.'

She held my eye for a moment, then shrugged. 'It was such a long time ago. We weren't much older than Ian is now.'

'He told me Felix killed himself,' I said and she blinked twice and then nodded. 'He also told me it was my fault.'

We looked at each other, two women on opposite sides of a history. A burning log wheezed in the hearth.

'There's two sides to every story,' Nicole said, wearily. 'I'd kicked him out. You didn't want him. The band broke up. It was probably just the end of the road for Felix. You know how he was, one hundred miles an hour into everything. Always dreaming of stardom and adoration. He didn't like normal life much. Who knows what it was that finally tipped him over the edge.' She sat back in the chair now, rested her head against the cushion. 'I've given up asking myself.'

'But it was tough on Ian,' I said, to keep her talking.

She nodded and looked at a photo on the mantelpiece. 'Nothing was ever good enough. Even his name now – Ivo indeed! What kind of nonsense is that? He always thought he was hard done by. He took everything I had and still wanted more. I hate to say it, but he's not a very nice person.'

A man pushed a pram past the house, its wheels creaking and cracking on the pavement. A young child ran along beside him, singing. The house felt very quiet after they'd passed.

'I'm worried that my daughter is in love with him,' I said then. 'He's persuaded her to throw in her university course and they're going travelling.'

'Travelling?' She snorted. 'Well, that's not going to happen, is it. When I call the police, they'll go and pick him up. The only place he's going is the local nick.'

'They have tickets for a flight tomorrow evening,' I said, to stress the urgency.

'I'll get on to the station now,' she said, but then put her head in her hands. 'Who'd have thought it would end up like this? Me calling the police on my own boy.' She wiped at her eyes but I had the feeling she was past tears with Ivo; it was more that she was bone-tired.

I breathed out slowly, feeling as though I'd just put down heavy shopping after walking up a hill. It would be over soon. I just had to make sure that I wasn't missing anything.

'I can't see him any more,' she said. 'He'll always be my son, but he's got Felix's darkness and none of his light. None of his father's charm or laughter, only anger and rot.'

'I think he's trying to hurt my family for what he thinks I did to Felix,' I said.

I told her about Dodge – the fact that he'd gone missing, the photo of Ivo pretending to hang himself with his lead. And then the incident on the ferry and David's broken leg, the bone poking white through his jeans. She made a small noise at that point.

When I'd finished, she closed her eyes. Suddenly I had a feeling that things were much worse than I'd imagined.

'Is he really dangerous?' I asked.

Nicole stood up, and then slowly lifted the bottom of her brown polo-neck jumper as high as the base of her bra, exposing her stomach.

A fresh and livid scar reached from one side almost to the other. The crimson line of stitches pulled her white skin into puckers, making her lopsided, lumpy.

I stared, open-mouthed, and then had to look away. I was horrified.

She tucked her jumper back in and sank back into the chair. 'That's what got him arrested.'

'My God,' I whispered, almost to myself. 'Why?'

'I told him I wasn't paying his rent in Bristol. He told me he wished I'd died instead of Felix. And then he did this.'

We looked at each other for a long moment.

A log fell in the grate and showered red embers into the ash.

'He told me you were dead.'

'No,' Nicole replied, turning back to me with a grim smile. 'Not yet.'

She stood, smoothing her jumper again over her scar.

I stood too, understanding that she wanted me to leave.

As I moved towards the door, I saw a photo that stopped me in my tracks. The three of them together: Felix, Nicole and Ivo. Felix with his son on his shoulders, chubby-kneed and cheeky, and his wife, arms wrapped round his waist. They were all grinning at the camera.

'Day trip to Southwold,' she said and as she did so I saw the pier in the background, the blue sky, the sea. I could almost hear the seagulls, the water clock, the tide.

Felix looked younger than when I'd first met him, shoulder-length hair in a ponytail. Eyes that lit up with laughter. Gorgeous. Happy. But more than that, he looked part of something. A group. A unit. A family. Something that I had totally disrespected.

I swallowed over a stone in my throat. I had to say something or I'd never forgive myself. 'Nicole, I'm truly sorry. For what I did.'

She looked at me, but whatever I was hoping she would say, she didn't.

As I left, she said, 'I'll phone the police now, then.'

It was already dusk by the time I got back in the car, despite it not being even 3 p.m. The London streetlights gleamed yellow in the gloom. I locked the doors and grabbed for my phone, desperate to hear the girls' voices, to know that everyone was safe.

I tried Morag first. I let it ring eighteen, nineteen, twenty times, knowing that her hearing was not what it used to be.

Nothing. I rang Jess next, not wanting to try Kit's mobile in case Ivo picked up. But nobody answered, whichever phone I rang. I left a message on Morag's mobile and home answerphone, saying to expect me soon after six.

As I turned the key in the ignition, Nicole stood at the front window, watching me. I nodded a goodbye to her and drove away.

I was exhausted by the time I took the Southwold turn almost three hours later. But every mile I got closer to home, the urgency grew in my chest. I'd been away a whole day. Anything could have happened. Nobody had called me back.

Eventually, I pulled up outside our house. The sky was clear and starry, a perfect winter's night. There'd be a frost later. But it was the house that caught my eye. The curtains were shut but the place was in darkness. No white fairy lights on the Christmas tree. Not even the outdoor light illuminated the way.

It felt wrong. I ran up the steps, breath pluming, and threw open the front door. It banged back against the wall. Nothing. The hallway ahead of me was empty, the kitchen black.

I snapped the light on, frightened of what I might see, but was met with emptiness. No coats hung on the bannisters. No trainers kicked off by the front door. The fridge hummed softly in the kitchen. They were all out. Of course – they'd gone to see David. I blew out my breath, let the fright go and pushed open the living room door.

A bang, shouting, a noise next to my head made my neck click reflexively to the right. I dropped to a crouch, put my hands up to my face.

'Surprise!'

Laughter, shouting.

The overhead light snapped on and someone shot another party popper in the air, as the streamers from the first one landed over my hair. When I looked up, through my fingers, Jess and Kit and Morag were all standing there, grinning. Ivo stood behind them, smirking at my reaction. A birthday banner was tacked to the wall. Helium balloons emblazoned with 'Fabulous at Fifty' were tied in bunches in the corners of the room.

'Happy birthday, Mum!' Kit said, pulling me to my feet and into a hug. I held her tight, breathed in her shampoo, clutched her waist. 'Blimey, don't break me!' she said, laughing, as she pulled away. Jess stepped into the void she'd left and I kissed her cheek and felt the softness of her skin against my lips. She whispered, 'Happy birthday, Mum' into my neck and a surge of love threatened to overwhelm me. When I let her go, Morag leaned in and gave me a kiss on the cheek and a hearty clap on the back. I squeezed her arm, genuinely pleased to see her, realising at the same time how little she was under her cardigan.

'How was your day at the spa?'

'So thoughtful of Dad. What treatments did you have?'

'Did you get a facial?'

The questions came thick and fast as Jess handed me a glass of champagne and Kit held out a present wrapped with a bow.

My hand shook as I took the champagne, and I sipped quickly to calm myself. It was sharp and cold and reminded me I still hadn't eaten. I put it on the table to resist drinking it down in one.

'Hope you like it,' Kit said, still proffering the gift. 'It's from all of us.'

The silky ribbon of the bow slid undone in my fingers, reminding me of the girls' plaits when they were younger. I pulled off the paper to uncover a book on wild swimming, the trendy name for it these days – all of a sudden, if you swam outside or out of season, you were a wild swimmer. The book was a collection of the top places to swim in the UK. I flicked through it, took in the lakes, the coastlines, the reservoirs.

'We looked through it and thought there were some brilliant places –' Kit said.

'So we chose our favourite one –' Jess said, flipping the pages to a bookmark they'd lodged at a certain point.

'And Gran chipped in with us and we booked you and Dad a couple of nights away in a B&B in the village –' Kit's words were literally falling over each other.

'Not until spring, so the weather should be nicer –' Jess was grinning and pointing at the pictures.

'And you and Dad can have a bit of a mini-break –' Kit said.

'All romantic –' Jess laughed.

'As long as his leg's healed by then, I suppose,' Morag added, keeping us on an even keel.

'It will be, Gran, it will be,' Kit said, tucking Morag under her arm and squeezing.

I looked at the location they'd chosen. It was a lake in the middle of woods, a sheet of water cascading from the low-level waterfall in the rocks above. They'd stuck in a booking-confirmation page for the B&B, which was a tree-house. The photographs showed wood panelling, a balcony in the leafy canopy with a view to die for. It was beautiful. All of it. My eyes got hot and I closed them, quickly. No tears allowed. Not on your birthday. It was an old household rule.

'I love it,' I said, fiercely, and they all looked delighted. 'Thank you.'

'It will do David good to get away too,' said Morag. 'After his accident.' I felt Ivo looking at me, and kept my eyes averted.

'Yes, how is he, Bella?' he asked and I faced him then. He did it more and more brazenly each time, taunting me. I made my eyes as hard as they could be.

'He's not in any pain. But he won't be home for a few days. It was a particularly nasty break, the doctor said.'

'I feel awful,' he said. 'If only I'd stayed sitting down it would never have happened.'

'Hopefully home for Christmas Day though?' Morag said. 'Otherwise it will just be me and you and Jess.' Nervous hope sprang inside me that actually Kit would be there too, and that Ivo would be gone. Under lock and key.

'Definitely home for that, Morag,' I said. 'Don't worry.'

'Wonder where we'll be for Christmas?' Kit said to Ivo.

'Christmas lunch in South Africa!' he said, a glint in his eyes. 'And then who knows where for New Year's Eve.'

'So exciting.' She laughed, jumping up and down on the spot like a kid going to a birthday party. It hit me then, how hard she would take Ivo being arrested. But it was worth it to keep her safe. To get him out of our lives.

'My turn,' Ivo said, handing me a boxed present wrapped in gold paper. 'Happy birthday.'

'Thank you,' I stammered. 'Maybe I should open it later?' But everyone groaned and Morag nudged me in the ribs, obviously thinking me rude.

I didn't want to take it. Or open it. The look on his face, his eagerness as I started peeling the paper off made my mouth dry. I uncovered an old shoebox and as everyone gathered around me to look, I lifted the lid. At the bottom, among white tissue paper, lay a CD in a case. I let my breath out slowly. I knew what it was already.

'It's The Hush, with my dad on lead vocals,' Ivo said to the others, and then to me, 'I thought it might take you back to your youth.'

Kit was already putting it into the CD player and pressing the button. I forced a smile, and thanked him publicly for the present.

'I had it transferred from an old cassette tape they'd made at one of their sessions,' he said, then silence fell on the room as we all waited. A bass guitar boomed suddenly, a cymbal crashed and everyone jumped and Morag clutched at herself like she was going to keel over. The sound must have been at full volume. We all covered our ears, blinking and gasping, unable to cope with the noise. Kit stabbed at the player with her finger frantically until the volume dropped and both girls laughed in relief. Ivo ignored us all, just slowly lowered himself into a chair and shut his eyes to listen.

Felix's voice filled the room. The husk of it, the low grav- elly tone that was so beautiful, so unique, so him. That voice had at times entertained hundreds of people and, at others, had sung only to me. Kit's eyes widened and Jess nodded in approval. Morag tapped her foot along awkwardly to try to show she liked it. I pressed my mouth tightly closed and tried to swallow a lump that suddenly filled my throat. Everything was too much. The memory. The day. The mess I'd made. His voice was so perfect. It was all such a waste.

As the song finished I felt Ivo watching me. His eyes burning into me from across the room.

'Amazing,' Kit fawned. 'Such a lost talent.'

'A very nice voice,' Morag agreed and patted his shoulder.

'Right. We'd better get ready, Mum. Didn't you say the table was booked for eight o'clock?' Jess said and I remembered the dinner table booked at the hotel. Dammit, I didn't want to go, I wanted to be here for when the police came. What would happen if we weren't at home? Would they wait?

'I'm actually pretty bushed,' I said, falteringly. 'Maybe we should give it a miss. It doesn't feel right without David,' I added, with a bit more conviction.

'Nonsense,' Morag said. 'He'd want you to go out and celebrate.'

'Yes, Mum,' Kit said. 'You only turn fifty once, you know!'

Jess stood and put her hands out to pull me up from my chair. She tugged me to standing.

'Come on,' she said. 'I'll come and help you choose an outfit.'

As we all stood to leave the room, Ivo turned the stereo up deafeningly loud and moved into the middle of the rug. With his eyes shut, he turned his face to the ceiling and started to jerk spasmodically to the music, a grimace on his face like he was in another place. Kit moved to dance with him but he was moving to something only inside his own head and was impossible to dance with as he dipped and bumped, no rhythm, no beat at all. She tried to take his hand but I could see it was limp in hers. I remembered Felix, leading me across the bedroom floor to dance, eyes on mine.

I'd followed him as if hypnotised. The bass had pumped through his hips as though he were part of the music. I turned away before Kit could see my face.

Jess stood in front of my open wardrobe and scanned the rails, then pulled out a blue silk blouse.

'Here,' she said, passing me navy jeans and white trainers to go with it, before flopping on the bed. I didn't have the strength or the inclination to argue and stripped off my jumper and trousers, let the silk settle round my shoulders. I zipped up the jeans and sat at the dressing table to fix my make-up.

The mirror showed me just how tired I was, although the shirt was a good choice; it seemed to bring some colour back into my face. My eyes were shadowed, my lips tight. I'd driven more today than I had in years. I'd found out things that frightened me to death. I just had to put a mask on for the evening and hopefully tomorrow things would get back to normal. I rummaged in my make-up bag, pulling out a blusher to add a bit of life to my tired face. Jess lay on her back and chatted about the shopping trip she'd had with Naomi, told me about a restaurant they'd found; I nodded and agreed when necessary and then a quiet descended. I caught her looking at me in the mirror as I dabbed concealer under my eyes, brightening them up.

'Everything okay?' I asked.

She looked upwards slightly, a signal that she was going to tell me something.

'Caught Ivo being a bit weird this afternoon,' she said.

I paused in my blending, checked her reflection.

'Why?' I asked casually. 'What was he doing?'

She swung to sitting, leaning against the headboard. 'Saw him outside in the back garden, marching up and down.'

I carefully applied the mascara to my eyelashes, focusing on the mirror.

'Maybe he was just restless,' I said out loud. Or planning, I thought.

'No. I thought he was on the phone at first, you know, hands-free, but then I realised he wasn't.'

I swept the brush through my hair, smoothing the tangles of the day.

'He was just walking about talking to himself.' She laughed uncertainly. 'Looked like a right idiot.'

The hairbrush caught on a knot, pulled at my scalp. I slicked on some lip-gloss and blotted my lips together, trying to relax my jaw.

'What do you think of him,' I said. 'Really?'

She tilted her head, side to side.

'He's all right,' she said. 'A bit intense sometimes.' She sniffed as though he really wasn't what she'd be looking for.

'Not your type?' I asked.

'No, Mum. Not my type at all.'

She held my eyes in the mirror. The moment stretched into a pause. Neither of us spoke. I waited. I could see a question in her eyes, or was it a decision? I raised my eyebrows just a fraction, encouraging her on, but she grinned suddenly and let the moment go. She flicked back to Ivo.

'I tell you what he looked like, Mum, when he was in the garden,' she said. 'Like he was rehearsing lines.'

I could imagine it: his brow lowered, his face concentrating. He took himself so seriously, like he was playing the main character on stage.

'Like he had something really important in his head,' she said, inspecting her nails. 'Maybe he's got an announcement to make,' she added, lifting her head to me, eyes wide.

We looked at each other again in the mirror. Her mouth dropped open and she said:

'Oh my God, Mum, maybe he's going to propose to Kit.'

The gasp from the doorway took us both by surprise; neither of us had seen or heard Kit come in. She clasped her hands in front of her chest, cheeks pink. Quickly shutting the door behind her, she flopped on the bed next to Jess.

'Do you think so?' she said, rolling to face her. Jess shrugged, looking horrified.

'Because if he did,' Kit said, hugging herself, 'I'd say yes.'

She looked at me, her face an open picture of hope.

'I'd say yes, Mum!'

The unnecessary place laid at the table reserved for us was dealt with deftly by the staff at the Sutherland House Hotel. One waiter pulled the chair out for me to sit at the head of the table while another whisked away David's setting and wine glass.

I'd have given anything for him to be there with me, making me strong, even if he didn't know what I was going through, what I was trying to do. I'd spoken to him on the phone before we left, the others waiting in the hall and making impatient noises, as I chatted, made sure he was okay. His voice was strong again, back to its normal tone, pain-free. He was upset about missing my birthday celebrations and worried about not seeing Kit before she left for her travels. I said I was missing him just as much and promised to take

Kit in to the ward in the morning so that she could say her goodbyes. I found myself crossing my fingers in my pocket, like some superstitious child. I hovered on the phone, wanting to tell David what I'd found out, but it was all muddled up in my head, which bits I could say and which bits would uncover my secret; and then Jess called through from the front door, 'Mum, we're going to be late,' and I had to say goodbye, listening as he hung up.

Now I had to focus on tonight.

Jess pulled open the front door and we all stepped out into the cold.

The sky glittered with stars as we walked across South Green. I walked the long way round, scanning the empty streets for the sound of sirens, the flash of a patrol car. The waves pounded the beach. They were normally enough to calm my mind, to soothe my soul. Not tonight. Now, all I could hear was Felix's voice, singing. All I could see was Ivo dancing like a puppet having its strings pulled too tightly. All I could feel was fear.

I sat at the head of the table. Kit sat next to me on the left side, then Ivo next to her. Jess sat on my right with her gran beside her. It felt weird, off balance, without David. Jess noticed me looking at his empty space.

'Ah, such a shame for Dad.' She took my hand on the table. 'And for you.'

'And me,' said Morag, as if anyone could forget her. Jess laughed and passed her a menu.

We all ordered drinks for ourselves and, at Kit's request, a bottle of champagne too. Initially I was touched that she wanted to toast my birthday – and then I saw her wink at Jess across the table, and say quietly, 'Just in case we need it,' and I realised she really *was* hoping for a proposal. I hadn't reacted earlier in the bedroom, not to her face anyway. I'd left that to Jess, who had snorted and told her sister to 'get a grip' and then reminded her, 'you've only known him five minutes,' and I'd never been more glad of her in my life.

The champagne arrived and the waiter popped the cork ceremoniously. Kit passed the first glass to me and then kept the next one herself, throwing significant glances at Ivo beside her.

'To Mum!' the girls said in unison, raising their glasses to me.

'Belle,' Morag said.

'Bella,' Ivo said and downed his glass in one, putting it down again too loudly, too fast.

'Steady on, Ivo!' Jess laughed. 'It's not tequila.'

'Maybe it's Dutch courage,' said Kit, with a wiggle in her seat.

Morag pushed her glass in front of him. 'I don't really like the taste of champagne. It's a bit dry for me. You can have mine.'

'I'll order you a good whisky instead, Morag,' I said and she treated me to a real smile as I waved at the waiter.

Menus were passed around and Morag put on her reading glasses. Everything sounded delicious; all the fish came with a 'jus' or a 'froth'. Vegetables glazed in herbs and butter, or chargrilled with garlic. Breads freshly baked, hot from the oven. My stomach rumbled, my mouth watered; but tonight wasn't one to linger over the table. I wanted to be home to see the blue lights flashing through the front window as the police arrived.

'Shall we just do main courses?' I suggested, to a groan of disappointment from the table.

'But I'm starving!' Kit said.

'You're joking, right!' Jess looked at me open-mouthed as if I was mad.

'The langoustine starters are rather good here...' Morag said.

Ivo just stared at me.

I had to keep things as normal as possible, and I knew I mustn't give Ivo any reason to suspect I was up to anything. So I gave in with a laugh.

'Okay, you've convinced me,' I said.

We ordered crab starters, and local fish dishes for our main courses. The vegetables came out in little white bowls, the sauces in tiny jugs. Waiters laid napkins in our laps and swept our places clear of crumbs after each course. The girls were on great form and Morag sucked langoustines clean of meat, smacking her lips afterwards with satisfaction. I ate my starter quickly, devoured two bread rolls along with it, remembering I'd hardly eaten all day.

Ivo, pushing food around his plate, was quiet, no matter how much Kit laughed or smiled or nudged him to join in. He was like a dark cloud at the table, and I saw the girls start to dart anxious looks his way every now and then.

'Don't you like it?' Kit asked eventually. He shrugged. 'Your meal?' she pressed.

'I'm not used to food like this,' he said, glumly.

Tense, I bit my lip; I didn't like his mood.

'We grew up on seafood,' Kit said. 'It's all locally caught and fresh round here.'

'I grew up on baked beans and jacket potatoes,' Ivo said, sharply.

I imagined Nicole cooking his tea, treating him with pizza and chicken nuggets to make him happy after Felix died. I wondered if he'd ever been happy, even as a child. Whether he'd have been nasty and selfish if Felix was still alive. I shook my head. I didn't want to be thinking about Felix anymore.

'We used to have langoustine in Scotland,' Morag said, 'by the bucketful. Perk of living by the coast, I suppose.'

'Perk of having two parents to pay for it too,' Ivo said, and Morag stopped chewing, taken aback, and tried to swallow her mouthful too soon.

The food caught in her throat and she coughed behind her hand, trying to be discreet, but her face grew red and she made choking sounds.

I grabbed the jug and poured her a glass of water, but Morag was panicking now, wild-eyed, as Jess clapped her on the back. Nothing happened and she waved her hand at Jess to do it again, which she did, harder. The thump sounded hollow on the back of her ribcage but this time I saw her cough something into her napkin. Her eyes were streaming and she sipped at the water I offered with a grateful nod.

'So sorry about that,' she said, and I thought she was meaning the choking, the spectacle of it, and I opened my mouth to reassure her. But Morag wasn't looking at us; she was talking to Ivo. 'Didn't mean to offend.'

He nodded but there was no smile in return, and Morag looked deflated.

'Just a fact of life,' he said, looking first at her and then at me. 'Nobody's fault.'

The dessert menu arrived and things moved on. The girls debated over eclairs and banana splits while Ivo slouched in his chair. I hoped that Kit might see how rude he was being, but the way she looked at him made it clear love was still blind.

At last we'd finished all three courses, and a yawn overcame me as the waiters cleared the plates. I was shattered. I just wanted to get home. I realised I hadn't checked my phone since we arrived, and wondered if Nicole had texted.

'Well, that was great,' Morag said with a surprisingly soft smile in my direction. 'Happy birthday, hen.'

'It was great, Gran, although I thought for a minute we'd be taking you to the hospital,' Jess said, putting her arm round her gran and giving her a hug. Morag winced slightly and shifted her chest. I wondered if her back was bruised from the thump earlier.

'Poor Dad, missing your birthday dinner, Mum – he would have loved this treat,' Kit said. Ivo began to drum his fingers on the tabletop beside his placemat.

'Especially the sticky toffee pudding,' I said.

Ivo shook his head, frowning at Kit. 'Oh, for God's sake,' he snapped, making my daughter recoil.

'What?' she asked, and I knew then it could only get worse.

'Your *daddy* has a broken leg,' Ivo sneered. 'And he's going to be fine.'

Kit put one hand to her mouth and one on her boy-friend's arm, shocked and peacemaking at the same time. She understood the implicit criticism in Ivo's controlling words, which I could see had been designed to make her compare having a father still alive and very much part of her life, and him not, and thus feel shabby about her innocent words.

Morag studied her napkin and Jess glanced at me, wanting me to step in. She hated confrontation, always had; but I knew I mustn't risk inflaming the situation further.

'Shall I get the bill?' Morag asked awkwardly.

'That might be a good idea,' I said and she hoisted herself from her chair and went towards the bar to find a waiter.

Jess glanced at me and made a little sign with her hand as though she were drinking from a bottle. She obviously thought Ivo was drunk. I thought she might be right. It seemed strange that he was confronting Kit like this if he was sober, especially bearing in mind their plans for the next day.

'I'm sorry if I said something wrong,' Kit said quietly to Ivo, still holding onto his arm. Her lip trembled.

I could barely watch.

Roughly, Ivo shook off her hand, and that was enough to tip her over the edge.

A flush burned two pink spots on her cheeks as her eyes filled with tears. She dropped her head, looking towards her lap.

I sat forward in my chair, convinced that now was the moment he was going to tell them all about me. I felt the pent-up energy surge inside him. Dark. Dangerous.

'You have no idea about me, Kit,' he murmured quietly, almost as if she wasn't there, and Kit looked devastated.

'Hang on,' cried Jess. 'Kit hasn't said anything bad. She didn't mean to upset you.' She leaned forward on her elbows, put one hand across the table to Kit, not quite reaching her. Kit flashed her a grateful look but didn't say anything.

'No idea at all,' Ivo repeated, and no one could mistake the nasty edge to his voice.

'Ivo, Kit really hasn't done anything for you to get upset about,' I said, and he looked towards me, lip in a snarl, as I continued cautiously, caught between wanting to protect Kit and trying to avert a shouting match, 'She really cares for you.'

'Yes, she loves you so much,' Jess said and threw a smile at her sister. 'I mean, only a few hours ago she was hoping you were going to propose!'

I couldn't believe Jess had actually said this, and nor could Kit, whose mouth fell open in embarrassment.

'Propose?' Ivo said incredulously, looking from Jess to Kit. 'Propose?' he asked again, his voice now threatening as he spoke directly to Kit.

She tried to laugh it off, make a joke of it. His leg was jigging under the table, making the glasses ring on the tablecloth.

'Why would I want to propose?'

Kit's head dropped, humiliated. Then her chair screeched on the parquet flooring as she pushed it backward quickly and stood. The diners at the table next to us all looked over as she almost shouted, 'I'm going home.'

She ran through the restaurant and out of the front door.

Jess gave Ivo a furious glare. 'What did you do that for?' she demanded.

He shrugged.

'I'll go after her,' Jess said to me.

'Take Gran,' I said, 'please. Get a taxi.'

'Arsehole,' Jess muttered as she passed Ivo.

He snorted and reached for Kit's half-drunk wine. He downed it in one.

So then it was just me and him, and I realised I no longer cared what he might do to me.

'Why would you behave like that?' I asked.

He reached for Morag's whisky. The gold of it shone in the candlelight as he raised it to his lips.

'She loves me,' he said, as if it was fact.

I nodded. 'So why not be kind?'

Grimacing, he drank. 'Karma's a bitch.'

He reached for Jess's glass. He kissed his fingers in a theatrical way and then pulled his man-bun free of its elastic band. He shook his hair loose to his shoulders, a small flash of pale scalp showing beneath the thinning top.

I realised that not only did I hate him, but I was repulsed by him.

'Bella,' he whispered, and then stared at Kit's empty chair. He wriggled nearer to me, his face too close. His skin was clammy-looking, pale. The candlelight hollowed his cheeks, shadowed his neck. He looked very like Felix, but where Felix was beautifully sculpted, Ivo was sinewy and mean, like a cheap copy. He didn't need to say he loathed me and he was taking Kit away as punishment; it was showing in every fibre of his being.

'Why Kit?' I asked. 'Why not Jess? Was it just because you were in Bristol and so was she?'

'Don't think I'm quite Jess's type, do you?' He laughed. 'I mean – I'm male, for a start.'

I kept still as I thought. It was as David and I had suspected. I'd been waiting for Jess to tell me when the time was right, and now this idiot was trampling over her territory.

'It seems your family has lots of secrets,' he slurred.

I thought back to Jess's face in the mirror earlier, when, I was sure, she'd been so close to confiding. Well, I'd still let her tell me in her own time.

'So that meant it had to be Kit,' Ivo went on. 'It's dangerous where we're going, you know?'

He swiped his finger through the candle flame towards me, fast enough not to burn, slow enough to feel the heat.

'Accidents happen,' he said threateningly then, holding his finger still in the flame.

My phone beeped in my handbag and I glanced at it. A text from Nicole assuring me the police should be on their way.

I took a deep breath. I hardly dared to hope that our nightmare might be over soon.

'Happy Christmas!' Ivo shouted suddenly to the whole restaurant, and I saw other diners look at me with pity in their eyes. He lurched up and clambered drunkenly onto his chair with mad eyes and wild hair, as he flung his arms wide and screamed, 'Happy Christmas, you fuckers!'

And there was something so unhinged about what I'd just seen that, as waiters escorted us from the restaurant and I glimpsed the maître d' standing with a phone in her hand ready to call the police, I understood without a shadow of doubt that Ivo was *never* going to leave my family alone.

He was going to destroy us all.

I had to be smarter. I had to work my way around him. I hadn't banked on him being drunk and unpredictable like this. I almost longed for the malicious, calculating, sober Ivo because at least I knew what I was dealing with then: a man who enjoyed prolonging the torture. Now he seemed impetuous and out of control.

The longer I kept Ivo away from my family until the police arrived, the more chance I had of keeping them safe.

'Shall we have another drink somewhere?' I said to buy time once we were outside, making my voice jolly as I banked on the lure of more alcohol. 'It is Christmas, after all.'

To my surprise, Ivo shook his head.

'Well, you can't possibly go without saying goodbye to your dad at his favourite spot,' I tried again, mumsy now. That got his attention. 'Let's go to the pier. To his plaque.'

He swayed as he looked at me drunkenly, but then he nodded.

The wind whipped icy down the high street as we turned to the beachfront. The promenade was deserted and the lights of a solitary cargo ship sat low on the horizon, heading north. The moon was half-hidden now behind patchy cloud, only occasionally casting its full light across the waves. The sea was black and rolling, then white-tipped and frothing as it hit the shore.

We walked in silence, leaning into the wind. Ivo staggered a bit every now and then. The water clock creaked, metal hinges squealing as strings of Christmas lights swung. The arcade machines were silent. We went out along the southern side, facing straight ahead to the sea.

At the end, I let him go ahead to the plaque. He stood with his hands on it, his head bowed, like he was praying. I could hear the odd word as he talked to Felix, fragments caught by the wind, but the rest was thrown to the sea.

I remained in the shelter of the white wooden pier shop, staying close to its back wall for protection, sitting on the frozen slats of the bench there, waiting, thinking. Ivo eventually turned back to me and threw himself down at the other end of the bench.

'You look like him,' I said. 'Seeing you there, it made me think of him so clearly.'

'Do I?' he asked, hopeful through his drunkenness.

And just like that, I had my way in.

'Definitely. I'm not sure why I didn't recognise you straight away. You're his double.'

'Mum used to only tell me I was like him when I was naughty.'

I laughed. 'Well, your dad *was* naughty too. That was what was so appealing about him,' I said. It was the truth: I remembered his smile, like the cat that got the cream, the mischievous way he crawled up the bed towards me.

Ivo moved an inch closer and I kept going.

'How much do you know about him?' I asked. 'Maybe I could fill in some blanks.'

'He was a singer. A loser.' He shook his head and a tic started beside his eye. 'Mum never had a good word to say about him.'

I wasn't surprised. Felix had had an affair when she was home with a young child, he never held down a job, and then he killed himself and left her to get on with it. Who could blame her?

'Ah, well, that's where your mother and I differ, Ivo,' I said. 'I only remember the good things.'

The force of the wind was moving the telescope on its stand by the railings, metal squeaking as it inched left and right.

'Me too,' he told me. 'I remember him running on the beach, chasing seagulls with me until we couldn't speak we were so out of breath. And we used to put the car radio up so loud that people on the pavement would stare at us and he'd wave at them and laugh.'

'He had such a sense of fun,' I said. 'Felix was the most vibrant person I'd ever met.'

As some bunting broke free at one end of the pier, I described the band, how Felix danced onstage. The way, when he laughed, he'd put his head back and howl at the stars. His fingers, always searching for the perfect rhythm, the best beat. His scribbling of words, poetry, thoughts. Always looking for the lyric that would sum it up, tell the world something special or encapsulate a feeling in a new way. I embellished the truth. I made Felix sound wild and creative – as he'd had the potential to be, but which he had lost along the way when he was wrung out with drugs and drink.

Ivo edged closer. His face relaxed as he listened, taking years off him, until he looked like a boy listening to a bedtime story. When I finally ran out of things to say, I leaned back on the bench. I sighed.

And then I made a mistake.

'I think your dad would want me to help you, you know,' I claimed.

He frowned.

Looking around me as if I could feel him, and then fixing my gaze on his plaque on the railing, I added, 'He'd want someone to care for you.'

Ivo's eyes widened.

'What do you mean?'

'He wouldn't want you to be messing up your life because he died.'

A muscle in his cheek twitched as he clenched his jaw.

'Plenty of people grow up without a dad, but they don't end up at nearly thirty and not going anywhere fast.'

Immediately I realised my error. He'd told us – or, more exactly, told Kit – he was twenty-four. I'd given myself away. How could I have been so stupid?

'Who've you been talking to?'

I paused. Then I decided to be honest. I'd lied too much already.

'I went to Bristol.'

'Why?' he said as a tiny speck of blood appeared on his lip where he'd pulled off a sliver of skin.

'I wanted to understand you. To see why you're doing this to me. To find your friends.'

'They're not my friends. I just live there.'

I nodded in agreement. He flinched and suddenly satisfaction flared through me at the pleasure of hurting him. I felt a buzz in my gut, anticipation of hurting him more, to give him a taste of his own medicine.

'Then I went to see your mum. Nicole. The mother you told me was dead.'

He licked the blood from his lip but it spotted again.

'She said you're entitled –' I lifted my thumb at him to show point number one.

'Mean –' my index finger joined the thumb.

'Weak –' my middle finger.

'Vile –' my ring finger.

I was scaring myself with how vicious I sounded. Then I rallied.

'Sounds like she'd rather you had died than Felix. Seems like Nicole and I have more in common than I knew.'

He stood, slowly, blocking my view of the sea.

'So Mum knows where I am,' he said slowly, much more sober now, as he obviously put two and two together.

I'd gone too far, given in to the urge to injure him.

He watched me closely, then grinned.

'You think you're so clever. But whatever the police do, I'll be back.' He bounced from one foot to the other, full of pent-up energy, wired with emotion. He stopped and bent towards me on the bench, his face frighteningly close. 'Just think, when you're least expecting it maybe, there I'll be. Behind Kit on a tube-station platform as the train rushes in. Next to Jess in a dark nightclub where it's easy to spike a drink. On a ferry with David. Beside you as you wait to cross the road.'

Spit foamed at the corner of his mouth. He ignored it as he pushed his chest out like a kid, before banging it with a clenched fist. 'You'll never get rid of me, you know.'

I had no alternative but to reach for the only straw I had left, the fact that his dad meant everything to him.

'I know you want to destroy me, Ivo. But you'd never hurt your dad, would you?'

He frowned.

'Then you can't harm Kit,' I said.

'Doesn't work like that.'

'It does, Ivo,' I said, exhausted. 'Kit is your dad's child too.'

The lighthouse beam swept over the pier, caught him in its searchlight.

Pinpointed the exact moment when he realised what I was saying. He gasped.

My stomach hollowed, knowing this was the biggest risk I could take, but I had to throw myself on the belief that knowing Kit was part of Felix would make Ivo feel differently.

'She's my sister?' he whispered.

'Half-sister.' I nodded.

For a moment there was nothing. He looked at the boards beneath his feet, letting it sink in.

'I'm not an only child?' he said. 'I've got twin sisters?'

I almost shook my head, but then thought better of it and said nothing. Maybe it was safer for him to think of them both as his.

'My whole life would have been so different.' He looked around him, held his hands out towards the promenade, as though imagining a childhood of beaches and donkey rides, ice creams and crabbing. He groaned so deep in his throat it sounded like a growl, low, animalistic.

'So you can't hurt her, Ivo,' I said again — a warning this time, not a question.

'Of course not,' he said as if I was stupid, and a flicker of something leapt inside me.

Was this the key to keeping them safe? I made sure to keep calm.

'I would never hurt them. My sisters.' He looked at me. 'My sisters!' Ivo bellowed into the wind.

And then I realised what I'd done.

'But you mustn't tell them either,' I said, quickly.

'Why not?' he said. 'Don't they know?'

'I only just found out myself,' I said, scrambling for thought.

'Then they have a right to know too,' he said.

'But you've been sleeping with Kit, Ivo.'

I watched it sink in, the realisation that he'd been having sex with his own sister. A tortured sound ripped out of him. He shook his head, backward and forward, horrified.

'It would scar her for life. She'd never be the same,' I said.

He pounded his own head with his fists, fighting whatever was going on inside. Slamming himself above the temples, catching his own eyebrow with his ring.

'So they're my sisters. But I can't have them?' he asked. I shook my head.

'They're better off being in the dark than facing that it's *incest*.'

There, it was out. The word that had been running around my head, the one I'd whispered on the dunes, heard as an echo through my dreams.

Suddenly Ivo sprang at me. His hand under my throat, holding me against the bench. His face only inches from mine. The smell of the wine still on his breath.

'You took my dad,' he said. He banged my head against the slats. 'Now you think you're taking my sisters?' He slammed me back again. My head cracked against the wood. 'You're evil!'

'No-no-no-no-no,' I moaned almost as one long word, holding on to Ivo now instead of pushing him away, gripping his coat. I couldn't let him go to them.

He ripped himself away from my clench. I grabbed him again and he lashed out, smacked my face hard enough for my ears to ring.

I lost sight of the moon for a second of blackness and then he was walking away, his back to me, heading back towards the shore. My feet made hardly a sound on the boards as I threw myself at his legs, and we both tumbled to the floor. He hit the deck hard with a grunt. With my face pressed flat to the boards, I saw a split second of the waves as they churned and crashed below.

I scrambled onto his back, trying to hold him down, but he roared and bucked me off. Then he straddled me, his full weight holding me down. I writhed and twisted, but it made no impact.

He laughed, face to the stars, and then put his hands to my throat, thumbs pressing into my windpipe harder, harder. I kicked and thrashed, and my eyes fizzed with white dots that became darker, darker as I started to run out of breath.

Then I found his face with my hand, but he only pushed deeper at my throat.

My eyesight was fading.

I felt the current taking me down.

I started to let myself go.

Suddenly there was a shout.

Ivo reared backward, and I saw him lash out at someone.

The cold air scorched my throat as I dragged in great lungfuls, bringing myself back to life.

Ivo crawled a few feet away from me, holding his head.

It was Morag who was there, leaning against the railing with blood running from her head as she clutched her shoe in her hand, which she'd obviously hit him with.

'Morag?' I said as I crawled to her. What was she doing here?

'I knew something wasn't right, so I came back,' she said, and in that moment I loved her. She said again, 'I knew,' as she pressed a hand to her front. It shook in the moonlight, but she looked magnificent.

I felt the sea spray hit my face through the railings, sting my sore skin. The beam from the lighthouse circled, illuminating the horizon, the black roll of the waves. The salt and tang made me feel alive.

'Mad old bitch,' Ivo said, rubbing his head.

Morag's breath rattled in her chest. The lighthouse torch showed the pallor of her face, a sheen of sweat on her forehead. She stood very still, her shoe still in her hand.

'She's not worth protecting.' Ivo tossed his head in my direction so that Morag would know he meant me. 'She's a liar. A cheat.' His bitterness sounded pathetic.

Morag reached a hand towards me with the other still clutched to her chest, right where her cardigan buttoned together, and then she grimaced hard, eyes squinted shut.

I only just managed to catch her as she slumped forward. She was tiny as a bird, lighter than the girls the last time I'd carried them. She glanced at me as though surprised. And then she died in my arms.

I knew it immediately. The fire that had driven this formidable woman for so many years wasn't there any more.

Gently I lowered her to the floor.

Her last act had been to save me. Her final instinct had been to protect her family. What a gesture of love. She sided with me when I needed her most, this woman who had been a thorn in my side for years, and she had died for me.

'Now look what you've done,' I said to Ivo in a low voice. 'You hit her. This time you killed someone.'

He shrugged as the wind whistled along the edge of the building, fanning his hair out behind him, the moonlight catching his bald spot.

'No,' he said. 'Morag died of shock after hearing the truth about you. Adulterer. Murderer.'

'But there's a body right here with your DNA on it,' I said.

He moved quickly and scooped Morag up in his arms. She looked tiny and fragile, and her arms hung towards the boardwalk limply. Before I could stop him, he flung her over the railing.

'There,' he said.

The shock of it, the callousness. Poor Morag's body sinking beneath the waves. My fight had gone.

I walked to Felix's plaque and touched it gently.

'I'm so sorry, Felix, for everything,' I said, and then I had one last idea.

I pressed my back to the pier railing, put my foot on the first rung and pulled myself up. I was now the same height as Ivo.

'If you tell the girls, I'll have nothing,' I said, desperation clear in my voice. I found the next level with my foot and pushed up again, climbing the side. My back was now completely clear of the railings, nothing holding me safe. I was now taller than Ivo by about a foot.

The wind buffeted my face as Ivo looked on in puzzlement.

'If David finds out what I did, he'll leave me...'

I pushed up again so that I stood with only a foot of barrier behind my calves, the rest of me precariously balanced, swaying in the wind.

'So come and finish it off, Ivo,' I said. 'You know you want to.'

He was on me in four steps. But I was ready.

As Ivo put his hands up to push me backward, to throw me to the mercy of the sea, I put my own arms round his head, his neck, and pulled him with me. Every part of me clung to him, every muscle held him tight against me like a limpet to a rock.

For one crazy moment, I thought it hadn't worked. That my momentum, my weight hadn't been enough to topple him, as I hung upside down, my legs wrapped round his chest, hands tangled in his hair.

But then it happened, and I felt the balance change as together we went over the railing and were no longer tethered to land.

We were falling, in slow motion, clinging to each other, towards the freezing black churn of the water, and in the moonlight I saw the glint of his desperate eyes searching for mine.

The promenade was two deep already with spectators by the time we got there, some people even sitting on deckchairs facing the pier as though it was seventy degrees in the sunshine and not ten degrees in the dark. Others sat on the cold stone of the wall, legs dangling over the beach. The annual November fireworks display was a real event for Southwold; the whole town turned out. Morag met up with her yoga class and they watched together. Kids ran up and down on the sand in the darkness with sparklers, shrieking with the sheer terror of being out in the moonlight. We were lucky with the weather; it was bone-bitingly cold, but dry. I was warm from the inside with beef stew and red wine, the combination making my cheeks pink. I paused to see where we might slot in, find somewhere to sit or lean, but David laughed and pulled me further down the beach.

'I've got the best spot, we'll have the best view.' He tugged my gloved hand.

The wooden beach huts stretched along the beach towards the dunes, a line of pastel-coloured sheds and decking. All named – CatNap, Windrush, Pennies from Heaven – slices of beach life for one family or another. They were extortionate in price; the locals joked you could buy a house somewhere else for the price of a hut on Southwold beach. Tonight some of the owners sat on their decks, lit their huts with fairy lights, wrapped themselves up in blankets, drinking flasks of tea or glasses of wine. David waved to them as we hurried past, urgency on his face to get to wherever he'd chosen for us to watch.

He'd got the promotion. We'd heard yesterday. The hard work and extra training had paid off and he'd bounded through the door to wrap me in a bear hug. To tell me to my face, rather than over the phone. I held on, so happy to have him after nearly messing every-thing up, ready to start our new chapter.

In the couple of weeks since I'd told Felix that he and I were over, I'd heard nothing.

Of course I jumped every time the letter box clattered, but whenever I checked, it was only mail on the mat. Whenever my phone showed the message icon my stomach dipped, but it was never him.

I saw him once, when I was with a friend having a coffee on the pier. He was standing at the end, looking out to the horizon. His shoulders hung. His hair blew. I prayed he wouldn't turn round as we paid and left. But Felix stayed there, stock-still, staring out to something only he could see.

There were no phone messages, no calls, and I started to enjoy my life again, terrified at how close I'd come to throwing it away. The more I thought about it, the more I put it down to a moment of madness. I'd never make the same mistake again. I couldn't live with the guilt. The hurt. Thank God it was behind me, this secret. I'd take it to my grave.

But what the affair had shown me was that I needed something – a buzz, a charge – to prove to me that I was alive. So one day, almost on impulse, I had walked down the beach and into the cold sea, much to David's amusement. Not equipped, in a swimming costume rather than a wetsuit, I'd lasted only a minute or two, battling to swim my way through the cold water shock. But it had been enough. The thrill of the icy water, its power, gave me a surge of endorphins and was exactly what I craved. I hit a high.

I'd gone in every day since.

'Where are we going?' I asked David now, but he just tapped the side of his nose.

'It will be worth it,' he said. 'I promise.'

The next stretch of beach huts were the last before the dunes, nearest to Gun Hill. They were in darkness; they were largely owned *by out-of-towners who just came for the summer season. He paused at the third one, striped blue and white, a black felt roof.*

'Wait here,' he said, glancing around him. He bounded up the three wooden steps and tried the door under the small porch.

I gasped. 'What are you doing?' I said, shocked.

'I thought we could watch the fireworks from here,' he said and beckoned me over his shoulder. I hesitated for a split second and then ran lightly up behind him. He opened the door and stepped into the darkness. I hovered on the veranda, scanned left and right. Surely someone would see us? It was so unlike him.

'Come in, quick.' David struck a match and bent to light a candle inside a jam jar and the flickering light illuminated the wood-clad walls, a cheap plastic card table set up with a stripy deckchair either side. A bottle of red stood between two glasses and a buffet of crisps and nuts sat in little bowls.

He grinned in the half-light and spread his hands wide.

'Welcome to our beach abode.'

I clapped my hands together, realising what he'd done. We'd always talked about buying one, something for our for ever life. We'd said coyly that it would be useful when we had children for buckets and spades, or for an inflatable dinghy so we didn't have to lug it up and down to the garden shed. Many a time on a walk, we'd picked out our favourite cabin names or colours. We'd pointed out shell garlands that people had hung over the doorways, or driftwood that sat on the steps and bleached white in the sun.

'You wouldn't call it spacious' – he laughed, turning round in the ten-foot by twelve-foot cabin – 'but you could call it "ours".'

I stepped in, ran my fingers along the tabletop, the grooves of the wood cladding. The back wall had hooks on it for towels and swimwear. A corner kitchen held a gas stove, a shelf for plates or glasses, a washing-up bowl on the single worktop; a faded curtain below hid a dustpan and brush, a bin. It was the cutest room I'd ever been in. Just the basics. Only what we needed. Just David and me. My grin was making my face ache. I kissed him, on the mouth, the cheek, the neck. He laughed and squeezed me till my breath went.

'Like it?' he asked.

'Love it.' I kissed him again.

'Right, let's get everything outside for the show.' He lifted one chair and I took the other one, placing them on the deck, side by side. He swung the bottle of wine between his fingers and balanced the glasses and the candle on the porch beam, before suddenly slapping his thigh and cursing.

'Forgot the bottle opener!'

We locked eyes and laughed, and then he was off before I could comment, bounding off up the beach towards a crowd gathered outside one of the huts about fifty yards away.

'I'll go and ask someone,' he said over his shoulder. 'Will be good to meet the neighbours!'

I watched his back. He was happy. I could tell by the way he bounced along on the balls of his feet. I settled into the chair, feeling the material bend and shape to my back, taking a moment to watch the surf, listen to the waves as they sucked the sand. I felt happier in my bones than I had done in ages. Life was good.

Felix stepped out of the shadows of the next hut, long black coat with the collar turned up, face hollowed out.

I scrambled out of the chair and pushed the hut door closed behind me so that he couldn't see inside, not even a peek of my life. I wanted him nowhere near it. I scanned the beach. David was still walking away and there was nobody else nearby. Still I felt eyes on me. Nobody was looking, but my skin prickled with guilt. Felix couldn't be seen here.

'How've you been, Bella?'

'What are you doing here?'

'It's a public beach,' he said. 'In fact, it's a party. You know I love a party.' He nodded towards the crowd on the promenade.

'You can't be here,' I said, folding my arms, resisting the urge to look towards David again.

'I've got nowhere else to go.'

'Go to your wife,' I said, nasty in my desperation to get him gone.

'She won't have me.'

He took a step towards me and the candle threw shadows under his eyes.

'I want you.'

A surge of adrenaline shot through me. I'd made a mistake. A stupid mistake. Looking at him now, I couldn't see the guy I'd thought he was. He was gone. This man before me was nothing like him.

'It's over, Felix.'

He flinched.

I glanced towards the pier, saw David in a crowd of people, shaking hands. He'd be turning back soon.

I had to get Felix away. I stepped to the handrail between us.

'There's still good times for us, somewhere.' Felix looked about him as though he might see something that would make me want to be with him.

'Never,' I said.

A quiver started by his left eye. It spread to his cheek and down to his jaw, until his whole head was trembling. Quivering. It seemed his face didn't know what expression to make, what emotion to apply, like it might fall apart completely. He opened his mouth once, but nothing came out. Eventually he whispered, 'There's nothing left.'

'You'll find something,' I said, heartless.

'I'll kill myself.' It was a statement. Not a question, not a threat.

I didn't need to say anything at all. But I did.

'Go ahead.'

And I pushed past him, shoving him with my shoulder as I ran away. I crossed the sand towards David and joined the group my husband was speaking to with a casual smile and a 'Hi, I'm Belle' as if nothing had happened at all.

It was only when the first fireworks shot green and gold into the sky and illuminated the beach in a flash of noise and light that I dared to look back.

But Felix was gone.

I hit the water thirty feet below on my back. It knocked a noise from me.

Ivo let go of me on impact, just as I'd expected. The shock of the cold water, let alone the drop, would dull his senses long enough for me to do what had to be done.

I pushed up, away from him, the weight of my coat, my trainers, like ballast holding me under. When I broke the surface, I pulled just a few strokes away to give myself space, and then pulled at my coat's zip, dragged my arms from the sleeves and let the sodden fabric go. I kicked frantically at my own heels, freed my feet of their trainers and then trod water for a few seconds to let my heart rate settle.

The waves lifted me, knocked me side to side. The tide was turning and I was further from the beach than usual. It was fierce, freezing. The pier loomed above us, black and towering. A current was forcing me closer to Ivo again, steadily moving me where I didn't want to go. It was then I realised the sea could help me.

He burst through the surface a few metres away, spluttering and spitting, and I knew he would have water in his lungs already. It would have been involuntary, a gasp under the water as his skin registered the freezing temperature. He coughed, thrashed around, turning left and right, panicking. His black hair was slicked back and a long tendril stuck to his cheek. I thought of the leather lace-up boots he was wearing. His heavy padded jacket, full of duck down that would pull him under.

I slowed my breath and summoned my energy.

The whites of his eyes caught the moonlight and he registered me there.

'Bella,' he gasped, his arms windmilling, waves slapping his face.

'This way, Ivo! Just follow me.'

I turned, swimming hard, leading him directly into the current, making him work harder than he had to. After a few seconds I checked. With the strength of youth on his side, he was following behind, in a lumbering crawl. He might be stronger than me, but I was resilient. And I knew he didn't have the cold-water acclimatisation I did. I put my head into the water, my face burning at the salt and sting, and pulled again, stretching into my own stroke, knowing I had to go further, faster. I kept the promenade to my left, checking my line every breath stroke, calming my mind with counting and breathing.

Twenty strokes before I looked again. The gap between us had grown; his stroke was slower. As I watched he raised his head to check where I was, wide-eyed, open-mouthed, coughing, spluttering. I put my hand up to him, encouraged him on.

Another thirty strokes and he was floundering. Arms like lead, only just tapping the surface, legs not kicking. I wondered if he even knew where I was. His left arm lifted, ineffectually.

I hesitated for a split second and realised I had to go back.

The current pushed me back to him with hardly any effort. He was almost motionless in the water when I reached him. Ivo opened his mouth to say my name, and then, instead of pulling him to me, I pushed him slowly down. His face submerged, the water running into his parted lips.

My hands were as pale as his face in the dark. His eyes were open, his hair like seaweed around his head. The shape of his head so like my own girls' heads, the square of the chin, the dimples. Suddenly it was Kit I was holding there, their faces merging into one. I gasped, cried out and for one brief second almost let go, terrified that it was Kit I was drowning. Then I remembered I wasn't killing my daughter, but saving her.

I pushed down harder until I didn't need to anymore, and I let Ivo sink to the rocks below.

I reached the beach, next to the pier. The sand sucked at my socked feet as I laboured out and threw myself down to rest. My breathing plumed white in the night air, my skin prickled and burned with cold. Shingle bit into my face, stuck to my cheek.

Ivo was dead. Drowned. He wouldn't hurt us again.

David need never know.

Kit was safe.

The girls would always believe they had each other, as twins.

My thoughts came thick and fast, in time with my rasping breath. I rubbed frantically at my arms, wrapped them round myself to warm up. We could go back to normal, just the family. Except that we wouldn't all be there. Not ever again. Morag was dead. And she was dead because she'd tried to save me; and I knew I'd grieve hard for the mother-in-law who'd been sharp and prickly, but who'd had the same sense of family as me, and had proven it right to the end.

Morag, dead.

How would the family recover?

What about me pulling Ivo off the pier? The fact that I'd been in the water with Ivo and not saved him?

Kit would never forgive me. David would never forgive me. It might all come out anyway as to why Ivo hated me so much. And then Morag would have died for nothing.

The sea pounded the pier legs near my feet, soaking me with spray where I lay on the sand. My body was suffering, but as always when I emerged from the water, my mind was clear. Sharp enough to remember something that would work in my favour. Just a little tiny thing, but one which meant that I could make things right. For my family. All of them. Again.

I scanned the beach, waiting. It wouldn't be long.

Boxing Day

Sea temperature: 8.5 degrees.
Air temperature: 5 degrees.

The Boxing Day Dippers wore Santa hats, or bauble earrings. They ran shrieking into the water, splashing, gasping, and submerged themselves. They only had to stay in for a minute for it to count as a swim. Their friends or family waited on the beach with towels, ready to wrap them up and pass them a flask of Christmas cheer.

Usually we were with them, all of us as a family, but not this year.

David sat on the prom in his wheelchair, medicated to the max, his broken leg jutting out awkwardly, pinned through with its metal brace. Jess leaned on the chair handles and I watched her lips move as she spoke behind his ear. He forced a smile but it was tired. Kit perched on the stone wall beside them, kicking her heels as she stared out to sea. She'd hardly spoken since Saturday night. She drifted round the house, room to room, as though she was looking for something but wasn't sure what.

I walked alone to the surf while they watched, 'cheering me on' as Jess put it, biting her lip. Nancy Barfoot appeared beside me.

'I'm so sorry about Morag,' she said, resting her gloved hand on my forearm. 'She always loved the Boxing Day Dip.'

'Thanks, Nancy,' I said, pulling my swim cap over my head and remembering Morag in her bright pink wetsuit as she strode into the surf.

'Such a lovely woman,' she said, and I smiled. Everyone said the same. And I had to agree with them, now. In the end, she had turned out to be exactly my type of woman.

'Anyway, hope you can enjoy some sort of Christmas holiday,' Nancy said and turned towards the water, duty done. She was better at it than some people, who just didn't know what to say when faced with the double tragedy our family had endured. They were at a loss for words. Easier just to smile and wave, or look away.

I was relieved to walk into the water again, to feel the sea around me. It drove the blood around my body, the thought from my head, the air from my lungs, and then it welcomed me like an old friend as I swam.

It had been as I sat under the pier that the solution had come to me. The light nearest to me on the promenade was out. So was another one along the beach. And the end-of-the-pier CCTV cameras were broken. I'd minuted it at the latest parish council meeting. All anyone could have seen was Ivo and me entering the boardwalk, followed by Morag. After that, nothing.

When someone found me on the beach an hour later, I was ranting madly and mildly hypothermic, shouting Morag's name at the sea, again and again and again. I was completely hoarse by the time the ambulance came.

Now, I turned in the water for my return leg and watched the Boxing Day Dippers running back up the beach, eager to go home to turkey leftovers, or to the pub for a festive drink.

I struck out: reach, pull, reach pull, heading in.

One of the few things that Kit had said to me since Saturday was 'thank you', for trying to save her poor depressed, deranged boyfriend when he threw himself off the pier. The fact that Morag and I had both jumped in to try to find him, to save his life, had meant more to her than anything.

'But why?' she sobbed. 'Why would he do that?'

I told her I didn't know but that he had behaved oddly in the restaurant after she'd gone, and, although I'd done my very best to keep him safe, Morag and I hadn't been able to save him.

Her questions were answered the next morning when the police turned up to rearrest Ian Carlyle, for stabbing his mother and jumping bail.

After they'd gone, Kit turned a broken face towards me and said he'd told her he'd worn the tag since getting arrested for smoking weed in the summer. That she hadn't said any-thing to me or her father for fear that we'd disapprove. Jess had known and had begged her to tell us. But Kit honestly – honestly – had no idea it was anything more than that. How could he have fooled her like that?

'Poor you,' I said. 'And Ivo too. He must have been very unhappy.'

Since then, she'd said hardly anything at all.

The news channels covered the story. I'd seen Kit reading them online, tears dripping off her chin. The tragic story of a young man who'd thrown himself from the pier in front of his dad's plaque. There were comments from the restaurant, the other diners. His odd behaviour. His outbursts. It fitted with the man awaiting trial for stabbing his own mother.

Now we had to wait for Ivo's body to wash up somewhere.

So far the current had not carried him in, and I couldn't help but see the fleshy remains of the baby whale in my head. I wondered what state he'd be in when the sea had done with him.

It was almost time for me to get out.

Morag's body had washed in the same night. Thankfully, unchanged by the sea. A blessing.

She was getting a hero's funeral. Half the town would turn out for the seventy-year-old woman who had once saved a young person's life, who died trying to save another one. When I told the police she had seemed to have a heart attack in the water, they said it was very likely. That's the danger of cold-water shock.

'I don't think she was thinking about herself,' I'd said. And that, at least, was true.

My feet found the seabed and I stood, water cascading down my body. The bite of the air made my skin tingle and burn as I walked out of the sea, feeling every cell of my body pulse with life. I licked the salt from my lips and couldn't help but smile as I walked back up the beach to my waiting family.

Wednesday 4 April

Air temperature: 17 degrees.
Water temperature: 13 degrees.

Five of the Southwold Sea-girls were already swimming, the number steadily increasing with the temperature. By May, if it was anything like last year, we'd be up to twenty every day. I saluted Nancy as she waited for me at the shore, and she waved back and headed in resolutely. The chill of the water sucked my breath as always but I steeled myself and steadily submerged, keen to be in.

The sea sparkled in the spring sunshine, the sky showed clear blue to the horizon. I calmed my breathing, struck out towards the pier. It was going to be a fantastic day. The start of a new phase in our lives.

Morag's flat was to be finished that afternoon. The last snags on the list should be completed, a chipped tile, a few paint strokes. Now officially known as 'The Granny Flat', it was to be marketed on all the holiday websites for Suffolk and let out to tourists. David and I had discussed it at length after her funeral and it seemed like the perfect option. We didn't need any more space ourselves, especially not with the girls off at university and then probably flying the nest, so it didn't make sense to convert the two properties back into one. And the uncertainty of selling the property as a stand-alone basement flat made us uneasy. What if we ended up living over somebody we didn't like? Maybe somebody a bit like Ivo, I thought. Eventually we decided to spruce the place up and rent it out, short term, to holidaymakers; they wouldn't stay more than a week or a fortnight, so it wouldn't matter whether we liked them or not. The income would pay the remaining small mortgage and more. It was a no-brainer and we'd both been happy with the plan.

The actual work had taken a few months, as David and I had been living there while he was still in his wheelchair. It had been the only way to have him home. And we'd needed him so much at the beginning. Not just me, but the girls too.

Naomi had turned up on the doorstep the moment she heard the news about Morag and Ivo, and she didn't leave. She wrapped Jess in a hug that was tender and loving and complete, and everything fell into place. I took them tea in the mornings and they were curled up like dormice, happy together. They woke smiling, brushed the sleep from each other's eyes. More than oldest friends. The secret she'd wanted to tell me before my birthday never really needed telling at all, it turned out.

Kit stayed home for weeks, wandering ghostlike from the sofa to her bedroom. Or sitting over a cold cup of tea at the kitchen table. Tired all the time, she slept in the afternoons but then I'd hear her floorboards creaking late into the night. She couldn't rest while she waited for a body, a funeral. It wasn't until the middle of January that a newspaper report announced Ivo was now 'lost at sea, presumed dead', which seemed to help her turn a corner.

One day Kit asked me to walk with her, and we headed towards Walberswick, just us and Dodge.

She paused, pulling at dune grass between her fingers as she looked out to the sea.

'Do you blame him,' she asked quietly. 'For Granny's death?'

I put my arms round her and pulled her into the tightest hug, feeling the guilt that she bore on his behalf. The thought that she had introduced him to our family and now her grandma was dead.

'No,' I said. 'I really don't.' And that was true. But my daughter didn't need to know that the person I blamed was myself.

It seemed to help Kit though, and the next day I came home from the parish council meeting to find the girls packing rucksacks, cramming their clothes into black sacks, announcing that it was time to get back to life. They were heading back to university. Kit had been in touch with her tutor and was picking up her course again.

'Giving it a go,' she said with a shrug.

As she hugged me goodbye, Jess whispered a promise in my ear. She would spend the first few weekends in Bristol, or get Kit over to Exeter. Nem was going down too and they'd look after her together. I squeezed her extra hard, my thoughtful girl. So like her father. And I squeezed Naomi too, and counted my lucky stars that Jess had someone so lovely in her life. I could only hope that Kit would find the same, in time.

When they were gone, I filled my days with work on Morag's flat. It kept me busy. It gave me a new focus.

The hardest thing for us to do was to remove Morag's possessions before the work began. I buried my face in the dressing gown that hung behind the bathroom door and inhaled the lavender of her scent. David stared at each of the pictures on the mantelpiece in turn, before wrapping them in paper for a box in the loft.

I went through Morag's desk, sorting out her finances, making sure I notified everyone in her address book. At the back of the drawer, I found her file, 'Family tree', full of birth certificates and timelines. I flicked through, thinking I would keep it in our attic. The girls might be interested in it someday. Some of the articles were copied from newspapers, some from library books. Our family line was worked through in detail, doodles and diagrams showing each stage in our history. I peeled through pages of death certificates and obituaries, marriage announcements and more. There was hours of research. It was a real labour of love.

Then I found a photo, stuck to the back of an ancient document. At first I didn't understand its significance in the family tree folder. In the foreground was Morag's friend, Rose Green, sitting in a pub garden. Nothing out of the ordinary; they often used to go on trips out locally and have a drink afterwards. But it was the background that chilled my body like ice. Felix and I were at a table near the hedge. I was leaning towards him, face uplifted, mesmerised. He had his hand in my hair. I remembered now, the pub, the day. I'd thought it risky going to The Low House in Laxfield, but Felix had reassured me with a squeeze of my hand, saying nobody ever went to such a tiny village pub on a Tuesday afternoon. I'd laughed away my doubt and followed him with a smile.

'I knew,' Morag had said, on the pier.

I thought she meant that she'd known Ivo was mad.

Now I could see she meant she had known something else.

It hit me like a punch. She'd been aware of my affair all along and she'd never breathed a word. She'd put family first, not wanting to do anything to jeopardise that. She and I were more alike than I'd ever realised. But now I had no chance to thank her. Morag. My mother, not just in-law.

I ripped the photo up into pieces too small to tear again and put them in the bin, before carefully transporting the file upstairs for posterity.

The rest of the refurb went smoothly. Although the place was immaculately clean, it had been stuck in the past with its decor and facilities. We had the carpets ripped out, the floors sanded back to their glory. Every wall was painted white, fresh and clean. Morag's rigid armchair and brown two-seater sofa were replaced with light-blue furniture, brushed cotton. We added cream wool cushions, dark-blue throws. The whole effect was beach-house modern, light and airy.

Today was the day it would be complete. Every last job ticked off. We already had bookings through to the end of August, with the first holidayers arriving for Easter in a few days' time.

Kit had been asking about the flat the other day on the phone. Joked that maybe she'd move into it herself one day, and I'd responded that if it meant she lived below us, I'd be up for that. Daily phone calls when she first went back to Bristol turned into every few days as she slotted back into life in halls. She still had down days, but lately she'd been more hopeful about the future. Talked about looking forward to summer and what the autumn might bring. I'd asked her whether she'd met anyone else but she'd just said no, it wasn't the right time for any of that. She had other things on her mind. I worried less about her as time passed and she mentioned Ivo less and less. Soon enough, I'd see her – and Jess. They were both due back for the Easter holidays. I couldn't wait to feel Jess's cheek against mine. Hear the lilt of Kit's laugh. Hold my girls. Not long to wait.

The spring sunshine didn't have enough heat in it to warm my skin as I walked up the beach. In the hut I changed quickly, efficiently, using the towel on the hook at the back, next to the candle in the jam jar we still kept there, for old times' sake.

George was signing for a delivery as I walked past the Red Lion. His T-shirt was too short or his trousers were too low; a white band of belly glowed shockingly white in the daylight.

'Saw you've got a reservation tonight, Belle,' he said, pen poised over the clipboard. 'Anything to celebrate?' He signed with a squiggle that ran off the page and handed the paperwork back.

'David's last physio today,' I said. 'Back to full working order, officially.'

George grinned.

'That's worth a pint on me.' He hitched up his trousers, to no avail. 'See you later.'

I headed down South Green, swinging my swimming bag beside me. Noticing the daffodils that swayed in the breeze, bobbing their yellow heads at the sea. It was a great morning for a walk and I was already looking forward to heading out with Dodge.

As I got closer to the house, I saw someone waiting for me.

Kit was sitting on the top step, leaning her back against the front door. Something inside me jumped in pleasure to see her there, earlier than expected. I felt the smile lifting my cheeks at the sight of her. Her face was turned up to the sunshine, her eyes closed. She looked perfectly content there, waiting. Happy even. An array of bags were piled beside her. She was home.

'Hello, darling,' I called as I neared, and she lowered her head, found me with her eyes. Those beautiful blue eyes.

A hesitant smile crossed her face making one dimple dance briefly on her cheek as she waved. It was as her hand dropped back to her lap that I noticed the ink of the tattoo, the same shape, the same position as Ivo's. A never-ending knot. Just like his.

My stomach dipped and my smile slipped. She hadn't told me about that. But I mustn't let it be an issue. Ivo was gone. Done with. He couldn't hurt us anymore. We could move on with our lives.

'You're early,' I said as I ran up the steps to hug her. 'How lovely.'

My daughter pulled herself to standing as if she'd been sitting for a long time, slightly stiff, uncomfortable.

And it was as she straightened that I saw the change in her body, the gentle curve of her usually flat belly. The unmistakeable bump of a baby.

A baby, which she cupped her tattooed hand over, protective already.

ACKNOWLEDGEMENTS

Thanks to everyone who made this book a reality. I still can't quite believe I now have two books on shelves and your help along the way has made a massive difference.

To Judith Murray at Greene and Heaton for your never-ending cheer and support.

To Jenny Parrott at Oneworld's Point Blank for your insight and wit. I'm lucky to have you as my editor. You're spot on with your insight and make me snort with laughter along the way.

To my early readers again – Sinead Nolan, Scott Taylor and Shayna Wilson – you're fab. I owe you a curry.

Thanks as always to my mum with her red pen and eagle eye. I'll try to make less grammatical mistakes next time. (Or is it fewer?)

To Frances Martin for her advice on having twins. I honestly don't know how you do it. You're a superwoman and a super friend.

To Euan for helping me through the 'this book is a pile of shite' days and celebrating with me on the 'actually, I think it might be okay' days. I love you.

To my boys, James, Ollie, Charlie and Harry. Thanks for keeping my CV diverse by adding taxi driving, cooking, relationship advice and cleaning, as well as any other such 'mum' duties as you may require at any time of night or day. I wouldn't have it any other way.

This book is all about family. So for my mum, Pat, my brothers, Richard and David, their wives, Grace and Ursi, my in-laws, Sheila and Ian, my brother-in-law Chris and Alison and all your lovely children: Riley, Erin, Carter, Emily, Lily and Sophia – I'm taking this chance to say that I'm glad you're in mine.

© Mark Rusher

JACQUELINE SUTHERLAND worked in corporate PR and marketing for over twenty years. Her debut novel, *The Coffin Club*, was first published in 2022. She lives in Guildford.